cupcakes
& crumbs

Berry Lake
CUPCAKE
POSSE

friendship · romance · cupcakes

BOOK ONE

MELISSA McCLONE

Cupcakes & Crumbs
Berry Lake Cupcake Posse
Book One

Copyright © 2020 by Melissa McClone

Cover by Cover Me Darling

ISBN-13: 9781944777-55-5 (paperback)
ISBN-13: 9781944777-54-8 (eBook)

Published by:

Cardinal Press, LLC
November 2020

get a free sampler

To receive a free copy of
Beginnings: A Sampler Collection,
join Melissa's newsletter.
Visit melissamcclone.com/join

🧁 dedication 🧁

For my family who listened to me talk about this series for years and gave me their full support (i.e. fed me and then left me alone) once I started writing it.

Special thanks to: Terri Reed, Elizabeth Bromke, Denise Stout Holcomb, Kevin McClone, Mary Moineau, Shari Drehs Bartholomew, Julie and Michael Harris, Tina Jones, Kimberly Field, Christa Haskell, Julie Trettel, Melanie D. Snitker, and the Heart Breathings Sprint Challenge Facebook group, especially Kyan, Lisa, and Rhiannon for hosting the live sessions.

In memory of Elizabeth Brooks
who was a friend, mentor, and surrogate aunt rolled into one.

chapter one

A S THE SUN climbed above the horizon, strokes of lavender, orange, and pink painted the awakening sky. Sunrise had once been Bria Landon's favorite time of day in Berry Lake, Washington, but that had been a lifetime ago. She was only up early this morning because fewer people would be out. If she hurried, she might make it to the cupcake shop before she saw anyone or vice versa.

Please let that be the case.

She wasn't taking any chances.

Since leaving her aunt's house, Bria focused on the sidewalk where grass grew between some cracks and dirt filled others. At least there were no bugs. Even if there were, she wouldn't look up. She didn't want to notice if someone exited Brew and Steep—the only place on Main Street open this early—and be forced to say hello.

Rude, probably.

But no one expected much from the once-chubby eighteen-year-old girl who'd left this town and her aunt behind fifteen years ago.

The prodigal niece.

That was what her aunt jokingly—and lovingly—called Bria.

Had called her, that was.

Ever since Aunt Elise's cancer diagnosis three years ago, Bria had tried to make up for not returning sooner by visiting as much as possible. She'd done everything she could for her aunt, and in the process, become reacquainted with people she'd long forgotten. But the idea of smiling or waving to anyone right now made her queasy. Forget about chatting for a minute or twelve—which was something else folks did there. That was beyond her.

Who was she kidding?

Everything Bria did lately was difficult, and she hated that.

And this day, of all days, might completely do her in.

The reading of the will took place tomorrow. Until then, the employees at the Berry Lake Cupcake Shop counted on Bria to make decisions regarding the bakery. No one knew what Elise Landon had decided to do with her estate, other than asking Bria to be her personal representative. Soon, everyone's question about the fate of the Berry Lake Cupcake Shop would be answered. But today, the staff looked to Bria for answers.

Today.

What would have been Elise's fifty-seventh birthday.

The only problem?

Bria hadn't a clue what to tell them. Not when her brain barely functioned. She wasn't sleeping or eating. What friendliness remained had been buried alongside the woman who was the closest thing to a mother she'd ever known. She wished people would leave her alone.

Not her aunt's employees, who needed her input.

Everyone else.

Some claimed there were no stupid questions, but Bria disagreed. How did people *think* she was doing when her heart was in pieces, as if sliced and diced by a skilled teppanyaki chef?

Forget replying with anything other than an "I'm fine" or "I'm okay" or "I'm doing better." No one wanted to hear the truth about how angry she was at cancer, at the doctors, and at her aunt. Especially Aunt Elise for stopping her treatments, throwing herself an over-the-top goodbye party, and leaving this world on *her* terms.

So typical.

But it sucked for Bria.

As she continued down Main Street, her shoes slapping against the cement, she rubbed her tired eyes.

Going along with her aunt's wishes had been the hardest thing Bria had ever done, but she loved Aunt Elise enough to let her go.

To say goodbye.

Even if fifty-six was too young to die.

Bria ignored the vise tightening around her heart. She had a feeling it would be like this for a while.

The countdown to Aunt Elise's last breath had been both painful and beautiful. Bria tried to focus on the beauty, but she didn't always succeed. Still, the final minutes with her aunt would be etched in her memories forever.

Live, laugh, and love for both of us, my sweet Bria.

I can do the first two, but you only added the third one to see how badly I'll mess up yet another relationship.

Guilty.

We both know I'll be like you, Auntie. Single, happy, and satisfied with the decisions I've made.

You know what I always say. Cupcakes are better than men, but a few good ones are out there. You might find one who's as sweet as buttercream icing.

There'd been a cheekiness to the curve of her aunt's lips and peace in her eyes—something missing since the cancer returned. At that moment, she'd known Elise was ready to say goodbye. But the knowledge didn't fill the hole her aunt's absence left in Bria's heart.

Her hands balled, so she flexed her fingers. If she gave in to the pain, it might consume her completely.

Just keep moving.

Everyone knew cancer would kill Elise Landon, including Bria, which was why she'd dropped everything when she'd gotten the call last month, taken family leave from her job as a CPA, and flown from San Diego to be with her aunt. What most didn't understand was the *knowing* hadn't made her aunt's death easier to accept. It hadn't prepared Bria for the onslaught of grief that ebbed and flowed like the tides back home, only on a less regular schedule.

Home.

She couldn't wait to return to San Diego. There, she was one more cog among many at the accounting firm. No one there cared about her aunt, this town, or Bria's past here. None of her neighbors, whose names she didn't remember, would fill her condo's fridge with meals. And the questions—the stupid, stupid questions—about her, her aunt's house, and the cupcake shop would stop.

Oh, how she wanted it all to stop.

If leaving after the funeral had been an option, Bria would already be gone. But she needed to attend the reading of the will and do whatever her aunt requested she do as the personal representative. After that, Bria would put this town and the memories of it behind her, once and for all. Until then, she would take it step by step, day by day, until nothing remained on her to-do list.

First up…

Should the cupcake shop celebrate their late owner's birthday or not? Aunt Elise had left instructions about everything else, but why not this?

Each year, her aunt celebrated her birthday by giving away mini cupcakes to every customer who came into the shop and offering significant discounts on other products until the inventory ran out. People visited the town specifically for the sale. It was chaotic, but Elise had thrived upon the craziness.

Keeping the tradition alive for their loyal customers made good business sense, but Bria worried about the shop's staff. The last few weeks, after Elise no longer had the strength to leave the house, had been difficult for the employees. They might not feel up to the madness the birthday celebration sale brought.

Should she take a vote?

That might be the best solution since the sale affected the employees most.

Bria crossed the street, making a beeline to her aunt's legacy, the Berry Lake Cupcake Shop. Even though a *Closed* sign hung in the front window, the lights were on in the kitchen, signaling the morning baking was underway.

She unlocked the door. As she opened it, a familiar bell jingled, and she stepped inside.

The scent of chocolate hit first. A kaleidoscope of memories sent her doubling over. She inhaled deeply, letting the aroma sink into her before standing upright. She closed her eyes and then opened them.

It was like stepping back in time. Nothing had changed, including the interior with dinged and scratched bistro tables and chairs and faded walls in need of fresh paint. Her aunt had planned a complete remodel—Bria saw the renovation plans—but that had been put on hold three years ago.

The glass display on the right side of the counter was empty, but sixteen flavors of cupcakes would soon fill the shelves. She glanced at the doorway to the kitchen, waiting for Aunt Elise to appear wearing an apron, a hairnet, and a bright smile.

Only that didn't happen.

And it wouldn't ever again.

A lump burned in Bria's throat. The corners of her eyes stung. She'd avoided this place for a reason, but she needed to be there now.

As she wrapped her arms over her stomach, she studied the framed photographs—more than twenty-five of them—hanging on the purple-painted wall. Each featured employees who'd worked there during a given year or specific season. Elise gave each group a nickname and engraved it on the frames: *The Crew*, *The Squad*, *The Mix*, *The Team*, the list went on.

One picture stuck out—*The Posse* engraved on the frame.

A smile tugged on the corners of Bria's mouth. She'd been so proud to belong to that group fifteen years ago. The photograph showed herself, Aunt Elise, Missy, Juliet, Nell, and Selena. They'd all worn the pink T-shirts they'd made with the *Berry Lake Cupcake Posse* in big block letters.

Bria laughed.

That summer saved her from a broken heart, humiliation, and tumbling headfirst into an eating disorder. Their group had been a mix of ages—seventeen to twenty-two—but they'd bonded as they worked together, talking about their futures and learning how to bake cupcakes with sprinkles of life wisdom thrown in by Aunt Elise, their fearless leader.

Missy Hanford never left Berry Lake. She'd been the youngest at seventeen and still worked at the cupcake shop. Nell Culpepper returned to town after a broken engagement and worked as an RN at the hospital. Juliet Monroe moved back last year with her wealthy husband. And Selena Tremblay, aka Selena T, was as famous as her hockey-player husband and lived in Seattle.

Bria didn't remember if any of them except Missy attended the funeral on Saturday. The day remained a blur, other than the knowledge that the one person who should have been there never showed up. Not surprising. Her father's relationship with Elise—his younger sister—had been strained for years. But Bria thought—hoped—her dad would come through this once. She guessed that meant he wouldn't be at the lawyer's office tomorrow morning.

Pans clattered.

"Missy?" Bria called out.

"I'm okay. Just dropped something." Three months ago, Missy took over running the shop for Elise, and her aunt made it clear she wanted Missy in charge long after she was gone. "Come to the kitchen."

Each step felt as if Bria were wading through marshmallow fondant. Her feet kept sticking to the tile floor. Not really, but she hated knowing her aunt would never bake in the kitchen again. Slowly, she trudged forward to where trays of unfrosted cupcakes sat on a wheeled sheet pan rack.

Everything looked the same as always—from the Hobart mixer to the double-deck, full-sized convection oven, yet the person who'd built this place from nothing more than her dreams was missing.

Bria cleared her dry throat. "Good morning."

"Hey. What a nice surprise." Missy wore the shop's all-white uniform, a hairnet, and a baker's cap. Plastic gloves covered her hands. "I didn't expect to see you here this early. Are you having trouble sleeping?"

Of course, Missy, who'd become a widow at twenty-three, understood. Bria should have remembered that. She nodded. "Does it get easier?"

"Define easier?" Missy stood at the stainless steel worktable and used an ice cream scooper to fill the liners with chocolate batter. "It's been nine years, and not a day goes by I don't think about Rob. But I cry less, sleep more, and no longer wish I wouldn't wake up."

Guilt coated Bria's mouth. "I'm sorry I wasn't here to help you."

"Your life was two states away. The same as it is now." The words came out in a matter-of-fact tone. A hundred-and-eighty-degree shift from the dreamy teenager all those years ago who'd talked nonstop about weddings, babies, and Rob. "I wouldn't have realized you were there, anyway. I was that out of it. But Jenny took care of me, and your aunt helped, too. Without them, my two cats, and this job, I'm not sure what would've happened to me."

"Thank goodness for your sister-in-law and Elise." Missy was a year younger than Bria. They'd known of each other in high school, but they hadn't hung out. Not until working together that summer. "But I should have come because we're friends."

"And we always will be." A timer dinged. Missy removed a pan from the oven. "Are you nervous about the reading of the will tomorrow?"

"Curious, but my aunt's biggest wish was for the shop to continue without her. That's why she made you the manager."

"Elise told me I always had a place here, but..." One side of Missy's mouth curved. "You could be the new owner."

"If that's the case, I'll be a long-distance one." Bria had left baking behind when she'd set off to college. "Which is why I'm so happy you're here. Elise trusted you to keep the bakery going, and so do I."

"At your service." Missy bowed. "I'll always be here for you."

"Thanks." Bria wished she could say the same thing in return, but another life—her real one—waited for her in San Diego. Now that her aunt no longer needed her, there was no reason to stay in Berry Lake. "I don't know what I'd do without you. Today..."

"I'm doubling the number of employees on each shift to handle the birthday sale. People will come in and out as their schedule allows, but that's how it's been in the past. I hope that's okay. I assumed you'd want to go ahead with the annual celebration."

Guess I've been worried for nothing. "If you and the others are okay with it?"

Missy nodded. "There might be some tears, but it's what Elise would want us to do."

"True." And that gave Bria an idea about how to decide things. She would ask herself what Elise would do in the situation. That would be better than second-guessing herself. "If my aunt were here, she'd put me to work today. What can I do?"

☕ chapter two ☕

OUTSIDE THE BERRY Lake Art Gallery, Juliet Monroe stood next to her husband, Ezra. No lights were on inside, and a *Closed* sign hung on the glass door. "The gallery isn't open."

"That sign is for the public. It doesn't apply to me." Ezra combed his fingers through his hair. The number of gray strands had taken over light-brown ones, and the creases at the corners of his eyes had deepened, but he was more handsome at fifty-five than he'd been at forty-two when they'd met. "Wait here. I won't be long."

"I want to go inside."

He blew out a breath. "We're not here to ooh and ahh over the pretty pictures on the wall, Juliet."

She forced herself not to cringe at his condescending tone. He must be tired from the extra hours he'd been working since last November. "I want to see Hope Ryan Cooper's new painting. It's supposed to be spectacular."

He rolled his eyes. "Are you kidding me? The only art you're familiar with features a mouse, a duck, or a castle."

His jab about her former job as a theme park princess was nothing new. Their first year of marriage, his words stuck to her like Velcro. Now after twelve years, the criticisms bounced off her as if she were made of rubber, though they still hurt. He appeared to forget that once upon a time, the tiara and gown she wore appealed to him so much he'd called her Princess. Occasionally, he still did, but this year, his workload as the newly promoted VP of sales had increased. Nothing she did pleased him. But he shouldn't take his job stress out on her.

Juliet crossed her arms in front of her until she remembered that might wrinkle her sleeves. She lowered her arms to her sides. "I just want to look at the painting. I'm not planning to analyze it."

"As if you could."

She counted back from one hundred in French to keep her anger from spiraling. Sometimes, he upset her so much she wanted to scream, but outbursts only led to him calling her weak and replaceable.

Replaceable.

A shiver shot along her spine.

Her biggest fear was for Ezra to divorce her. He'd made her sign a prenup. She'd been so ridiculously in love with him she'd only skimmed the document. She'd never once considered consulting an attorney. Big mistake. The agreement was one hundred percent in his favor. And since they had no children—he hadn't wanted any—she would receive a limited alimony and only a few assets.

Which was why she spent her days and nights trying to keep him happy.

What other choice did she have?

Juliet hadn't worked in nearly a decade. Her only skills were being a trophy wife and a theme park princess. No way could she afford a house on her own. Rent would be impossible to pay without a job. Her grandmother, Penelope Jones, owned the Huckleberry Inn, but Juliet didn't feel right asking her for help or even advice. She didn't want to disappoint her grandma, who believed in the sanctity of marriage.

Ezra's intense gaze bore into her. "Why do you even care about some painting?"

Juliet didn't lower her eyes or step backward. That would only draw more negativity from him. "I met the artist in Brew and Steep. Hope moved to Berry Lake after getting married a few months ago."

"What's her husband's name?"

"Josh Cooper."

Ezra sneered. "That football has-been is nothing but a drunk."

Josh, who was a year younger than Juliet, had been the golden boy of Berry Lake. Every girl—including her—crushed on him, in high school and beyond. An injury forced him to retire from football and become a sportscaster. He'd hit rock bottom after being arrested and finally realized he needed to turn his life around. "He's sober now."

Her husband scoffed. "How long do you think that'll last?"

Forever, because Josh has his career and a wife he doesn't want to lose, but those words would be lost on her husband, so she shrugged instead.

Ezra adjusted his silk tie. "You can see the painting another time."

"Fine." She'd learned early in their marriage that getting upset only worsened a situation. Appearances meant everything to Ezra. He expected her to dress, act, and talk a certain way, especially in public. And she did. On rare occasions, however, she wanted to push him. Today was one of those days. "Unless you wouldn't mind me taking a selfie with the Sasquatch."

The gallery's Bigfoot sculpture provided a prime photo opportunity in town. There was usually a line to pose with it, but she wouldn't have to wait this morning.

Ezra grimaced. "Do as you're told, and don't move."

He jerked open the door, jingling the bell hanging from the handle, and hurried inside.

Juliet balled her hands until her manicured nails dug into her palms.

What was his fascination with art about, anyway?

It had started in December. Since then, he'd purchased dozens of paintings, but he hadn't allowed her to hang them in their house.

An investment, he'd said of the artwork, with a stern warning not to touch them.

She hadn't, but paintings propped against the walls in his office didn't seem like the proper way to store something of value. Then again, her postsecondary education consisted of learning how to do a royal wave, embody the princess mystique, and forge the signatures of the park's original princesses. To this day, she wrote the loopy and heart-inspired script without a second thought.

"Good morning, Juliet." Charlene Culpepper's heels clicked on the cement. As usual, the fifty-something-year-old event planner was dressed to the nines. She carried gorgeous bouquets of vibrant mixed flowers. "Isn't it a beautiful Monday?"

"Yes, it is." Juliet inhaled the sweet floral scent surrounding Charlene. "I didn't have time to speak with you at the reception on Saturday, but you did a lovely job with Elise's funeral."

"Thank you." Charlene's genuine tone contradicted her reputation for being a pain in the neck—and other parts of the body. "I worked with Elise for months to make sure I knew exactly what she wanted. She pre-paid, so her niece wouldn't have to deal with anything."

Guilt coated Juliet's mouth. She'd seen Bria Landon, teary-eyed and exhausted, at the funeral, but Juliet hadn't offered her condolences. So many people had crammed into the church and the reception afterward, it had been difficult to move around, and Ezra had wanted to leave early.

"Is Bria still in town?" Juliet wanted to see Bria before she left.

"Through the end of the week, I believe." Charlene motioned to the flowers. "Don't these remind you of Elise?"

"They do." The woman had been as colorful as the varied blossoms. Beige wasn't in the baker's vocabulary. "What are they for?"

"Elise would have turned fifty-seven today. I'm making a birthday bouquet for the cupcake shop."

Juliet's heart dropped to the tips of her Brian Atwood flats. How had she forgotten the day? Elise had been her boss and mentor a long time ago, but since Juliet moved back to Berry Lake last year, they'd become friends. "Is the cupcake shop celebrating?"

"I don't know, but if not, people will be disappointed. That's what Elise did on her birthday." Charlene half laughed, staring down Main Street with gleaming eyes. "Guess this isn't the year, after all."

"The year for what?"

"For Bigfoot to make his appearance finally."

People swore Bigfoot lived on the edge of Berry Lake. Despite the rumored sightings and reality TV shows who searched for the creature in the surrounding area, no one had taken any photos or videos of the Sasquatch. Even the local business that took tourists on day trips and overnight search parties had only found footprints and heard calls in the wee hours of the morning. But the folklore grew, and the town capitalized on the interest. Thousands of Bigfoot fans attended the Bigfoot Seekers Gathering this past summer. For the first time, the attendance surpassed that of the annual Huckleberry Festival, which surprised everyone except for Buddy Riggs, who owned Sasquatch Adventure Tours.

"Why would Bigfoot appear today?" Juliet asked.

Charlene's expression softened. "Elise always said someday Bigfoot would walk down Main Street on her birthday."

"You and Elise were close."

"We were. For almost our entire lives. Well, hers." Charlene sniffled before straightening. "I'd better get these flowers arranged and delivered before the day slips by."

It wasn't even ten, but Juliet wouldn't mention that. Everyone was mourning the town's beloved baker in their own way. "Good luck. And I'll have a cupcake later to celebrate Elise's birthday."

Charlene adjusted the bouquets in her arms. "I'm planning to do the same. Maybe I'll see you at the shop."

With a nod, Juliet turned her attention to the art gallery. A single light was now on, but she didn't see Ezra, the owner, Sal DeMarco, or two of his stepchildren who worked there.

That was odd.

Ezra said it wouldn't take long. So, where was he?

As Juliet opened the door, a bell rang. The place, however, appeared empty.

"Hello?" No answer. "Ezra, are you still here?"

The gallery remained silent.

Each time she'd been there before, music played. Then again, all the lights had been on then, too.

At least a minute passed.

Her husband rushed through a doorway, straightening his tie. "I told you to wait outside."

"Where were you?"

"Looking at a painting that arrived yesterday." His tone was impatient, one word coming on top of the other. "I'm a premium customer, so I'm allowed to view them before anyone else."

"I thought that's what exhibit previews are for."

"Stop trying to pretend you know anything about the art world, Juliet." Spit flew out of his mouth along with his words. "Go put on a tiara and smile at the mirror. That's the only thing you're capable of doing."

She raised her chin. "You used to like when I did that."

"You were younger, then. Thirty-five is too old to play princess."

Remy Dwyer, a young twentysomething, entered the gallery through the same doorway Ezra used. Her leopard-print miniskirt, black crop top, and gold stiletto heels were something to wear to a club, not work. Her messy bun only added to her unprofessional look. She waved a cell phone. "You forgot this."

He took the phone. "Thank you, Remy. Your diligence is noteworthy."

Remy beamed. Seriously, the girl's face glowed.

Had Juliet ever been that young? And then she remembered. She'd been twenty-two when she met Ezra. He'd showered her with attention, affection, and expensive gifts. She hadn't stood a chance against his looks, money, and charm.

Allowing a pretty young thing to flirt with her husband wouldn't help their marriage problems. Juliet tapped her toe. "Are you finished, Ezra?"

"Yes." He focused on Remy. "Please contact me when the next shipment arrives."

Remy batted her mascara-caked eyelashes. The dark color contrasted with her blond hair, and not in a good way. "Of course, Mr. M."

Ugh. Juliet hated the way the woman practically purred his name. She touched Ezra's arm, a calculated, territorial move. "Don't you have a meeting at the bank?"

Ezra muttered under his breath. "I forgot."

"It's a good thing you have me, then." She laced her fingers with her husband's. "Let's go."

Once they were outside the gallery, Ezra shook off her hand. "Don't do that again."

"What?"

"Disobey and embarrass me in front of people. I told you to wait outside."

"And then you disappeared."

"I told you—"

"Are you sleeping with her?" As soon as the question slipped out, Juliet wanted to take it back. His answer would change everything.

His eyebrows furrowed. "Who?"

"Remy."

Ezra's nostrils flared. "I can't believe you'd accuse me of cheating."

"Your sudden interest in art and visits to the gallery coincide with her starting work here."

He shook his head. "You're letting your imagination run wild. I'm interested in art as an investment to set us up for the future. No other reason."

Juliet wanted to believe him, except he hadn't answered her first question.

Ezra tucked a strand of blond hair behind her ear. "Have I ever given you any reason to doubt me?"

Other than cutting me down every chance you get?

She shrugged, noting he'd answered with a question of his own.

"You know I haven't." He placed his arm around her. "While I'm at the bank, you run to the cupcake shop and buy dessert for tonight."

She'd planned on that anyway, but now she wouldn't be forced to explain her purchase or spend an extra hour on the elliptical machine or the Peloton bike since he'd suggested it. "Today is Elise's birthday."

"All the more reason for you to go there. You miss her."

Not trusting her voice, Juliet nodded.

He pulled her closer. "Buy a dozen if it'll make you feel better."

"A dozen will go straight to my waist and thighs, but I'll pick up a few." She might be overreacting, but things had been strange since the beginning of the year. Last December, even. She hoped the man she'd fallen in love with reappeared. She leaned against him. "I love you, Ezra."

"I know you do, Princess." He kissed her forehead. "I know you do."

chapter three

MISSY HANFORD DIDN'T know which was worse—the sweat dripping down her neck or the clothes clinging to her skin. The temperature in the bakery's kitchen kept rising, but stepping outside and cooling off wasn't an option. The line of customers was out the door, and they kept running low on items. That meant she had cupcakes to make. If she met the demand, the shop might recover the revenue they'd lost from closing on Saturday for the funeral.

As Top 40 hits from the seventies and eighties—Elise's favorite music—drifted in from the front of the shop, Missy filled baking cups with vanilla batter. The scent tickled her nose. The grumbling of her stomach reminded her she'd skipped her break and lunch. And her tastebuds whispered *mine* at the same time she imagined Elise shouting, *Why eat plain vanilla when there are more flavorful combinations?*

Missy laughed. Even though plain vanilla cupcakes with vanilla icing were foundations for other flavors, Elise hadn't

19

sold them except for special orders. Missy, however, enjoyed vanilla cupcakes. Dare she say they were her favorite? The simplicity appealed to her in a way the more creative fillings and toppings didn't.

Elise had claimed Missy hadn't found her favorite yet.

She disagreed. *Why mess with perfection?*

Her boss, however, had been on a mission to find a recipe Missy would prefer over "plain" vanilla. Only now, there would be no new recipes created to tempt her away from her favorite. Not unless she wanted to come up with them herself.

Tears pricked her eyes.

Not now.

She would cry later.

At home.

While she ate a vanilla cupcake.

Elise would have laughed at that or given her the stink eye.

Missy kept working. After filling the last cup, she placed the pan in an oven and grabbed another pan with cups to fill. Hunger was easy to ignore. Her dry throat, not so much.

"Keep going."

She'd been telling herself that for hours. Those in the front dealing with customers eager for a freebie and a discount had it worse. They also had air-conditioning, which meant something must be broken with the vent system—one more thing to add to the to-fix list.

Bria stuck her head into the kitchen. A hairnet covered her auburn hair, and her eyes were no longer as red-rimmed as they'd been this morning. "You okay?"

"I'm fine." Missy continued scooping the batter. "Sounds busy out there."

"Madhouse, but I think it's what I—all of us—need." Bria's gaze softened. "Did you eat lunch?"

"I will later." If Missy got too hungry, sweet treats surrounded her. Of course, she'd crash later from all the sugar, but sacrifices had to be made sometimes.

"Please do." Bria glanced over her shoulder. "I can't afford for anything to happen to you. Seriously, Missy. Without you, this place would shut down."

Missy stood taller. "Nothing will happen to me. Promise. I just need to get more cupcakes finished."

Bria opened her mouth but then closed it. "Okay, but yell if you need help."

"I will."

Bria side-eyed her.

"I've got this." Missy half laughed. Bria was more like her aunt than she realized. "Stop worrying. If I need help, I'll ask."

With that, Bria disappeared.

Missy hadn't been lying. She had things under control—somewhat.

All she had to do was stop staring at her water bottle like a woman who'd gotten lost in the nearby Gifford-Pinchot National Forest with nothing to drink for days. Okay, she was exaggerating, but she was thirsty. Unfortunately, if she took a sip now, she would need to wash her hands yet again, and that would take time she didn't have. The tray needed to be filled before the timer dinged.

Then she would guzzle the entire thing.

Of course, she'd been telling herself that for an hour, and it wasn't close to closing time. But as long as people wanted to buy cupcakes, they wouldn't close until nothing remained. That was how Elise ran the shop. Missy would do the same.

"Just think how relaxing a shower and then sitting in front of the television will be."

Her feet nearly sighed in relief. Okay, it wasn't *that* bad. She was used to the chaos Elise's birthday celebration brought each year, but today was the first with her in charge. Everyone, from the employees to Bria, looked at Missy to get the job done. No way would she disappoint them, but…

She glanced up at the ceiling. "How did you do this?"

Missy didn't expect her boss to answer, but if anyone could, it would be Elise Landon, who had been the definition of a dynamo. She was both boss and friend to each employee who stepped through the door at the Berry Lake Cupcake Shop, regardless of gender, age, or orientation. She expected her staff to work hard and follow the rules. Nothing she hadn't done herself. Oh, chemo had flattened Elise several times, but she'd kept going until she couldn't and asked Missy to take over.

"I won't let you down."

For the last three months, she'd been running the cupcake shop. After working there for so long, Missy didn't have to think about what she was doing. Her muscles and mind knew what needed to be done. Thank goodness, because her heart missed her boss and her friend.

The timer dinged.

She pulled out a pan, placed it on the rack to cool, and then slid the next one inside the oven to bake.

Sheridan DeMarco entered the kitchen. She wore an apron, and her hair was covered with a hairnet. "We're running low on red velvets."

Missy did a double take. She hadn't seen Sheridan since

December when she filled in for three weeks. They'd known each other for what seemed like forever, though.

"I was about to fill another tray." Missy grabbed the ingredients. "I thought you were in Asia."

"We were, but I wanted Michael to see Berry Lake. We also wanted to get some wedding planning stuff done before we fly off on another adventure. I'm sorry I wasn't here sooner to say goodbye to Elise."

"She understood why you didn't want to return to Berry Lake."

As Sheridan laughed, warmth filled her gaze. "Elise should have called this place Cupcakes and Counseling."

"She gave better advice than any bartender in town."

Sheridan nodded. "So, red velvet?"

Oh, right. Missy didn't have time for distractions, but she hadn't expected to see Sheridan.

"They're up next." As she grabbed the bowl of batter, she looked closer at Sheridan, whose face glowed and not from the heat. Missy recognized the look because she saw it daily reflected on her sister-in-law Jenny's face. "Being in love suits you."

Sheridan beamed brighter. "No complaints except I wish Michael would agree to elope."

"Wedding planning has you down?"

"Not really." Sheridan washed her hands. "Charlene is the coordinator, so we don't have to do much."

Charlene Culpepper ran the only event-planning business in town, and she also enjoyed poking her nose into everyone's business. They didn't call her Berry Lake's busybody for nothing. Even though she was the only party coordinator option, she was also the best in the surrounding area. "She'll do a wonderful job."

"For sure. But being here is stressful."

"Sal and Deena?"

Sheridan rolled her eyes. A common reaction by anyone when Sheridan's father and stepmother were mentioned. "They're upset Michael didn't invite them to watch him propose in Indigo Bay."

Those two were always complaining about something. Sal DeMarco had been a nice guy until he married Deena, who had so many ex-husbands no one could keep track of her last names except for her first one—Dwyer. But since the two married last October, Sal had joined his wife in the race to be known as the town's villain.

"Did they forget about giving your job at the art gallery and your apartment to Remy?" Missy asked.

Remy Dwyer and two of her brothers were their mother's minions. It was almost comical how the three did whatever their mom said. Ian was a senior in high school, but the twins, Remy and Owen, were twenty-four, old enough to know better. The oldest sibling, Dalton, who was a year older than Missy, left for college and never returned to town. Smart move, given his family.

"I guess so, but I haven't forgotten. They aren't invited to the wedding. Nothing will change my mind. I asked my mom to walk me down the aisle, and she's thrilled to do that." Sheridan motioned to a tray of unfrosted chocolate cupcakes. "Want these frosted?"

"Did Bria send you back?"

A sheepish expression formed. "She asked me to check on you."

Missy swallowed a sigh before nodding. "If they don't need you up front—"

"They don't."

She wouldn't turn down an extra pair of hands. "Fill them with cherry first."

A grin lit up Sheridan's face. "Oh, I love filling them. That was one of my favorite jobs when I worked here. Are these Black Forest cupcakes?"

"Yes, but you don't have to do this." Missy fought the urge to wipe her face. "It's cooler up front."

"I want to help you." Sheridan put on gloves. "Elise hired me last December based on your recommendation. I didn't work here long, but this is the least I can do today."

Sheridan sounded like her mom, Sabine Culpepper, who ran the local animal rescue. Both women had strong work ethics and compassion. Sabine was married to Charlene's ex, Max. Life in a small town. At least the three got along, which was more than could be said for Sabine and Sal. "Be sure to clock in."

"Nope."

Missy laughed. "Guess the rumors about your fiancé might be true."

"Rumors?" Sheridan shook her head. "Let's hope they're better than the ones Deena spread about Sal's reasons for firing and evicting me."

"I heard your fiancé is loaded." Missy filled the scoop with more batter. "Your engagement ring tells me that's true. It's gorgeous."

"Thanks." Sheridan stared at her glove-covered left hand with a dreamy look in her eyes. "Michael is wealthy, but I fell in love with him before I knew about his money."

"He's lucky to have you."

"I think so." Sheridan grabbed a cupcake corer. "So, what else?"

"Someone said you're only with him because of his money."

"That's my stepmother, not me."

Missy would have laughed, except it was one hundred percent true. Since Paul Dwyer's death sixteen years ago, Deena married and divorced wealthy men as if it were a game. The goal—increase her net worth as much as possible. So far, it had worked well. Somehow, Sal DeMarco hadn't heeded the warnings. Now, he'd turned his back on his own daughter and allowed two of his stepchildren to work at his gallery. People bet as to how long the marriage lasted—two years appeared to be the average—and most assumed Deena would end up with the gallery after the divorce.

"When I met Michael Patterson, he was unemployed, and that didn't matter to me. I didn't have a job, either." Sheridan didn't sound offended. If anything, she appeared amused. "Did you hear anything else?"

"Only that your fiancé is forcing you to sign a prenup, and you said no, so the wedding might be canceled soon."

As Sheridan laughed, she made holes in the tops of each cupcake. "I offered to sign one, but he told me no, much to the chagrin of his attorney."

That's true love. "Oh, I forgot another one. I heard you're both homeless."

"That one is correct."

Missy nearly dropped the scoop into the bowl. "Seriously?"

Sheridan nodded. "But only because we can't decide whether to buy a big place in South Carolina and a vacation home in Berry Lake or vice versa. We stay at all sorts of places, but most are four or five stars."

"Now, that's my kind of homeless."

"Right?" Sheridan filled each cupcake with cherry pie filling. "I sometimes have to pinch myself because I'm living a dream."

"Enjoy it."

For as long as it lasts.

Missy, however, would never say those words aloud. But the way Sheridan and Michael traveled pleased her. She'd believed she and Rob would have time for vacations and kids, but that hadn't been the case.

"I plan to." Sheridan inhaled. "It smells so good in here. Michael and I are coming in for a tasting, so we can decide what flavors of cupcakes to serve at the wedding. We're also having a small cake because Charlene said we needed one to cut into for the photographer."

"She's right." As Missy recalled her own wedding, she felt a pang, but it wasn't as sharp as it used to be. *Progress.* "You want those photos."

"That's what Charlene said."

Charlene had helped plan Missy's wedding to Rob. They'd been so young, eighteen and newly graduated from high school, and hadn't been able to afford much. Her dress had come from a consignment shop in Portland, compliments of Rob's parents since hers hadn't agreed with the marriage and didn't attend, let alone offer to pay for anything. The reception had been in the church's basement. But it had been perfect for them.

"Trust her."

"Nell says she's crazy."

Nell was Sheridan's stepsister and one of Missy's closest friends. Not that she spent much time with anyone other than Jenny, Dare, and little Briley. "Most people think that about their mother. Charlene enjoys meddling in other people's lives, especially your three stepsisters, but she could go head-to-head with the top event planners in Portland or Seattle. She won't steer you wrong, but if you're not sure about something, ask me. I helped Jenny and Dare with their wedding in Indigo Bay, so I have some recent experience."

"Thank you." Sheridan raised the pastry bag filled with chocolate frosting. "Is this the right one?"

"Yes."

Sheridan frosted the cupcakes as if she'd been working there every day. "What have you been up to?"

Missy raised her hands, careful not to drip any batter. "This place."

"Mom said you'd cut back volunteering at the rescue."

"I help when I can, but I didn't have time to foster and bottle-feed kittens, with Elise needing me here. I stopped working for Jenny, too. Her husband took over."

"Do you think you'll have more time now?"

Now that Elise is gone remained unspoken.

Missy straightened. "Elise said she wanted me to manage the shop after she was gone, but it depends on what's in her will. I'll know more soon. I want to foster again, though. My two cats miss having the others around."

"Is it exciting to run this place?"

"I'm getting there." Missy's chin itched, so she rubbed her face against her shoulder. "At first, I was terrified I would make a mistake and ruin everything Elise had built. It was also hard to accept knowing I was in charge because of her cancer."

"And now?"

"I'm nervous, but I'm up for it." After three days of managing the shop on her own, something had changed. It was as if a switch inside Missy flicked on, and she was ready to face the challenges head-on. Uncertainty remained, but that didn't stop her from thriving. The cupcake shop, too. "Elise's trust gave me a new sense of purpose. It's been… good for me."

As close to perfect as Missy expected to get.

She no longer filled her days with a part-time job at the bakery, another with her sister-in-law, and any extra time spent volunteering at the rescue to keep from having too much time on her hands. The longer hours here meant keeping her mind occupied, even after she left. She was too tired to think about Rob and the life they'd dreamed of having when she arrived home each evening. "All I want to do is turn Elise's plans for this place into reality."

"You will." Curiosity filled Sheridan's eyes. "So, your professional life is going great. What about your personal life? Are you dating anyone?"

"Not right now." That had become Missy's stock answer.

"Were you dating someone before?" Sheridan pressed.

"No." Missy wouldn't lie, and she should have expected the question since they'd only exchanged a few comments on social media over the last nine months. She'd gone out for coffee with a few guys, but that was it. "I haven't met anyone I've wanted to see again."

"It'll happen when you least expect it." Confidence filled Sheridan's voice. Typical of someone in love and happy. "That's when I met Michael. The timing was so bad, but it turned out to be the best thing ever."

Missy nodded. That was easier to do than tell the truth—that she'd known Rob her entire life and fallen in love with him in middle school. No man would ever take his place. She'd given up trying. She wore her wedding ring and Rob's dog tags around her neck to keep him and what they'd shared close. How did she explain that without those things, she would be lost? "Jenny tells me that, too."

"It's true."

"I've seen it happen. You, my sister-in-law, and even Josh Cooper are proof." But that didn't mean it would happen for Missy.

"If you're up to meeting someone new, a new vet is joining the animal clinic. My mom met him during his interview. She said if she was single and thirty years younger, she'd ask him out."

That sounded like Sabine. Missy grinned. "She probably wants a discount on vet services for the rescue."

Sheridan laughed. "Probably."

"I'm always up for appreciating some eye candy." *Look, don't touch* was Missy's motto. "My two are up to date on their shots and visits, but I might have to volunteer to transport spay-and-neuter animals once he starts."

"You should," Sheridan encouraged. "My mom misses you."

"I miss her." *And fostering and helping out with the cats and dogs.* Missy didn't care about meeting a handsome vet, but she should visit the rescue on her day off. She loved her two cats wholeheartedly. Mario and Peach were her world. But she enjoyed cuddling and falling for the cuddly fur babies who passed through the rescue.

And let's face it. Falling in love with animals was all she was capable of doing now.

chapter four

NELL CULPEPPER STOOD at the nurses' station in the emergency department of the Mount Adams Regional Hospital. Her twelve-hour shift was almost over, and she was ready for quitting time. A cupcake had her name on it. Possibly two.

Nothing unusual.

A trip to the bakery on the way home from work relaxed her, and today was the perfect day to continue her habit of eating dessert before dinner.

Well, as long as her mother didn't find out. If she did, the meddlesome Charlene Culpepper, aka Mom, would add carbs and sugar to the list of reasons Nell didn't have a boyfriend. Not that big of a deal. She'd been dealing with her mother's meddling for thirty-seven years, even if she didn't remember the first few. But a cupcake wasn't the only thing waiting for her at the shop. Missy would be there and most likely Bria Landon. Nell hadn't been able to say more than a few words to Bria on Saturday. She wanted to see her before she returned to San Diego. For her old friends, Nell would face whatever consequences with her mom.

Gurney wheels sounded, and people rushed by, sending a gust of air across her face and arms, but she remained focused on the monitor. Nell prepared the discharge papers for the hiker who'd used poison oak for toilet paper. She cringed, thinking how much that would hurt. She didn't want to hold up his release, given his now-ruined backpacking vacation. The guy had been through enough.

"Is the patient in four ready to go?" Cami asked, efficient as ever. She yawned less now that she worked days instead of the third shift. Graveyard had been hard on the single mom of twins, but then again, it hadn't been Nell's favorite, either, and she only took care of herself.

"Almost." She grabbed the pages from the printer, double-checking each before stapling them together. "His drive home to Portland won't be fun."

"No, but it's a lesson learned, and let's hope he'll think twice before heading into the wilderness without being prepared." Cami, who looked younger than thirty-two, adjusted her ponytail. Her thin blond hair never stayed in place, but she kept it pulled back. "What happened is better than him ending up dead. Given how clueless the guy is about anything he can't look up on his cell phone, he should have never set out by himself to backpack for a week."

"True." Nell wasn't big on being outdoors. Watching a movie without buttered popcorn was her idea of roughing it. Not that the patient in exam room four appeared to know much more. Cami's comment about his cell phone was on point. His only preparation for his trek into the forest had been to stop at REI on his way out of town.

Nell hadn't hiked or camped in more than two decades, but she knew better than that. She also recognized poison oak. What was the rhyme her dad had taught her?

Leaves of three, let them be.

It was something like that.

Nell handed the paperwork to Cami. "Here you go."

Cami read the top page. "I'll discharge him."

"Thanks." Nell glanced at the board. Today was surprisingly light. Not that she would complain about a lack of patients, but the day passed by slower.

"Hey, Nell." All six feet two inches of Welles Riggs stood at the counter. His brown hair had been recently cut, so the strands no longer touched his collar, but the ends still curled. Thick eyelashes surrounded his blue eyes. "How's your day going, Nurse Nell?"

"Fine, Paramedic Welles." Too bad she had nowhere to be. Not that anything was wrong with him. He was a friend—a neighbor, even. But at times, he grated on her nerves. "Are you dropping off a patient or picking up?"

"Dropping off."

The man oozed sensuality. He was four years younger than Nell, and the only thing that had changed since high school was his uniform. Then, it had been a jersey, shoulder pads, padded pants, socks, and cleats. Now, he wore bunker gear.

His face and body screamed heartbreaker. That big red flag told her to stay away from the sexy paramedic. Not that he tempted her. She would always see him as a kid she'd babysat one summer when his dad was working, and then as an annoying freshman.

"First time here today?" she asked.

"Nope. You were at lunch the last time." He leaned closer. "Miss me?"

"Not really. To be honest, I thought I might get a day off from you."

His laugh wasn't only rich but also attractive. *If* she went for his type… except, she didn't.

"You wound me." He placed his hand over his chest. "Any word on that car accident patient from yesterday?"

A guy had crashed his tiny hybrid car into a semi on the highway. When would people learn that texting and driving were akin to playing Russian roulette? One moment of inattention and *bam*. He was lucky to be alive. "Transported upstairs for surgery. That's all I know."

"No news is good news." Welles flashed her a crooked smile. "So, tomorrow and Wednesday are my days off this week. You're off on Wednesday, right?"

Relentless was the only way to describe him. "Who told you I'm off?"

He wagged his eyebrows. "I have my sources."

Most likely other nurses he flirted with. Perhaps some said yes. "I will neither confirm nor deny their accuracy."

"Aw, Nell. This game of yours has run its course."

"Game?"

"Playing hard to get."

"I'm not playing anything." She didn't miss a beat. "You're the one who came up to me."

"I have a reason for that."

Of course, he did. The guy asked her out all the time and had for years. Okay, decades.

"Then how about we get together on hump day?" he continued. "Picture a romantic picnic on the shore of Berry Lake followed by skinny-dipping. I'll even bring clean towels."

Nell didn't know whether to applaud his perseverance or tell him to get lost once and for all. They lived next door to each other, so she wouldn't be rude, especially since he'd loaned her his wet vac twice. Every six months, he also asked to change the batteries in her smoke detectors. "Someday, if I ever say yes to a date, what will you do?"

"Pocket a twenty from Pierce and use it to show you a good time."

His words sank in before she frowned. He had some nerve. "I'm low maintenance, but that offends me."

"Then, please keep saying no, Nell." A smiling Jordan Pierce, an EMT, sauntered over. While Welles was a pretty boy, Jordan was ruggedly handsome with brown eyes and dark skin. Most of the nurses had a crush on one or both men, though only Welles was single. "I need that twenty for my son, who keeps wanting to buy tokens for some game he's obsessed with these days."

Welles shook his head. "That money isn't leaving my wallet. Nell will give in."

"Maybe in your dreams." Jordan snickered. He and his wife, Mikayla, were from Vancouver—or Vantucky as Portlanders called the town across the Columbia River. They'd moved here for Mikayla's job. She was the principal at Berry Lake Elementary School.

"Your money is safe, Jordan." The two teased each other more like siblings than colleagues. Nell wondered how Mikayla put up with her husband and his friend. They acted like teens trying to outdo the other. "I promise."

Jordan nodded once. "Good, because you deserve a better date than this sucker."

"Hey, this sucker is a great date." Welles winked at her. "If you say yes, you'll find out for yourself."

She gave the guy props for trying. "Not today."

"Or any day," Jordan added before high-fiving Nell. "How long has he been asking you out?"

She tried to remember how long she'd put up with this. Not quite forever, but close. "Welles was in elementary school. I was in middle school. He even made up a rhyme about Welles and Nell."

Jordan shook his head. "Dude—"

"The rhyme was clever for a kid. Our names kind of rhymed." Welles shrugged. "And what can I say? I enjoy older women. It wasn't so bad when I became a freshman and Nell was a senior."

Jordan clucked his tongue. "I thought you were smarter than this, Riggs. She's friend-zoned you." He glanced at her. "Am I right?"

"You're not wrong," Nell admitted.

"We're friends. Neighbors," Welles agreed. "But haven't you heard of friends becoming more?"

Jordan snickered. "Friends with benefits."

No way. Nell wouldn't let the discussion drift into sex. She made a T with her hands. "This conversation is deteriorating. I have things to do, so go back to that fancy red rig of yours and do whatever it is you do out there."

Welles patted the spot on his chest above his heart. "I miss you already."

"Do something about him, please," she told Jordan.

It was Jordan's turn to shake his head. "I tried drowning him when we went waterskiing at the lake. I fear it's hopeless."

Welles broke out into a song from the musical *Hamilton*, but he changed the lyrics to hopeless.

"I'll just remove him from the premises." Jordan put his hands on Welles's shoulders and pulled him away from the desk. "Have a nice evening, Nell."

Welles didn't stop singing.

Once he was out of hearing range, she laughed. She wouldn't egg him on, or he might put on daily performances.

Cami returned to the station. "That hottie needs to find a woman to extinguish his fire."

"From your lips to God's ears. Unless you're volunteering."

"No way. I have two kids, and Welles Riggs has commitment-phobe written all over him. That goes for anyone over thirty who isn't married."

"I'm thirty-seven and single."

"I meant never been in a serious relationship. Welles hasn't, but you were engaged, right?"

A lump formed in Nell's throat. She didn't discuss that part of her past. Though she might have stalked her ex-boyfriend on social media only to see his lovely wife, their two beautiful children, and photos worthy of a magazine layout.

That was supposed to be *her* life—marry the handsome doctor, have babies, and live happily ever after. She'd met Andrew at college. He'd gotten into medical school in Chicago, so she'd found a job nearby. When his residency took him to Boston, she followed. On her thirty-second birthday, she'd expected an engagement ring, not to have him ask for a month apart before he proposed. But she'd been his first serious girlfriend, so she agreed. Four weeks was nothing in the grand scheme of a life together. At least she'd thought that, until he met someone who worked at Pottery Barn and married her in Las Vegas two weeks later.

The worst part was seeing photos from his wedding on social media. He didn't text her until two days later, asking her to move out of their apartment. The lease had been in his name, so she hadn't had a choice. When she handed over her keys, Andrew didn't apologize. He told Nell that he had loved her, but something was missing in their relationship—something he found with his wife.

Overwhelmed and devastated, she'd quit her job and returned to Berry Lake. Most of her friends had moved away, but Missy had still been there. And Elise, who plied Nell with cupcakes, offering a shoulder to cry on, and ears that never stopped listening.

As Nell wrapped her arms around her stomach, she nodded.

"Then you're not a commitment-phobe," Cami added.

If only that were the reason Nell was single. All she ever wanted was a family—a husband, kids, and pets—but since wasting those years on Andrew, who'd told her how much he loved her every day they were together, she didn't think she would ever trust another man. Elise had told her not to judge all men by one, but that was easier said than done. "My mom would disagree with you."

"It's a mom thing."

She thought about Cami's ginger twins—a boy and a girl. "Guess you would know."

"Yes." Cami sat and pulled up a file on the computer. "But if I ever turn into your mom, promise you'll do an intervention or shoot me."

Nell recalled her mom's last visit, how she waxed on about the new "single" vet who would join the animal clinic at some point.

Sabine, Nell's stepmother had mentioned him to her mom. The man hadn't started working there, nor did Nell own a pet, but her mom had suggested taking an animal from Sabine's rescue for an appointment.

So not happening. "That won't be a problem."

Cami raised a brow. "You sound certain."

"I am. Trust me. The world can only handle one Charlene Culpepper."

chapter five

SELENA TREMBLAY GLANCED at the Berry Lake Cupcake Shop. The line wasn't out the door like earlier, but she wanted to finish her caramel macchiato before going inside. Elise never allowed other food and drinks in the shop unless the *Closed* sign was out, and caffeine was crucial right now.

Selena had been up half the night dealing with a... situation. She would call it a nightmare or a cluster-you-know-what—and had—until her team corrected her, saying those words would mess with her high vibe.

High vibe, right?

Given that she was peeling herself off the ground today, whatever vibe she possessed was at its lowest frequency. Never mind that having a high vibe wasn't a goal of hers, anyway. But her team had latched onto the buzzword in the personal-development field.

Her team.

She loved the women and men who worked for her. She'd hired each one, believing they embraced her mission statement. She'd trusted them implicitly, only to have one betray her.

And that hurt.

A deep, raw, cutting hurt.

Two teenagers wearing ripped jeans and crop T-shirts approached Selena. Both had long brown hair that fell past their shoulders with bright eyeshadow on their lids and highlighter on their forehead and cheekbones. The shorter one nudged the taller to go ahead.

She glanced at her friend before facing forward. "You're Selena T?"

"I am."

Both young women sighed. The shorter one moved closer. "We listen to your podcast. It's great."

"Wonderful." Selena eyed both. They couldn't be more than seventeen. "You'll be ahead of the game when you go off to college."

The two shared a glance. The first who'd spoken pointed to her friend. "That's what her mom told us."

The friend nodded. "She bought us each a copy of your book."

"You have a smart mom." Selena tucked her cup between her arm and body before digging into her purse to find bookplates and a pen. "What are your names?"

"I'm Gigi." The shorter one seemed to have found her courage. "And this is my best friend."

"Belle." Her cheeks turned pink. "I'm Belle."

"If you peel off the back, you can stick these in your books." Selena signed the bookplates and then handed them to the teenagers. Both squealed with delight. *Was I ever that young?* "Keep listening to the podcast and listen to your heart every day."

Both girls nodded. "Thank you."

The two walked away in a daze, staring at the autograph as if it were a golden ticket to wherever they wanted to go.

Pride made Selena straighten. She really had put the past behind her.

Few saw a girl who grew up living in a double-wide trailer outside this small town.

Now, she was the multimillion-dollar life coach who fixed problems and made women's dreams a reality. Too bad she didn't have someone like herself to call when she had a problem.

A text notification sounded. Selena pulled out her cell phone.

> **Hanna:** *Legal is handling the broken NDA. Still no response from Caledonia. Everyone has tried to reach her. You're trending and not in the way you want.*

Selena groaned, nearly crumpling her coffee cup. *So much for embracing light, love, and kindness.* There were times for positive thinking, but this wasn't one of them. She would need cupcakes—lots and lots of cupcakes—to get through this mess.

Yesterday, a former team member—whose name Selena would no longer speak unless the police or her lawyer required it—quit, claiming the opportunity of a lifetime dropped in her lap. She'd also asked if she could forgo giving two weeks' notice. Selena hated to see the woman leave, but she'd agreed and then told her assistant, Hanna, to change the passwords on shared programs, apps, and sites they used.

No biggie.

People moved on, even though Selena wished they wouldn't. Except…

The same teaser graphic for her upcoming launch showed up yesterday afternoon on a new manifestation coach's social media. The colors were from Selena's branding, which was different from Caledonia's, a rising star. When Selena reached out to her, the woman said a new employee created the graphic. It turned out to be Selena's former employee who'd resigned that morning, but Caledonia wouldn't remove it. She said the graphic was hers and posted a scathing message about Selena and her team.

That wasn't the worst of it.

When Hanna checked the shared folder containing all the files for the upcoming launch, including the workbook, they were all gone. Someone had deleted the files from the backup drive and cloud, too. Without the original files, it was Selena's word against Caledonia's, and the other woman had the promo and course materials in her possession.

Selena knew better than to hold in her emotions, so she let them out.

Big-time.

And then the turmoil inside her settled, and something happened—a random thought popped into her mind about Logan. She remembered downloading the folder onto her husband's laptop when she wanted to show Logan the upcoming course. No one else on her team knew that.

Now, it was time to take action.

But redeeming herself brought no glee. Only more sadness over what Selena had to do, but she needed to fix this. The ten people who worked for her needed their paychecks. She wouldn't let them down. Caledonia and her team had made their choice, and they would face the consequences of that decision.

She downed the rest of her coffee before tossing the cup into a nearby garbage can. Then, Selena typed a reply to her assistant.

Queen: *Is everything ready to go?*
Hanna: *Yes. I'm waiting for you to tell me when.*
Queen: *Publish.*

Forget revenge. Selena was salvaging her reputation and business. She'd never been the Mother Earth type—nurturing, soft, and warm. Selena T was known for being a savvy businesswoman who'd fought for every success.

A boss babe.

Caledonia shouldn't expect Selena to let this go. Oh, she'd considered it until a new range of attacks happened an hour ago. Then, her heart demanded she take care of her business, her team, and herself.

Given "listen to your heart" was her tagline, she would do just that.

At this moment, Hanna was publishing everything from Selena T's upcoming course—the graphics, the workbook, whatever else had been sitting on Logan's laptop.

All of it would be available for free.

Her team thought she was insane, given she would have charged close to a thousand dollars for the new program, but she'd listened to her heart, and this was what she'd heard.

Sure, people would miss the actual lessons—live or taped—with her, since she hadn't recorded any yet, but the workbook and extras might entice them to sign up and pay for those. Her bank account would take a hit, but she considered the amount to be an important lesson learned. No one would profit from her and her team's hard work.

> **Hanna:** *Done.*
> **Queen:** *Thank you. I wish it hadn't come to this, but we bring situations like this into our lives to teach us what we can't or fail to see. We have a lesson to learn, so this doesn't happen.*
> **Hanna:** *Caledonia just replied with an apology. She wants to talk to you.*
> **Queen:** *She missed her chance today. Tell her I won't be available until next week.*
> **Hanna:** *Got it.*
> **Queen:** *Hope things aren't too chaotic for you.*
> **Hanna:** *We're used to it with your launches.*
> **Queen:** *Then, I'll leave you to it. It's time for a cupcake.*
> **Hanna:** *Enjoy.*

Selena planned to savor each bite. She opened the door, stepped inside, and stood at the end of the line. She'd done this a thousand times when she was growing up in Berry Lake. Only now, her breath caught in her throat.

The place hadn't changed that much.

She hadn't been there in more than a decade, but Elise had visited her several times in Seattle. The last time, they'd spent the day together—eating, shopping, and discussing updates to the cupcake shop. Selena had also introduced her to an interior designer to help with the plans. Only, Elise had gotten sick, and the shop hadn't been renovated.

That still hadn't been enough to bring Selena to her hometown.

She'd left Berry Lake to prove herself, to show everyone she was more than the poor girl with big boobs who lived in a double-wide on the outskirts of town. She'd done that by becoming a brand name and marrying an All-Star hockey player. Her life was better than she dreamed it would be. But she shouldn't have stayed away for so long.

It had been Selena's turn to visit next, but she'd been too busy, and now it was too late. She would never hear Elise's laughter and be embraced in the woman's loving hugs again.

The bell jingled. Someone stood in line behind her. She glanced over her shoulder.

Another face she didn't recognize. *Guess I've been away from Berry Lake longer than I realized.*

AC/DC's "Thunderstruck"—her husband's ringtone—played in her purse. She eyed the menu board before stepping outside to take the call.

"Hey, baby," she said. "Everything okay?"

"I'm good but missing you." Logan's rich voice washed over her. "When will you be home?"

"Wednesday at the latest." It depended on when she could be unavailable to her team for the four-hour drive to Seattle without too much impact. "Do you need me there sooner?"

"No, but I miss you. How was the funeral?"

"Nice." Except they'd discussed that on Saturday.

"Have you caught up with your friends yet?" Logan asked.

They also had talked about how crowded the service and reception had been, so Selena hadn't been able to speak with everyone she'd wanted to. "No, but I plan to before I leave."

"I'm sorry I'm not there."

"You had practice today."

"I'd rather be with you."

"Aw." She'd found the perfect guy when she fell in love and married Logan Tremblay. "I'll bring cupcakes home."

"Now you're talking." He laughed. "That'll make up for the empty spot in our bed."

Uh-oh. That wasn't like Logan at all.

She adjusted the phone. "What happened?"

Silence greeted her, which confirmed her suspicions.

"You sleep without me on road trips," she continued. "So, tell me what's up."

"We have rookies practicing with us."

They always did before the season started. "And?"

"One called me 'old man' today. Another called me 'daddy.'"

The hurt in his voice kept her from smiling, even if one tugged at her lips. At thirty-eight, with a beard and a sprinkle of gray hairs, she saw where the "daddy" came from. Logan would be a sexy silver fox someday. But this wasn't the time to tell him that. "They're young. Trash-talking kids trying to make it in the big league."

"They *are* young. One is half my age." He didn't sound happy about that.

"Age doesn't matter. You play on the same team. Rookies think they know everything, but they're clueless. Use your experience to help them adjust. That youngest one probably misses his family and girl if he left one at home. Remember when you were that age?"

"I do, but…"

"What?"

"Do you think they're right? Am I too old to keep playing?"

"They're dead wrong. Seattle needs you on the ice." Logan might be one of the oldest players in the league, but… "You had one of your best seasons last year. Your coach and the front office support you one hundred percent. I can't believe some players' chirps are making you doubt yourself."

"I'm tired of people asking me if this is my last season."

So, it wasn't only the rookies. "Tell them it's none of their business."

"What if this is my last year?"

Logan exuded confidence and strength. He was strong, mentally and physically. The vulnerability in his voice, however, made Selena want to drive home tonight.

"Then it is," she said in a matter-of-fact tone. "You've had a Hall of Fame career. You've played the game with integrity, grit, and heart. It's your decision when you retire, no one else's."

"I'm one injury away from…" His voice trailed off.

"Sweetie. You've been one injury away from never playing again since you stepped on the ice, like every other hockey player who straps on skates and picks up a stick. All you can do is keep going. Your career isn't over."

"That's easier to believe when you say it."

Her heart swelled with affection for the man. "Then I'll say it as many times as you need. But get those thoughts and feelings about your age and hockey out of your head. Hit your punching bag or go for a run. If the emotions get stuck inside you, they'll hamper the way you play."

He blew out a breath. "I'm not one of your coaching clients."

"A good thing. I'm expensive. But you're lucky I find you irresistible, so I'm at your beck and call twenty-four seven," Selena teased.

He laughed. "Are you giving me affirmations next?"

"No, you know all this. You just need to hear it again."

"You're right. I love you, Selena."

"I love you, too. Anything else?"

"No, but did that work thing you mentioned yesterday get resolved?"

"I'm working on it." She didn't want him worrying about her business during training camp. "Talk to you tonight?"

"Definitely."

No matter whether or not they were together, they spoke each night before bedtime. "I'll speak to you then."

"Bye, gorgeous," he said before hanging up.

Selena placed her phone in her bag. *Should I leave town tonight*? Logan needed her. Who was she kidding? Everyone needed her—her team, her coaching clients, her readers, her social media followers. But one question kept resonating through her.

What do I need?

Nothing was the quick answer.

She had an adoring, devoted husband and made millions on her own. Together, they had more money than they could ever spend. She was living the life she'd always wanted. So, how come it felt as if something was missing?

"Going in, stranger?" a woman asked.

"Nell!" Selena hugged her friend. "What are you doing here?"

"Cupcakes to celebrate Elise's birthday. You?"

"The same. I can't believe she's gone."

"She was ready, but that doesn't make it easier on the rest of us." Nell glanced at the shop's door. "Bria is struggling."

"Is she here today?"

"My mom texted me that she was working with Missy this morning. Not sure about now."

Selena nearly laughed. "Who would have thought Missy would be the lifer?"

"This place saved her. When Rob died, it was… bad. I wasn't here, but when I came home for Christmas"—Nell shook her head—"Missy was different. I thought I'd seen everything working in the emergency department, but she acted like the walking dead. Her eyes were dim and her face pale. She was going through the motions, not really living."

A pain struck Selena's heart. "I'm sorry I never came back."

"Don't be." The words rushed out. "No one else did. Don't forget, Missy was the only one who stayed in Berry Lake, and she holds no grudges. She might be the youngest, but she's always been an old soul. Elise used to call her that, remember?"

"I do. An old soul who was giddy in love."

"We were the two old ladies."

"Only you were in love," Selena reminded.

"We all make mistakes." Nell's gaze ran the length of Selena. "Being rich, famous, and head over heels in love agrees with you."

"Thanks. It does." Nell had cut her hair much shorter than what she'd worn in college. She also dressed super casual. "You look great."

"I appreciate that, but great is pushing it. You appear to be ten years younger than me. If I hadn't come straight from the hospital, maybe I'd say seven," Nell joked.

Oh, right. Selena and Nell were the same age. "Three tops."

"Five, and I'm only agreeing because I'm four months older." Nell opened the door. "After you."

Selena stepped inside for the second time. Only, being with Nell gave her a sense of homecoming. The line was shorter than when she'd walked out to take her call. "Do you know what you're ordering?"

"Salted caramel to eat here, but I'm buying a dozen to take home."

When they worked here together, Nell took the rejects home for her family. That suggested she had people—or a person—she wanted to share these with now. Not surprising, since Nell was a caretaker. Selena was curious if her friend had found love again. "For your coworkers or do you have a boyfriend you haven't mentioned?"

"No guy. And these aren't all for the hospital. I'm keeping some for myself." A smile lit up her face. "They freeze well."

Selena hadn't expected to hear that. It pleased her to see Nell put herself first, finally. "Good for you."

Nodding, Nell patted her hips. "My waist and hips might disagree in a few days."

"You have nothing to worry about." Nell had never been thin, but she appeared to be in better shape now. "Do an extra workout."

"Extra implies I work out, which I don't." Nell glanced around. "I wanted to make sure my mom isn't nearby. She thinks I should join a gym to find a husband."

"It's where I met mine." Selena stepped forward in the line. "Well, an apartment complex gym."

"Shh." Nell placed her finger at her lips. "Don't give my mom any ideas, or she'll pay for my membership herself."

Selena's jaw dropped. She'd assumed Mrs. Culpepper mellowed over the years. She'd nearly driven Nell to the brink in high school and college. "Your mom is still meddling in your life?"

"The meddling and matchmaking don't stop." Nell sounded resigned. "It's one reason I left town."

Until the breakup.

Elise had mentioned Nell's devastation. "You had your reasons for returning to Berry Lake."

Something flashed in Nell's eyes, but whatever it was vanished quickly. "I did, and I took your advice from a podcast and told my mom I was happy with my life and choices. It only worked for a few weeks, but those were pleasant and quiet days, so thanks."

"I'll see if I can come up with something else for you to try."

"It's fine."

"Hey, I'm always looking for content. Lots of women have issues with their moms. It's a topic I should address again, so thank you for bringing it up." She typed a note on her phone. "I'm jotting it down, so I don't forget."

"I appreciate it."

They moved closer. Selena didn't recognize anyone working the counter. Bria and Missy might be in the kitchen.

"What are you ordering?" Nell asked.

Selena glanced at the menu board. "Double chocolate. I'll grab more on my way out of town."

Elise used to say cupcakes made everything better.

Selena was counting on that today.

chapter six

AN ENDLESS STREAM of customers wanted a free cupcake. The door barely closed before someone else entered. Bria had no complaints because that was what today was all about. Most people left with more than their freebie, too. A win-win.

The work kept her mind focused on the tasks at hand, which she appreciated. Silence gave her time to think. Something she'd done too much of these past few days. She relished the noise surrounding her, grateful for those eating cupcakes there, and the conversations between customers waiting in line.

The only negative?

Bria's feet hurt. Her fault for not wearing a better pair of shoes, but she hadn't been thinking straight when she packed her suitcase three weeks ago. At least, she wouldn't stand behind this counter for *that* much longer.

She handed a box filled with a dozen red velvet cupcakes to a man she didn't recognize. He must have arrived in Berry Lake after

Bria moved away, or he was from out of town. She'd seen many new faces today, but for all she knew, they might have been at the funeral.

"Have a nice day." As the man left, another customer stepped up, but Bria focused on the cash register drawer, ensuring she'd closed it. Her attention wasn't as sharp this afternoon, but that didn't stop her from pasting on a smile. "Welcome to the Berry Lake Cupcake Shop. Please take a free mini cupcake."

The words came so automatically she had a feeling she would say them in her sleep for days.

"What do you think?" a familiar voice asked. "Try the free one and then decide?"

Bria's gaze jerked up to see two old friends standing on the other side of the counter—Nell Culpepper and Selena Tremblay. The two women had been close friends in high school, even dressing similarly, but now they were total opposites.

Selena's style was a mash-up of elegance and hip. Her body was toned and showed off her designer clothes. Her flawless makeup and straight blond hair appeared professionally styled. She'd claimed to play second fiddle to Juliet in the looks department, but that wasn't the case. Selena turned heads wherever she went. She just worked harder at it.

Nell was soft curves, big smiles, and warm hugs. She exuded kindness. Her shoulder-length brown hair complemented her natural wave and pretty face. She must have come straight from the hospital because she wore no makeup, not even a hint of lip gloss, and sweats.

Seeing them sent a burst of energy through Bria. "It's great to see you. Juliet was here this morning."

"I'm sorry I missed her." Selena grabbed a freebie and popped it into her mouth. "Delicious."

Nell's eyebrows drew together. "You look tired, Bria. Have you been here all day?"

Bria laughed. Nell had always been the caretaker of their group. Not surprising since she'd wanted to be a nurse. "Yes."

While Nell and Elise had taken each day one at a time, Bria still focused on the future. But it was with a feeling of impending doom, as she waited for the next bad thing to happen. That was all she knew, given her mom took off when she was two and her dad preferred chasing his latest get-rich-quick scheme to raising his own daughter. At least Aunt Elise had been there for Bria.

"I am tired, but that's normal for the birthday sale." She hadn't seen Nell in a few days, but being an RN gave her some kind of sixth sense. Her friend would know if she was untruthful. "But business is booming, so it's worth it. I can rest later."

"You better," Nell added without missing a beat. She ate a chocolate mini cupcake. "Yum. Looks like you're not close to running out yet."

"Missy has been baking since before sunrise." Bria had sent Sheridan back to help earlier. "I don't know how she does it. As soon as we run low on any flavor, a new tray comes out."

"That's Missy for you." Nell tilted her head. "Oh, you've got Elise's mixtape going."

Bria nodded. "A blast from the past."

"Elise always claimed we had no taste when it came to real music." Selena's forehead creased. "Is this the Bee Gees?"

"Andy Gibb," Nell answered. "I know that because my mom and Elise had big crushes on him."

A memory popped into Bria's head. Elise and Charlene had attended a concert in Oregon. "Rick Springfield, too."

Nell nodded. "I've been hearing many of her Elise stories this week."

"Charlene mentioned a few things this morning when she stopped by." Bria had been grateful to hear how Butterscotch was doing. Elise had thought her cat would prefer living in a house with more room than a condo. "It's so great seeing you both. I'm sorry I was out of it on Saturday. Days have blurred into each other. I'm not sure if that's because of tiredness or self-preservation."

"A combination of both, and no apology is necessary." Selena used her life coach podcast voice. "You can't rush grief, but these first weeks may be foggy as you deal with the business side of death."

Bria sighed. She couldn't help it. "I have an appointment with Mr. Carpenter tomorrow about my aunt's will."

"Wait." Selena's nose crinkled. "Wasn't Mr. Carpenter the stooped-over lawyer with white hair who came in right before closing time to try to get discounts on his cupcakes since they'd just be thrown away?"

"That was the elder Mr. Carpenter," Nell explained. "His son, Marc, took over when his dad retired, and now his grandson, Elias, works there, too."

"Are you ready for the appointment?" Selena asked Bria.

No, because it'll make everything seem more permanent. As if a funeral wasn't enough... "I'm getting there. I know I'll have things to do for the estate." Bria's stomach churned. "It's one of those things I have to get over, so I can move on to the next thing."

"There's no rush." Selena's voice was gentle. "You have time."

"I'm leaving on Sunday," Bria countered.

"It's only Monday," Selena teased.

"True." Bria had no idea how Selena made common sense sound like a nugget of gold. But then again, that explained why the woman was rich and famous. People soaked up every word she said. Those who followed Selena and put what she taught into action provided amazing testimonials about their successes. "I'll try not to stress."

Nell chuckled. "You're always stressed."

Selena whipped out her phone. "I'll send you a link to one of my guided meditations. Do it first thing in the morning and see if it helps."

"Oh, great idea," Nell agreed.

"Thanks." Bria didn't know if listening to her friend's voice would do anything, but it couldn't hurt. The line of customers was about to reach the door again. She didn't want people forced out onto the sidewalk. "I'd love to catch up, but I can't right now. Let me take your orders. I'll try to sneak away for a few minutes after that."

"I have a better idea." Nell's eyes sparkled. "Why don't we get together for dinner? You and Missy will be too tired to cook."

"I would love that." Dinner with old friends would be better than heating up food from her fridge. "Thanks. Are you free, Selena?"

"I was thinking of driving home, but Logan knows I wanted to catch up with you guys." She typed on her phone. "Do you think Juliet would want to join us?"

"I'll text her. Does seven o'clock work?" Nell asked.

As Bria nodded, her chest filled with warmth. "It'll be like old times."

With a nod, Selena glanced at the wall of photos. "A Cupcake Posse reunion."

Aunt Elise would have loved that, especially on her birthday. *If only she were here…*

Emotion tightened Bria's throat. She swallowed. "I'm in, but Missy might have plans."

Nell made a face. "Seriously? I love Missy, but her life revolves around this place, Sabine's animal rescue, and Jenny. I guarantee, if Missy has plans, she'll be able to change them."

Selena tilted her head. "And you know this how?"

"Because it's Missy," Nell answered without missing a beat. "She's the one constant in our lives. Always has been. She stayed in Berry Lake after all of us left."

"I haven't seen Missy since her wedding," Selena admitted. "Juliet, either."

Nell squeezed Selena's shoulder. "We have a lot of catching up to do tonight, then."

They did. Bria readied her order form. "Tell me what you want before the customers behind you mutiny."

"I'll take a mixed dozen." Selena peered into the display case. "No duplicates, please. Everything looks delicious."

Bria handed the order to a high school kid who had stopped in to help out. His name escaped her, but more than once, he teared up when a customer mentioned Elise. "How about you, Nell?"

"Six double chocolates and surprise me with the other six." Nell pointed to the display's second shelf. "I'd like a salted caramel and an unsweetened iced tea for here."

As Bria rang up the first order, the kid placed Selena's box on the counter.

Selena gave him a hundred-dollar bill. "Put the change in the tip jar. Everyone deserves it today."

Bria hadn't announced the total yet. "Selena—"

"Don't fight me on this, or the line might get rowdy."

Bria was too tired to argue. She took the change—well, bills—and added them to the jar. The tips would be split among everyone who'd worked today. "Thank you."

Nell paid next with her debit card before pulling out a few dollar bills and slipping them into the tip jar.

Bria sighed. "Your mom already dropped off the beautiful flowers. You don't have to do that."

"I want to." Then she added more money.

"Any requests for dinner?" Selena asked before Bria could say anything else.

"Carbs." The word burst out. Bria didn't care about eating healthy tonight. As long as she filled her stomach, she would be satisfied. But carbs would help. "The more, the better."

Nell tucked her wallet into her purse. The teenager handed Nell her cupcakes. "Anything else?"

"Wine?"

Selena raised her perfectly shaped eyebrows. "Now we're talking."

"No casseroles, please." Bria looked forward to a meal that she didn't have to heat or fix herself. "People have been so generous dropping off meals. They've been tasty and just what I need, but a break from casseroles and roasted chicken would be nice."

Nell tapped her chin. "How does Italian sound?"

"Delicious," Bria said. "Especially if there's garlic bread."

"There will be. And dinner is my treat," Selena said without missing a beat. "I'm not at home, so calories don't count. Which is why there will be dessert and wine with our pasta, too."

"Glad I'm not home, either." Bria's mouth watered thinking about the menu. But she would gladly eat another casserole if it meant spending time with her old friends. "Thanks."

Someone in the line cleared their throat.

Oops. Bria shouldn't keep customers waiting any longer than necessary. "See you tonight."

🧁 🧁 🧁

At a quarter after six, the last customer exited the shop. Bria quickly locked the front door before anyone else entered. With a deep exhale, she relaxed. Each muscle unwound after spending the day coiled tightly. Even her feet hurt less. The place was quiet except for the playlist that had looped all day. "We did it!"

Missy and Sheridan cheered. Of the various employees who'd filtered in throughout the day, only those two remained. The others had left with a thank-you and a free box of cupcakes. Tips would be sorted into envelopes and passed out at their next shift. That was what Elise had done, and Missy had agreed they should continue the tradition.

"Congrats on a fabulous birthday sale. I've only experienced these as a customer. I had no idea the madness behind the scenes." Sheridan hugged Missy and then went to Bria. "Do you need help cleaning up?"

"Nope. You've done more than enough." Bria motioned toward the door. "Go home. Or to wherever you're staying."

"Thanks." Sheridan grabbed her purse from beneath the cash register and slid the strap onto her shoulder. "Michael is waiting for me at the café. We're giving my mom and Max a break tonight."

"You were a lifesaver today." Missy hugged Sheridan again. "Thanks so much for your help."

"Don't save me a share of the tips, Bria." Sheridan picked up her box. "I didn't do this for the money. The cupcakes are reward enough. Michael will be thrilled I have dessert. And there's plenty to share with my mom and Max."

With that, Sheridan left.

"She's a hard worker." Bria was surprised how many hours she'd put in for free. "If she needs a job..."

"I'd hire her on the spot. But a job is the last thing she needs. Her fiancé is loaded. They've been traveling the world, going to art museums and eating at the best restaurants. He spoils her rotten, and she deserves every bit of it."

Bria wiped tables with a damp rag from the bleach-solution bucket. "Good for her."

Missy nodded. "The best part is how angry Deena gets whenever anyone mentions how well her stepdaughter is doing."

Thankfully, the woman hadn't come in today. "Deena DeMarco makes the evil stepmothers from movies and cartoons look like congeniality award winners. I feel so bad for Sheridan, but it sounds like things are working out for her."

Missy nodded. "Elise never liked Deena. I don't know why, but things worsened between them after Sheridan worked here in December. Elise tried to protect her as best as she could."

"That sounds like my aunt."

Missy cleaned the display case. "Elise would be thrilled over how well the sale went today."

"I think we broke a record."

"Given the number of cupcakes I baked and how few remain, I'm sure we did." Missy glanced around the table area. "Cleanup was quicker than I thought it would be. But the floors need to be mopped."

Bria nodded. "Not until after dinner."

Missy's nose scrunched. "Dinner?"

"The Posse is bringing food at seven."

She inhaled sharply before a wide grin spread across her face. "Everyone?"

"I don't know if that includes Juliet, but Nell was letting her know."

"We all haven't been together since my wedding—not counting Saturday—but we all weren't together there." The words flew from Missy's mouth. Her excited tone matched her sparkling eyes. "This is the perfect way for us to close out Elise's birthday. We were her favorite."

"She said that to each group."

"Yes, because I've been in many others over the years, but she told me the Posse held a special place in her heart."

"That makes me happy because all of you meant—mean—a lot to me. Even if we haven't stayed in touch the way we said we would."

"Same, but don't forget it was a different world then and we were different, too."

"We were oh-so young." Bria's gaze narrowed in on all the photographs. She rubbed her eyes. "I miss her."

"Me, too, but Elise left her mark on this place. That'll remain, even if she isn't with us." Missy touched her arm. "Your aunt was ready to go. She's no longer in pain."

If only Bria had been ready for that. "I know."

"You have a lot to do this week, but when you're in San Diego, slow down and grieve. There's no timetable, but it'll be okay. Not tomorrow or next week. Maybe not for months or years, but eventually, the hurt won't stop you in your tracks, and the tears won't come as quickly."

"Thanks. I needed that." Bria wanted to feel normal again, but she had a feeling that might not happen. No matter how much time passed, the loss would always be there. "I'd invite you to San Diego, except Aunt Elise made you the manager and expected you to run this place."

Missy laughed. "That's okay. Two years ago, I went to Indigo Bay on the South Carolina coast for Jenny and Dare's wedding. That trip filled my vacation quota for the next ten years. I'm too much of a homebody to travel. I'm happy staying right here in Berry Lake."

"You've always wanted that."

She nodded. "This was where Rob and I planned to live when he left the Marine Corps. Though he would have hated living in his sister's backyard."

"Your guest cottage is adorable."

"The cats and I love it." Missy glanced at her apron. "I'm going to change out of these clothes."

"Do you need to run home?"

"I have stuff upstairs."

The second floor of the bakery had an apartment that Elise had converted into a storage area, employee lockers, a staff bathroom, and her office, which now belonged to Missy.

"There's time for a shower if you want. And please take the tip jar up," Bria said. "I'll push the tables together so we're ready when they arrive."

"I sure hope Juliet makes it tonight."

Bria had been so rushed this morning, so they hadn't spoken long. "Me, too."

A Cupcake Posse reunion was long overdue.

chapter seven

AS JULIET READ the text on her cell phone for the fourth time, dread replaced her initial excitement.

Nell: *Posse reunion tonight at 7!*
Nell: *Selena's bringing Italian food for dinner.*
Nell: *I'm taking care of drinks.*
Nell: *Cupcakes for dessert.*
Nell: *All you need to do is show up. Bria wants to see you. All of us do.*
Nell: *See you at the cupcake shop.*

Juliet wanted to see everyone. A few minutes chatting with Bria this morning hadn't been long enough, and she hadn't seen Selena in over a decade. Not in person, anyway. She'd watched several interviews with her, but that wasn't the same.

It was after six, and Juliet hadn't decided what she should do. The pan of moussaka was ready to go into the oven. The Greek dish was one of Ezra's favorites. She'd made it after upsetting him at the gallery. Though, her gut told her something was going on between him and Remy Dwyer that had nothing to do with art.

As Juliet's upper teeth sank into her lower lip, she stopped herself. That would ruin her lipstick, and if Ezra happened to arrive home, he would notice.

She glanced at the messages again. If she didn't plan on going, she should let Nell know.

I want to go.

The thought resonated through Juliet. She didn't ask for much these days—other than a kind word from her husband and time with her grandmother—but she wanted tonight with her former coworkers and friends.

Ezra hadn't called or texted to say he was working late, but he didn't always give her advanced notice. For all Juliet knew, she would end up stuck alone again, waiting for him to get home when she could be out with her friends.

That gave her an idea. Okay, a reason to call him.

I shouldn't need one to call my husband.

Juliet knew this, yet she found herself trapped with a verbally abusive husband. At times, she wondered if it would be better if he hit her. Then, her love for him would completely disappear, and she might find the strength to leave her comfortable—albeit unfulfilling—life.

Mustering her courage, she hit his number.

The phone rang. Once, twice…

"What do you need now, Juliet?"

She flinched. The way he snapped suggested he hadn't had a good day.

As long as he doesn't take it out on me.

"I want to know what time you'll be home." She hated how weak she sounded. His words didn't leave bruises and cuts on her skin, but they left scars—invisible ones she feared would never heal. "I made one of your favorites, but it takes an hour to bake."

His drawn-out sigh would power a hill full of windmills in the Columbia River Gorge. "I'm working late. I meant to text you, but I've been busy."

Yes!

"That's fine. I know how hard you work." She kept her voice neutral. "We can have what I made tomorrow."

"Whatever." He might as well have said *meh*, given his lack of… Well, anything except disdain for her.

"Since you won't be home, is it okay if I see Bria tonight?" Juliet held her breath.

"I thought I let you see her at the cupcake shop this morning?" That snappish tone returned.

Not the answer she wanted. "Only for a few minutes. She had customers to help."

"Is the house clean?" He spoke with a rush of impatience.

"Yes." She didn't hesitate to answer. The house was always clean because he expected no less. The one time she'd forgotten to dust a bookcase he'd nearly burst a blood vessel in anger.

Something tapped in the background. His pen against the desk? Unless the noise came from his brain working extra hard over whether or not to allow her to go out. "The kitchen?"

That was part of the house, but she kept herself from saying anything. "Yes."

The tapping continued as if he were searching for a reason to say no. "Laundry?"

"Folded." And then Juliet remembered. "Your shirts are ironed, too."

Silence filled the line. No more tapping, but a popular game show theme played in her mind.

"Then," he said finally. "I suppose you can go."

She fought the urge to cheer. "Thank you."

"I want you home when I get there."

"When will you be home?"

"Ten or eleven."

Yes. That gave her almost three hours.

"I'll be home by ten. Thank you." She wiggled her toes. "I hope you get lots of work finished tonight."

He hung up without replying. For once, Juliet didn't care. She typed a reply to Nell.

> **Juliet:** *I'll be there at seven.*
> **Nell:** *Great! See you soon.*

Anticipation made it impossible for Juliet to sit still. She kept glancing at the clock.

Time moved so slowly. The way it had since they'd relocated to Berry Lake from Los Angeles.

A year ago, returning to her hometown had sounded like a dream come true. Ezra thought Juliet should spend more time with her eighty-three-year-old grandmother, Penelope Jones, who owned the Huckleberry Inn on Main Street. That seemed so opposite to his plans for the future, but she'd missed her grandmother and friends.

Now, she wondered if they should have stayed in Southern California.

Ezra allowed her to visit her grandmother a few times a week, but she rarely saw Nell or Missy—her only two friends still living in town. Other than trips grocery shopping or appointments at the hair and nail salon, her husband wanted her to clean, cook, and wait on him—both to come home from work, and then once he was there.

They'd had a housekeeper in California, but he'd told Juliet she needed to contribute more to the household. What that meant was turning her into *his* maid. She never expected to live a real-life Cinderella story, only with Prince Charming as the villain and no forest creatures to help her clean.

It hadn't been like this before they moved, but now, Ezra treated her like his domestic staff with benefits. Thanks to his exacting standards, she lived in a pressure cooker, never knowing when things would boil over. Even when they traveled to Portland or Seattle for a work event, she wore clothes he picked out for her.

It was… infuriating.

Each time she brought up his controlling ways, he shot an IED of criticism her way. The heat-seeking precision of his words hadn't missed their mark in months. A person could only take so much.

You could leave him.

Except her life was comfortable, and no marriage was perfect. This was better than starting over at thirty-five with nothing. Besides, Juliet was all Grandma had left. She wouldn't disappoint the only person who still loved her by getting a divorce.

So what if her husband's views about marriage and his wife were out of date?

Juliet had *almost* everything she wanted in life. If she tried harder, she might convince him to see her as more than his housekeeper and cook. He might remember their first seven years together where every day had been more magical than the last.

Juliet checked her reflection in the mirror. Her blond hair fell to her midback. She'd spent an hour straightening it this morning before Ezra woke. He no longer liked the natural wave in her hair. With a skilled hand, she touched up her makeup and made sure her nail polish hadn't chipped or cracked.

Pretty as a princess.

Except keeping that up was getting harder each day. She was thirty-five and didn't look it yet. But Ezra made her use a daily skin routine that took forever. He didn't believe her when she told him good genes helped keep her looking young more than expensive facial and neck creams.

As she picked up her keys, she remembered what her grandmother had ingrained in her—never show up to an event empty-handed. Juliet grabbed a bottle of red wine from their cellar. This would go with Italian, but champagne would be better.

Tonight was a celebration.

A Posse reunion.

Oh, how she needed this.

Them.

She kept up with Missy when she visited the cupcake shop. Occasionally, she bumped into Nell, but the ER nurse kept in touch via text whether or not Juliet replied. Even though Juliet had only lived a couple of hours away from San Diego, she'd never met up with Bria. Selena, who'd always been a shooting star ready to launch, occupied her own universe, high above the rest of them, living the dream she'd shared when they were younger.

The only difference?

Selena hadn't married a billionaire but a hockey player, who adored her, with a multimillion-dollar contract.

Juliet half laughed. *Rough life.*

But she would love to trade places if only for a day—or a few hours—to see what being so adored felt like.

A few minutes later, she parked on Main Street. Most everything except the café was closed. Once Labor Day hit, businesses shut down earlier because the tourist season was over.

The handwritten *Closed* sign hung on the cupcake shop's door, but the lights were on inside. Three women stood around tables pushed together.

It was like old times. Elise had always locked the door at closing and then unlocked it right before everyone was set to arrive.

A weird shiver ran through Juliet. She'd grown up with these women, yet part of her wanted to turn around, get in her car, and drive home. Even though only a dark, empty house waited for her. That made no sense when she'd been looking forward to seeing everyone.

Stop being ridiculous.

Ezra would tell her that if he were here.

With a deep breath, she forced her feet to move and entered the place that had been her second home years ago. The music caught her attention. It was the same that had played earlier in the day. "Hello, everyone."

Bria greeted Juliet with a hug. "I wanted to do this earlier, but the counter was in the way."

"I'm glad it's not now." She squeezed tightly for herself and for Elise, who'd adored her niece. When Juliet let go, she handed over the bottle of wine. "Nell told me she was taking care of drinks, but I wanted to bring something, too."

Missy laughed. "A Penelope-inspired action."

"Guilty," Juliet admitted. "But if she hears about tonight, and we know she will, my grandmother will ask what I brought."

Bria showed everyone the wine. "This will go perfectly with dinner."

"And wine is a huge step up from the lemonade or iced tea we used to drink when we had dinner here," Missy reminded them.

"Selena and I were old enough to drink, but Elise wouldn't let us buy you guys alcohol." Nell's gaze appeared unfocused. "Remember when Penelope stopped by one of our dinners to give us an etiquette lesson?"

Bria's eyes widened. "Oh, yes. How could I forget? She wanted to make sure us heathens didn't make Berry Lake look bad when we set off for college, but she scared me."

Missy nodded. "She didn't want people to think Berry Lake was full of unmannered hussies."

Laughter exploded through the shop.

"Unmannered hussies!" Nell rubbed her eyes. "That was it."

Juliet nodded. "I'm sure she called us heathens at one time."

"I'm sure she did." A thoughtful expression formed on Missy's face. "But I must admit some of your grandmother's lessons came in handy over the years."

Juliet appreciated hearing that. Penelope Jones wasn't the give-cookies-and-milk-to-the-grandkids type. She was an elegant and refined East Coaster who'd ended up in the Pacific Northwest because of her husband's real estate investments. But she'd made the most of it. She'd single-handedly put Berry Lake on the map with her inn and the annual Huckleberry Festival she founded.

Not all appreciated her grandmother's lessons or advice, but the woman's heart had been ripped out and flattened by her children, one of whom had been Juliet's father. That was where her hardness and tough love, I-don't-want-you-to-screw-up-your-life-like-your-parents stance came from. Sure, it would've been nice to have a softy for a grandma, but in Juliet's eyes, her grandmother was her hero. Without her, she wouldn't have had the guts and the money to move to Los Angeles after college. That was why Juliet never wanted to disappoint her grandmother the way everyone else had.

"I took Penelope's lessons to heart." Nell nodded. "Of course, if I ever forgot one, my mom reminded me."

Bria motioned to the bouquet on the counter. "Charlene dropped off those flowers this morning."

"The bouquet is beautiful." The flowers looked even prettier than when Juliet had seen them earlier. "Your mom did a lovely job with the arrangement."

"She misses Elise," Nell admitted. "But now that the funeral is over, I fear her attention will be back on my sisters and me. She already wants me to meet the new vet when he moves to town."

"Sheridan mentioned him to me today." Missy raised her glass of wine. "I'm happy to let you have him."

"No, thanks. He's all yours." Nell scrunched her face. "I'll never date another doctor. It doesn't matter if they treat people or animals. Not doing that again."

Juliet winked at the only other single person there. "Then, that leaves you."

"Not me." Bria held up her hands as if to ward off vampires. "I'm leaving town on Sunday. Besides, Charlene took Butterscotch, so I don't have a pet."

"Selena is married and petless," Nell said.

"I'm out." Juliet waved her left hand in the air. Colorful prisms from the diamond engagement ring shot around the room. "The new vet will just have to do without one of the Posse. His loss."

The door opened.

As Selena Tremblay entered with bags in both hands, a hush fell over the room. It had been that way when they were younger, too. She was an inch shorter than Juliet's five-five, but Selena carried herself as if she were the Queen of the Amazons. That might be how she'd been named the "Queen of the Internet."

As far as Juliet knew, this was the first time Selena had returned to town since Missy's wedding. But that didn't surprise anyone. Selena had been vocal about leaving town and not looking back.

No one blamed Selena for saying that, given her upbringing. She'd been poor—dirt poor. Her family had lived on a dirt lot outside of town in a double-wide trailer. But that hadn't stopped her from dreaming big and wanting to do better.

Both her parents had dropped out of high school and tried to convince Selena to do the same so she could work a full-time minimum-wage job and bring home money. She hadn't. Instead, she attended community college and then transferred to Central Washington University, where she graduated with honors and student loans.

Selena had always been pretty, but the hand-me-downs that never fit right, home haircuts, and cheap makeup, if any, hid her true beauty. But all of them had recognized it.

Now, she was—in a word—perfection.

No wonder the woman made millions as a life coach extraordinaire. Selena T had a charm—a magnetism—that was palpable.

Juliet's stomach burned. She shifted her weight between her feet, feeling underdressed for the first time in... forever. She wished she could have an ounce of Selena's confidence.

It's not a competition.

Whereas her husband believed everything was, including when they were in bed together.

Don't think about him.

Selena set the bags on the table. "My favorite women in the world are in this room. Look at us all."

Missy's face glowed. "We're all grown up."

"Only some of us," Nell quipped.

Hugs followed with everyone talking over one another, like old times.

Nell whistled. "We have all night to catch up. Why don't we eat before the food gets cold?"

Missy winked. "Yes, Mom."

Juliet went to the table and removed the food from the bags. She opened containers of ravioli, chicken fettuccini, spaghetti, mini pizzas, calzones, garlic bread, and salad. The scents of basil and tomato made her stomach grumble. Next, she set out the paper plates and plastic utensils. "We have quite the buffet for five of us."

A regular person would have shrugged. Not Selena. "A Cupcake Posse reunion requires lots of food, and I wasn't sure what everyone ate. I skipped the lasagna because I didn't want anything that resembled a casserole."

"Thank you." Bria gave her a thumbs-up. "Everything smells delicious."

"My stomach's doing backflips," Missy said.

Nell shook her head. "That's what happens when you skip lunch."

Fifteen years later, Juliet found comfort in the way Nell still looked after everyone because she no longer felt like the same rising college senior, dreaming about being an actress and living happily ever after.

Juliet surveyed the table. The bottle of wine she'd brought was there, but no cups. "All we're missing is the beverage service."

Nell snickered. "You sound like my mom or your grandmother."

"What can I say?" Juliet aligned the paper napkins. "Us hostesses speak the same language."

Bria carried two open bottles of wine and a liter of sparkling water tucked under her arm. "I need to grab cups."

Missy bolted into the back and returned with plastic ones. "I've got them."

Soon, everyone had their plates and cups full.

"I wasn't sure if we'd ever do this again." Missy's gaze traveled around the table. "It's great to have everyone back together."

Except one person was missing. That was the elephant in the room—er, cupcake shop.

No one said anything, causing the atmosphere to change, thicken.

Juliet needed to fix that. "Elise would have loved seeing us together. She loved the Posse. Part of that was having Bria be a part of the group, but Elise told me we were different from the others."

Nell nodded. "She told me that's because we listened to what she had to say."

"Cupcakes are better than men," they said in unison.

As if on cue, each of them raised their glasses.

"To Elise," Juliet said.

"To Elise," the other women repeated.

"She visited me in Seattle a few times." Selena took another slice of garlic bread. "She gave the best advice, especially when I was starting my business. My husband, Logan, was supportive, which I needed, and I bounce ideas off him all the time, but he makes millions playing a game, so it wasn't the same. Whenever I hit an income threshold, I called and celebrated with Elise. I wouldn't be where I am without her."

"This morning, Sheridan told me Elise should have named this place Cupcakes and Counseling." Missy picked up a piece of garlic bread. "She's right. I sure got my share here."

Bria touched Missy's shoulder. "We all did."

Juliet remained quiet. Elise hadn't liked Ezra. She'd offered to help her with anything she might need, but Juliet had turned her down, saying everything was fine. It hadn't been the right time. She doubted there *would* be a right time.

Bria sniffled.

"You okay?" Nell asked.

"Having all of you here is what I needed. Thanks." Bria set her fork on the plate. "We should have done this a long time ago. But I was so busy in San Diego—"

"What's your life like there?" Selena sipped her wine.

"It's good. I have a job I love, and a condo that's perfect for me. I finally have a place to call home."

Missy's brows creased. "What about Berry Lake?"

Juliet had been about to ask that same question.

Bria shrugged. "I consider this my hometown, but it was hard with my dad coming in and out of my life, sometimes taking me with him, then dropping me off with Aunt Elise again."

"I don't remember that," Missy admitted.

"Elise wouldn't let him take me after I started high school," Bria explained. "She said I needed stability for the next four years."

Nell nodded. "Elise knew best."

Juliet hated the past tense. "She did."

"I wasn't sure if I could manage the bakery for her." Missy stared over the lip of her cup. "But Elise kept telling me I was the right person for the job. And she was right. I love it."

"That makes you the lifer among us," Nell teased.

Missy grinned. "One of us had to be."

"Elise never liked Andrew." Nell twirled pasta around her fork. "We visited the cupcake shop each time we were in town, but nothing he did or said swayed Elise. In private, she told me I deserved better, but I was too blind to see it. I should have listened to her."

Juliet's breath caught in her throat. Elise had told her that Ezra wasn't the man Juliet thought he was and to be careful. She swallowed. "You were together for years, right?"

"Ten years too long," Nell joked, but the hurt shone in her eyes. "My mom had told everyone I was going to marry a doctor, and I'm not sure she's over that."

"Typical Charlene," Missy muttered under her breath.

Nell nodded. "Now, she just wants me married. It doesn't have to be a doctor. Any guy who is breathing."

"I can introduce you to some of Logan's teammates," Selena offered. "Hockey players are so hot."

"Especially if they have all their teeth," Missy teased.

Selena raised her glass at Missy before turning her attention on Nell. "I enjoy living in Seattle. It rains more there, but it's a cosmopolitan city. The top hospitals in the Northwest are located there. You could find a job easily."

"Thanks, but I'm happy being single and living here."

"If that changes, you know who to call." Selena took another sip of her wine. "So, Juliet, what have you been up to these days?"

The question made her squirm. "I got married when I was twenty-three. Ezra and I lived in Los Angeles and then moved to Berry Lake last year so I could spend more time with my grandmother. I don't have a job, other than taking care of my husband."

Nell refilled her wineglass. "That's a full-time job with overtime, according to my mom."

"It depends on the man," Selena said.

"Ezra is high maintenance, but I... I love him."

"You got that happily ever after you always wanted," Bria said.

"Yes." The word came out a little too quickly. Especially when it didn't feel that way to Juliet. She thought happily ever after meant more, and there'd be more emphasis on the happy part. But at least she was with her friends again. That counted for...

A lot.

"I've missed you all." Bria's voice cracked. "I'm sad it took Aunt Elise's death to bring us together, but I don't want to lose track of you again."

"I agree," Selena said. "We should have an annual retreat or girls' weekend."

"I'm in." Nell finished her slice of garlic bread.

"That would be amazing." If Ezra allowed Juliet to go. She would have to find a way to convince him.

"Once everything is settled with the cupcake shop, I'm in," Missy said.

Bria nodded. "I just need to build up my vacation time."

"Great." Selena raised her cell phone. "Let's use a group chat to keep in touch. And if anyone needs anything, including a shoulder to cry on, know we're here to help each other. That's what Elise would want. Agreed?"

Everyone said yes, but Juliet's sounded a tad more desperate than the others'.

Missy put her hand out. The other four did the same. "The Cupcake Posse forever."

"The Cupcake Posse forever," everyone repeated.

For the first time in years, Juliet didn't feel so all alone. Her eyelids prickled, and she blinked. Tears would mess up her makeup and draw questions from Ezra. But this—these women—might be the lifeline she needed.

☕ chapter eight ☕

TUESDAY MORNING, BRIA sat in the lawyer's office full of dark wood and leather furniture and books— shelves of them. Framed diplomas hung on the wall behind the wide mahogany desk. The smell reminded her of a library except for the scent of coffee from the cup she held. In the hallway, muted voices sounded.

Is that her aunt's attorney, Marc Carpenter?

A few minutes ago, his assistant had led her to the office, brought her a coffee, and said he would be in shortly.

Bria didn't mind waiting. After sleeping through her alarm clock, she assumed she would be late for their meeting. For once, her need for punctuality hadn't sent her into a panic, because last night had been the best night of sleep she'd had in weeks. She had her friends to thank.

She enjoyed catching up with everyone. They'd filled their stomachs and emptied the wine bottles. The five of them might be older, and they weren't the same as they'd been years ago, but they'd picked up right where they left off. The food had been delicious, but the company had been better.

The Cupcake Posse forever.

This time, they would stay in touch. Bria had promised to do her part because she wanted to see them again. No matter where they met—in Berry Lake or somewhere else.

A clock hung on the wall. Each tick of the second hand echoed in the office.

A glance at the door showed a slight crack, but no one was in the hallway.

She adjusted her position in the wingback chair, but she couldn't get comfortable. It didn't take a psychology degree to know why.

She didn't want to let her aunt go. Oh, wishing for Aunt Elise wouldn't bring her back, but Bria wanted to cling to what she could for now.

Who am I kidding?

She wanted to run out of the office, bury her head against her aunt's pillow, and pretend the past weeks—okay, three years—had all been a nightmare. The reading of a will, or whatever this meeting was called, sounded so…

Final.

Permanent.

Yes, Aunt Elise was dead.

Nothing would change that.

Even if Bria would give everything she had to bring her aunt back for five more minutes.

Five seconds.

But being in this office made her aunt's death suddenly more real.

And she hated that because she wasn't ready to move on.

The door behind her hit the wall.

Bria waited for Marc Carpenter to greet her, but he said nothing. She glanced over her shoulder and did a double take.

Blinked.

But *he* was still there.

Her throat tightened. "Dad?"

"Hey, baby doll." Brian Landon kissed the top of her head.

He was fifty-eight, but he kept his hair dyed, worked out, and used Botox on his facial wrinkles so he appeared younger. His suit was top-of-the-line and tailored, which fit his fake-it-till-you-make-it motto perfectly. When Bria had been in college, she glimpsed his credit card statement. Seeing a six-digit amount owed had rocked her world. Okay, it had made her sick. She'd thrown up, twice. She'd never understood his finances since he didn't have a job at a company. But with some accounting and business courses completed, she realized how he leveraged his lifestyle, and that her aunt had been the one supporting Bria financially.

He plopped into the chair next to her. "You doing okay?"

Dumbfounded, Bria had no idea how to answer him. "Why are you here?"

"For the reading of the will. Marc Carpenter reached out to me."

That surprised her, but she and her dad were her aunt's only relatives. Aunt Elise might have left him something because he was family, but Bria couldn't imagine what since they weren't close. "Why weren't you at the funeral?"

"I had a pressing matter." His voice remained flat, with no sign of emotion, including regret.

She clutched her hands around the arms of the chair, digging her fingers into the leather. "More pressing than your sister's funeral?"

He shrugged before adjusting his already-straight tie. "We said our goodbyes the last time I saw Elise. She's dead, so she doesn't care who was there or not."

"*I* cared," Bria blurted. "I would have preferred not dealing with everything on my own."

"I'm sure you handled everything well. You always have."

That didn't make her feel better. Missy and Charlene had been around, but Bria had thought her dad would show up. "It would have been nice to have you there."

He wiped his palms on his pants. "I'm here now."

Bria didn't understand why. She and her aunt had once joked about him chasing after the proverbial pot of gold at the end of the rainbow. That proved true with his last venture, involving a sunken ship rumored to carry gold coins somewhere off the coast of Florida. His blowing off his sister's funeral completed the caricature.

He followed one get-rich-quick scheme after another. Over the years, a few had paid off, which kept him going. The same way casinos kept slot machine players pushing the button until their credits disappeared.

But knowing a sunken treasure or whatever he'd been doing was more important hurt Bria's heart. She shouldn't be disappointed; she'd never been a priority to him. Still, she'd clung to a sliver of hope. That was all she had left when it came to her father.

His gaze narrowed. "You look tired."

"I am." Bria shouldn't, but she had to ask. "Did your pressing matter get worked out?"

"Not exactly, but that happens. I'm working on something else."

He always said that. Her father had been trying to make a fortune since before she was born. After her mother left when Bria was two, he'd become maniacal in his attempts to be wealthy. And over the years, nothing had changed. He'd gotten worse in his tunnel-vision pursuit of profit—one reason she'd spent more and more time with her aunt.

Bria could tick off the major events of her life he'd missed for work or some deal that would change everything. Sure, he'd claimed to do this to provide for her future, but she would have preferred he attend her high school and college graduations, or spend Thanksgiving and Christmas with her and Aunt Elise. As the years passed, his calls came less often, and his promises remained unfulfilled. Now, they rarely spoke, and she didn't mind. He'd disappointed her too many times for her to want him back in her life.

Marc stepped into his office. "Sorry I'm late. I got stuck on a conference call with my partner, who happens to be my son."

Bria remembered Elias Carpenter, who had been a brainiac in high school. He'd also been captain of the debate team.

"You do important work, and your time is valuable." Her father leaned back in his chair. "So, why don't you cut to the chase and tell us what Elise left me?"

His tone was calculated, greedy, and rude.

Bria flinched. Once again, her father had proven what mattered to him. It wasn't her or his sister. "How do you know she left you anything?"

He smirked. "If I weren't a beneficiary, Marc wouldn't have invited me to this meeting. So, tell us what's in the will."

"I'll get to the will shortly. There's no rush." Marc glared at her father.

The two men were around the same age, but the attorney was the kind of man her father strived to be—successful, respected, and well-off. She'd only met the attorney a few times, but he'd shown more kindness and compassion in those few minutes than her father had in years.

"How are you, Bria?" Marc asked.

"Tired and trying to figure things out." She knew Elise and Marc went way back to when they were kids. People might leave Berry Lake when they were eighteen to head off to college or the city, but many returned years later. "The house is so quiet, especially with Butterscotch at Charlene's house."

"Be grateful you didn't get stuck with that fat orange cat." Her dad sneered. "Not sure why Elise wanted a pet when she spent so much time at the cupcake shop."

Bria bit her tongue. Butterscotch was one in a long line of cats who'd come before. Her aunt had a type when it came to felines—orange and big. Though the "big" might have come from the beloved cat being spoiled by his devoted owner.

Marc opened a manila legal-sized folder sitting on his desk. "My wife stopped by the cupcake shop yesterday and bought a dozen at the birthday sale. She said it was as if Elise were still there."

With a nod, Bria blinked to keep the tears at bay. "Missy did a fabulous job running it."

"You both did her proud," Marc said.

"Thank you." Bria's voice cracked.

Marc turned his attention to her father. "When did you arrive, Brian?"

"I flew into Portland last night and drove here this morning. I didn't want to hold up the proceedings."

"That was thoughtful." Marc shuffled through the papers in the folder. "I'm sure Bria needs to return to the cupcake shop, so I won't draw this out any longer. Elise's final requests were simple. She updated the will two months ago."

Bria straightened. She must have done that after seeing how well Missy was managing the cupcake shop. "I'm sure she had her reasons."

Marc's eyes widened. "Didn't she speak to you about the changes?"

Bria shook her head.

"That's odd." As Marc pressed his lips together, he steepled his fingers. "She told me she would. Unfortunately, I can't tell you what she said."

The lawyer seemed to make a big deal out of whatever had been changed, especially if her aunt had left the cupcake shop to Missy. But if that were the case, why wasn't Missy at the meeting?

Bria's stomach churned.

Her dad shifted in his chair. "Can we get on with this?"

"There's lots of legalese. I have copies I'll give both of you, but here's the part you want to hear, Brian." Marc held up a page and read. "One hundred percent of my personal assets, which includes a house, vehicle, investments, and bank account, go to my niece, Bria Landon."

She didn't care about Elise's stuff, but Bria appreciated her aunt doing that. What really mattered was for the cupcake shop to keep going for Missy, the other employees, and the town.

"Your aunt wanted you to be her personal representative for the estate." Marc picked up a pen. Not a blue- or black-capped ink pen, but a fancy one made of wood. "Do you accept the assignment?"

Aunt Elise had mentioned *this* to Bria. She had to go to the county courthouse in Goldendale to be appointed. That was also where the paperwork for the estate would be filed. "Yes, I accept."

Her dad leaned forward. "Keep reading."

Marc frowned. "This isn't a race."

"No, but you charge by the hour," her dad countered.

With a not so subtle eye roll, Marc returned his attention to the page. "I leave fifty percent of the Berry Lake Cupcake Shop, which includes the Main Street building, equipment, and other business assets, to my niece, Bria Landon."

Will Missy get the other half, even if she isn't here for the reading?

Oh, that would be perfect, after what they'd discussed and planned over the past weeks. Missy would continue to run the cupcake shop, and everything would continue as Aunt Elise had wanted.

"I leave fifty percent of the Berry Lake Cupcake Shop, which includes the Main Street building, equipment, and other business assets, to my brother, Brian Landon."

What?

Bria didn't know if she'd said the word aloud. She didn't care. Her hands balled. "I don't understand."

"What's to understand? Your aunt wanted both of us to have the cupcake shop." Her dad slapped his palms together before hollering a cheer. "Elise did us right, baby doll. We're in the money now."

No. The word echoed in Bria's head.

Her fingernails dug into her skin.

This made no sense—none whatsoever.

Aunt Elise had loved her brother, but she'd given up on him, too. How could she not? He'd dumped his only child on her for weeks or months at a time. He also wanted nothing to do with the bakery. He'd never helped out once. Over the years, all he'd done was make fun of it and eat free cupcakes. Oh, except for the time he'd asked to use the bakery's building as collateral for a loan so he could invest in one of his "sure things." Elise had said no. A good thing, since that crazy scheme turned out to be illegal, and more than one person involved landed in prison.

Why would my aunt do this?

"There's more." Marc flipped to a new page.

Bria braced herself. Not that it could get any worse.

"If the two parties can't agree on business decisions regarding the Berry Lake Cupcake Shop, attorney Marc Carpenter will assign a mediator," Marc said. "The decision of the mediator shall be final. If one of the parties decides to relinquish his or her ownership in the Berry Lake Cupcake Shop, the other owner has first right of refusal."

A mediator?

Bria sat stunned. That told her Elise had thought about this decision. She'd known Bria and her father hadn't gotten along for years. But how would this partnership work when they both knew her father didn't care about the business? All he wanted was to make a fast buck.

"We won't need a mediator." Dollar signs shone in her father's eyes, reaffirming his only motivation in life—money. "This is unexpected, but I shouldn't be surprised. Elise was the best sister ever."

Bria cringed. "She was your only sister."

"Which makes her the best." Her dad rubbed his face. "This will make us rich, baby doll."

Of course, his mind went there. The inheritance was likely his most significant windfall in years. "I did Elise's books and taxes. She lived comfortably, but she wasn't rich."

"We're not Elise. There's the cupcake shop and the building. If we do things differently, we will make money. A whole lot of money."

Ugh. That was what Bria was afraid he would say. He acted as if Elise's death had been something good, not a tragedy.

"No." Bria used a firm tone in case the word itself wasn't strong enough. There had to be a way to get her father away from the cupcake shop. A diversion. Or give him a reason to sell his share to her. Well, if Bria could afford it. "This isn't a way for you to leverage a big payoff. The bakery was your sister's passion—her heart and soul—not a way to make a fortune."

"You're still grieving. Give it a couple of days." He treated her as if she were a child, but the last time they'd spent more than a weekend together had been when she was in eighth grade. "We'll talk in a day or two when your head is clearer."

Her jaw tensed. She parted her lips to keep from grinding her teeth. "Your sister is dead. The woman who was the closest thing I ever had to a mother is dead. It might take time for my head to clear."

"Then return to San Diego. That's where your life is," her father said in a nonchalant tone. "I'll deal with the cupcake shop. I can't buy you out, but perhaps Marc could arrange for you to give me power of attorney."

"I can." Marc fidgeted with the pen. "But that's Bria's choice." His tone implied *not yours.*

She wanted nothing more than to leave Berry Lake, but she couldn't. Elise had told her what she wanted with the cupcake shop—to have Missy run it and make the changes and upgrades they'd been planning before she got sick. Bria had no idea why Elise had changed her will or left her brother half of the bakery, but someone—namely Bria—had to protect the cupcake shop from her dad.

She would never leave her father to deal with the cupcake shop on his own. Forget having him do things by proxy or with a power of attorney. She didn't trust him—hadn't for over a decade.

"I have things to do as Elise's personal representative." She lifted her chin. "I'm here until Sunday. We'll have to figure out a plan before that."

"We can do that," her father agreed.

Of course, they could and would. What other choice did they have?

Her dad combed his fingers through his hair. The man might be two years away from sixty, but he squirmed like a six-year-old. "I'm staying at the Huckleberry Inn. I thought you'd prefer privacy during this time."

At least he made the right decision there. "Thank you."

"You have my number."

One she hadn't used in months other than to let him know Elise had died. Bria nodded.

"We'll set a date and time later." Her father didn't notice her unease. Instead, he stared at his phone.

So typical.

His attention was always focused on something else.

Was that why her mom left them so many years ago and never looked back?

All her life, her dad had only given Bria crumbs of his time and his attention. It hadn't been enough in the past. It wouldn't be enough now.

And don't even get me started about Aunt Elise.

Bria tried to understand why her aunt had done this. Tried and failed.

Marc handed each of them a stapled document. "These are your copies of the will to keep."

Bria clutched the document, not wanting to see the actual words the attorney had read. At least not yet. She needed time to process it all.

But no matter what the will said or what her aunt had done, Bria had promised her aunt to oversee her estate. And unlike her father, she never broke her promise.

She took a deep breath and then another. "So, what's my first step as the estate's personal representative?"

🧁 chapter nine 🧁

A S A LOCAL radio station played, Missy relished the stillness in the cupcake shop. A few customers had come in, but it was nothing like the chaos from yesterday. Most regulars had stocked up during the birthday sale. They wouldn't return for a few days or until next week. It was like this every year, and why she'd arrived an hour later than usual—sixty extra minutes of sleep made a huge difference—and hadn't baked the full inventory of products. Why let the cupcakes go to waste?

The day after the birthday sale had been a regular day off for her, but not any longer. She didn't mind. This place was her second home.

Standing at the front counter, she reviewed her notebook. It contained ideas for things Elise had planned on doing once she kicked cancer's butt again. Only she hadn't gone into remission for a second time. Now, it was up to Missy to make Elise's plans happen.

Missy closed her eyes, imagining how the shop would look once all the work on her list was finished. The faded paint would be bright and fresh. New tables and chairs would replace ones that always broke. A new menu board would hang behind her—one that featured not only the regular flavors but specials. They would try new recipes to see if any favorites or bestsellers arose.

Tingles raced through her.

This place was great, but soon, it would be... awesome.

They just needed to go slow and stay within budget.

Missy giggled. She sounded like Bria.

Whereas Nell sounded like a mom when she gave advice or a caution, Bria was in full-on accountant mode with what she said. She calculated the credits and debits, weighed the pros and cons, and analyzed the costs and profit. Figuratively, yes. But Missy wondered if Bria had a secret spreadsheet she used before making any decision. That was how thorough she was about everything.

Elise had needed her niece to keep the bakery profitable. Bria's favorite phrase might be "not in the budget," but when Elise had wanted to buy a day bed for the office so she had a place to rest—an unexpected expense not in the budget—Bria ordered one online and had it delivered and set up.

Missy hadn't reconciled her bank statement in years. She would also rely on Bria's accounting and money skills to take the bakery to the next level.

The bell over the door jingled.

Missy opened her eyes to see Bria in a pair of black pants and a pink button-up shirt with her auburn hair pulled back in a ponytail. "Hey."

Bria nodded, her gaze traveling around the cupcake shop as if she were avoiding making eye contact with Missy.

Uh-oh. Bria didn't look good, either.

Last night, her face had been flushed from laughter and wine. She hadn't stopped smiling. Now, her complexion was pale, her eyes troubled.

Concern gripped Missy. She closed her notebook and placed it beneath the counter. "Are you okay?"

Bria blew out a breath. "Not really."

"Sit." Missy went to the closest table and pulled out a chair. "I'll be right back."

Nell was better at nurturing people, and Juliet was the hostess with the mostest, but Missy had come a long way. Before Jenny fell in love with Dare, one of Missy's jobs as her assistant was to make sure the bestselling thriller author ate more than chocolate, drank more than caffeinated beverages, took breaks away from the computer, and slept in her bed during deadlines. Missy would never admit it aloud, but her niece was easier to babysit.

In the kitchen, Missy placed two cupcakes on plates, grabbed two napkins, and filled two cups with coffee. She put the items on a tray and carried it to the table. If the traffic pattern continued, she didn't expect another customer for thirty minutes. "Break time."

As Bria reached for a drink, her hand trembled.

Something must have happened—something terrible.

The worst thing had already happened—Elise dying. *So, what could it be?*

Missy wanted to ask. Questions sat on the tip of her tongue, waiting. But she hated when people pushed her to talk. She wouldn't do the same to Bria.

Instead, she studied her friend, who was a year older. Elise had called her niece the oldest teenager she'd ever met, and that had nothing to do with her age. Bria's childhood dream had been to find a good-paying job with benefits and buy a place as soon as she could afford one since the mortgage interest was deductible. No one was surprised when she became a CPA—talk about a recession-proof job—or made an offer on a foreclosed fixer-upper condo in her mid-twenties.

Bria peeled the paper liner from the cupcake, but she didn't take a bite. She sipped her coffee again.

During high school, Bria had been quiet, shy, and oh-so-smart. Kids begged to copy her homework. Others, especially the jocks, wanted her to tutor them. If teachers needed something done, they asked her. She was on time, responsible, and cautious. Bria wasn't a fan of surprises, spontaneity, and change, but she handled stress well. Elise's death had gutted Bria, but the only other time Missy had seen Bria so upset was at the end of her senior year when the boy she loved humiliated her.

Until today.

The fear in the depths of her eyes practically chilled the room.

So unlike the woman who'd returned to Berry Lake when Elise was first diagnosed with cancer and taken charge, making sure her aunt received the best care. That grown-up Bria was no longer the mousey smart girl. She was professional and confident. Vibrant and beautiful. Like Selena, Bria was living her dream life and had everything together.

Seeing her now, however, shook Missy to her core.

Bria set the cup on the table, removed a stack of papers from her purse, and tossed them on the table, barely missing the cupcakes. "I was at Marc Carpenter's office this morning."

"The meeting about Elise's estate."

"Yes." Bria's voice cracked. Tears filled her eyes, spiking her long eyelashes. "My aunt left equal shares in the cupcake shop to me and... my dad."

Huh? Elise never mentioned her brother. Missy had only met Mr. Landon a handful of times, which said a lot since she'd worked there for years. He hadn't been at the funeral, either. "I don't understand."

Bria sniffled. "Neither do I. My aunt never said a word about bringing my dad into this. She knew my dad and I are…"

"Estranged."

Missy's parents had disowned her when she married Rob after high school graduation instead of going to college. A few months later, her mom and dad moved without telling her where they were going, and she hadn't heard from them since. Not even after Rob died. But thankfully, the Hanfords had become her new family.

Bria nodded.

Okay, but Missy still didn't understand why Bria was so upset. Thinking she might inherit everything and making plans based on that assumption would be a shock. Still, the plans were in place—plans Elise had told them herself. They would need to discuss those plans with Mr. Landon and maybe change a few things, but he would want his sister's cupcake shop to succeed, right?

Missy must be missing something. She might as well ask. "What does this mean for the cupcake shop?"

And for me.

"I don't know, and that's the problem." Bria rubbed her eyes. "My dad sees his share of the inheritance as a windfall. A way to get rich."

Missy scratched her cheek. "With this place?"

"I told him that wouldn't happen with the bakery, but he says we don't have to run things as Elise did."

Missy gripped the edge of the table. "She's what made this place successful."

"I know, and I'm afraid he's not interested in the cupcake shop but the overall worth of the business."

"What's worth more than the bakery?"

"The building." Bria glanced around the shop. "Elise bought it when the town was nothing more than a stop for fishermen on their way to Berry Lake. She owns it free and clear. Given the prime location and the upstairs apartment, it's worth much more than the cupcake business."

Talons gripped Missy's heart and dug in deep. "You think he wants to sell…"

The rest of the words wouldn't come. She bit the inside of her cheek.

Without the cupcake shop, Missy would need another job. When she'd taken over for Elise, Missy had turned over her remaining tasks as Jenny's author assistant to Dare, who was able to work with little Briley around. Missy received a monthly DIC payment from the VA because of Rob's death during active duty, but she couldn't live on that. She had savings from the death gratuity the military paid and Rob's supplemental life insurance policy, but she planned to use that to move into a place closer to Main Street. She loved living with Jenny, but her sister-in-law had her own family now. They didn't need Missy living in the backyard's guesthouse and always being around. But if things changed or the cupcake shop ceased to exist, there weren't many jobs—if any—for bakers in Berry Lake, especially an untrained one.

"I don't know, but my dad goes from one get-rich scheme to another. This place turns a profit, but it won't make anyone rich."

Only comfortable and happy and secure.

Which was all Missy needed for herself and her cats. Tears pricked, but she wouldn't cry. Bria had lost her aunt and now this. Even though Missy had everything to lose if the cupcake shop closed, she would stay strong for her friend. The way she had for Elise.

Squaring her shoulders, Missy swallowed around the lump in her throat. "We'll figure this out. If we can't, we ask Nell, Juliet, and Selena for help. I have no idea why Elise did this."

"Marc said she changed her will a couple of months ago. She might have added my dad then. Did she mention anything to you?"

"No, but I have a notebook of ideas she and I brainstormed for this place. She told both of us what she wanted to see happen. She wouldn't have done that if she thought the place would close."

Right? Missy hoped she was right.

Bria wiped her eyes with the napkin. "You're right."

Thank goodness. Missy blew out a breath.

"My dad wants to discuss things. I couldn't today with the way I'm feeling, but tomorrow should work. I'm only here until Sunday. I can't put this off too long. I just…"

Missy touched her friend's hand. "What?"

Bria stared at the wall of photographs. "I thought I knew Elise, but I'm so confused by what she did. I'm sure Marc knows why, but he won't tell me."

Missy went over and hugged Bria. "Lawyer-client privilege. I saw it on a TV show."

"I forgot you watched those crime ones."

"I love them." Missy eyed the will. "Remember, Elise never did anything without a reason."

"True, but what was it? She changed the will a couple of months ago. If she added my dad then, that gave her plenty of time to tell me. Either by phone or in person. I was with her twenty-four seven those last three weeks."

"She was dying." Missy tried to be gentle, even though she felt betrayed, too. She'd given up her second part-time job with her sister-in-law to manage the cupcake shop full-time. Why had Elise asked Missy to take over if she would only end up jobless? As Bria said, it made no sense. "Your aunt might have forgotten to tell you."

Bria hung her head. "True, but she could have put it on the list she gave me or in a letter. Something. I feel blindsided."

The unflappable accountant looked it.

Missy's heart ached for her friend. There had to be a way to figure this out. She took a sip of coffee, barely tasting it. Something from another crime show popped into her mind. "Do you mind if I look at the will?"

"Go ahead. I haven't been able to read it."

She flipped through the will until she reached the page with signatures and the notary stamp. The familiar, sharp script sent grief slashing through her heart. That, however, wasn't the one she was looking for. It was the other two—the witnesses—she wanted to see.

One of those signatures blared from the page like a neon light. *Bingo.*

Missy turned the paper so Bria could read it. "Mr. Carpenter can't explain Elise's reasons, but perhaps this witness can." Missy pointed to the name.

Bria's lips parted. "Charlene Culpepper. She was my aunt's best friend. If anyone knew the reason for including my dad, Charlene would."

"Go see her."

Bria bit her lip. "Would you come with me? You have more to lose with this than I do."

Missy nodded. "Someone is coming in to work the lunchtime hours. We can go then."

🧁 🧁 🧁

At eleven thirty, Missy and Bria walked to the end of the commercial portion of Main Street. Few people were out, but it was a Tuesday in September, and the sky was overcast. Missy waved at Penelope, who stood on the porch of the Huckleberry Inn with a watering can in hand. Even with a full staff, the woman enjoyed taking care of the garden and potted plants.

Across the street from the Victorian sat a quaint cottage with a white picket fence. A small sign that read *Events by Charlene* hung on a post.

Bria touched her purse with the will inside. "I hope Charlene knows the reason."

"Me, too." Missy used the brass-plated knocker against the front door. The sound boomed. "I wasn't expecting that."

As the door opened, a wave of floral perfume surrounded them.

"Oh, girls." Charlene placed her hand over her heart. She wore a burnt-orange skirt with a matching jacket. A strand of pearls graced her neck, but she was barefoot. "What a lovely surprise to see you."

"We wanted to ask you a question about my aunt." Bria pressed her lips together. "If you have time."

Charlene motioned them inside. "I always have time for the two of you."

The inside smelled like an entire bottle of Charlene's perfume had been sprayed around. More likely, the event planner was working with flowers. It had smelled that way when Missy and

Rob came here to ask Charlene to help them with their wedding. They'd both been so nervous and clung to each other's hand, afraid Charlene would say no since they didn't have much money, but they'd received an enthusiastic yes. The wedding had been lovely, and Missy had wondered if Charlene lost money on the event. The town busybody was also kindhearted, even if few saw that side.

"You just missed Selena." Charlene sat on a Queen Anne chair upholstered in a gray damask fabric. Behind her in the dining room, wedding invitations covered a large table, and a rainbow of ribbons laid next to them. "She stopped by on her way out of town. Please sit."

Missy did. Bria took a seat on the floral print love seat. Charlene crossed her legs at the ankles. "What's your question?"

Bria hesitated.

"Go ahead," Missy urged. They both needed an answer, but for different reasons.

"I met with Marc Carpenter this morning to discuss Aunt Elise's will." Bria removed the document from her purse. "My father was there."

"Brian is in town?" Charlene sounded surprised.

Bria nodded. "He arrived this morning."

Charlene rolled her eyes. "Not in time for the funeral."

"No." Bria's hands trembled.

Missy touched her friend's arm. "You okay?"

"Yes." Bria inhaled deeper than before. "My aunt changed her will two months ago. I have no idea what the change was, but my dad and I are the beneficiaries of the cupcake shop. I don't understand why my aunt left half to my father."

Charlene stared at the will, but she said nothing.

Bria's eyes gleamed.

Missy knew that look all too well. Tears would fall soon. Time to step in. "Both of us are confused right now. Hurt, too. We know what Elise wanted for the cupcake shop and at no time did she mention Mr. Landon, so we want to understand her reason for what she did."

Bria blinked. "I honestly hoped my aunt had left the cupcake shop to Missy. But now I can't help feeling betrayed by the one person I thought loved me unconditionally. If you know anything, would you please tell us why Elise left the cupcake shop to my father and me?"

"Elise loved you, Bria. You, too, Missy." Charlene grabbed a box of tissues from a side table and placed it in front of Bria. "She knew the cupcake shop would be in good hands with you two."

Bria sniffled. "Then why did my dad get half?"

Charlene clasped her hands on her lap. Her posture was ramrod straight. "Elise was worried about you. After she died, you would only have Brian."

"So?" Bria sounded defensive. "He's made his priorities clear for years."

"Yes, but Brian is still your father, and he felt the same way Elise did. A couple of months ago, he called her with his concerns. He suggested she leave the cupcake shop to both of you. That way, you would have something in common, something to work on together, so you could become closer. Your aunt did this *for* you, not to hurt you."

Bria's jaw dropped. "My dad *knew*?"

Charlene nodded. "As I said, it was his idea."

Bria buried her face in her hands. "He acted surprised today. But all this time, he knew what Aunt Elise had done because he'd asked. Yet, he still didn't come to her funeral."

Missy placed her arm around Bria. "I'm so sorry."

She slumped. "I can't believe he did this to his sister. My father doesn't care about the cupcake shop. He only wants money."

Charlene tsked. "He'll be disappointed, then. The cupcake shop isn't worth that much. But please, don't underestimate him. You are his only child. He may surprise you."

Bria's lower lip quivered.

Missy would help her out. "I don't know how much Elise mentioned to you about the cupcake shop, but the business isn't worth that much compared to the building."

Charlene inhaled sharply. "Brian wouldn't sell—"

"He wants a big payoff," Bria interrupted. "He said so in Marc's office."

Charlene shook her head. "Brian knows how important the shop was to your aunt."

"I wish that were the case." Bria sighed. "If what he implied at the meeting is true, we'll end up fighting each other over what to do with the bakery."

"Oh, no. That wasn't supposed to happen. Elise believed him when he told her this would bring you together, but she may have miscalculated." Charlene rubbed her fingers against her thumb. "I told her to be careful. That she couldn't get her way from the grave, but she wouldn't listen."

"She never did," Missy muttered.

Charlene nodded. "Elise didn't, but she was so happy when he reached out to her. She trusted Brian to do the right thing."

Bria scoffed. "He's never done it before."

"This time, Elise wanted him to do it for you. If she believed he would want to sell, she would have never changed her will.

That's why she added him as a beneficiary—because she was so worried about you being on your own."

"I'm not alone. I have friends." She squeezed Missy's hand. "Here and in San Diego."

"Yes, but no family. Elise wanted your father to be more involved in your life. She had good intentions to go along with his idea, I promise you."

"Good intentions won't help Missy or the other employees if my father wants to sell the building. If he and I can't agree on what to do, a mediator will decide the fate of the cupcake shop."

"Marc had her add that. Elise hadn't believed you'd need one. She was sure this would work."

"I wish she would've told me herself."

Missy nodded.

"And what would your reaction have been?" Charlene pinned Bria with a stern gaze. "You would have been upset and tried to change her mind."

Bria straightened. "Yes, because that would have been the smart thing to do if my aunt wanted her business to thrive."

"I agree." Missy didn't want to argue, but she also wanted to support Bria. "It's like her dad is trying to pull a fast one."

Bria nodded. "He already did. My dad scammed his own sister."

Missy rubbed circles on Bria's back. "Talk to him and find out his intentions. This might be a big misunderstanding, and you're worrying for nothing."

Charlene gave them an encouraging smile. "I agree," she said. "Brian Landon is many things, but he would never con his sister."

Bria sighed. "I hope not."

Her defeated tone, however, suggested she had doubts.

Anger seethed inside Missy, but she kept herself under control for Bria's sake. "He has questions to answer."

"Yes." Charlene picked something off her skirt. "But before you let your emotions spiral out of control and go all worst-case-scenario thinking, allow your dad to explain his side."

What Charlene said made sense, and Missy agreed. But that didn't stop a dark cloud of doubt from squashing her.

She prayed Bria had misunderstood her father, and they would laugh about this tomorrow.

If not, Missy's job—her *future*—would be completely up in the air. Just like after Rob's death. And she didn't want to go back to that uncertainty.

She couldn't.

☕ chapter ten ☕

SELENA PARKED HER car in front of Juliet's house and sent Logan a text, telling him she needed to make one more stop before heading home and would let him know when she left Berry Lake. He didn't reply, but she hadn't expected him to. He was at practice, most likely on the ice.

With a yawn, she slid out of the SUV. She should've slept better after Caledonia fired her new hire and publicly apologized for the "misunderstanding" about the stolen files. Negative posts had also dwindled to a stream of avatars either behind on the news or trolling her. But that hadn't stopped Selena from tossing and turning, which was the reason for her visit now.

An elegant walkway split the manicured lawn into two carpets of green. Neatly trimmed shrubs were artfully placed around the yard. The garage and driveway must be on the side or in the back. She saw neither from the front.

Selena's heels clicked against the pavement. She quickened her step, driven by worry over her friend.

Last night, Juliet had seemed off—her mannerisms, even her voice, were stilted. She'd said the right things, but what she left out bothered Selena.

She'd last seen Juliet at Missy's wedding. Juliet Jones had glowed, bubbling over with excitement about her new job as a theme park princess. It was how she'd been in high school, too, except there'd been something more—contentment, as if she were finding her place finally.

Last night, Juliet hadn't been like that. She'd changed and not in good ways. She was still gorgeous. Her clothes were no longer from big box stores purchased on a day-trip shopping excursion to Portland, but not even the designer label pieces and expensive shoes hid the truth. Juliet Jones Monroe was no longer the vibrant woman Selena remembered.

She wanted to know why.

She studied the house located on the corner of a street lined with custom homes on large lots. The housing development hadn't existed when she lived in Berry Lake. If it had, this would have been the prime trick-or-treating spot. There'd been a few wealthy folks in town, but the place had grown as a vacation spot for those who kept a second home there and as a full-time residence for those intrigued by small-town life or wanting to get away from the city. A few, like Juliet and Nell, had returned to their hometown for their own reasons.

The architect had designed the house's two-story covered entryway with a fancy hanging light to impress. Urns of orange and yellow flowers sat on either side of the massive front door with an ornate door handle.

Selena had always pictured Juliet living in a castle or a quaint cottage, but the way she'd dressed last night fit this home.

The only problem?

The outer package didn't always match what was inside.

Call it intuition or experience, Selena thought that was the case with Juliet.

This wasn't a shot in the dark. Selena had learned not to ignore those little twitches, twinges, or in this case, niggling thoughts. Through her one-on-one clients and millions of followers, she'd met people from all walks of life. Some were what they appeared to be, but others didn't show their true selves. The reasons varied, but the result was the same—unhappiness, discontent, restlessness, sadness, frustration, the list went on. That was no way to live, but some didn't even realize how they'd put on masks or wore costumes to hide what was inside them.

Most times, it was a useful skill to possess. She loved helping others, unraveling the emotions and traumas they'd stuffed deep inside. It was just harder when people she knew were doing it.

But she had to help.

If she didn't, who would show them how to peel the onion?

That was how Selena explained what her clients needed to do—remove the outer layers to reach the core of what was holding them back, making them want to hide, pretend, or ignore. Sometimes, a combination or even all three. Then, they could address, and if need be, heal the root cause, and embrace and show the world whom they were meant to be. Strong emotions were difficult to face for many—most cried through the process—which also related to the onion. Not the strongest analogy, but it gave her a starting point in explaining the process.

Selena wanted to be wrong about Juliet, and there was only one way to find out. She pushed the doorbell.

No one answered.

She tried again.

"Who is it?" Juliet asked from the other side of the closed door.

Given the low crime rate in Berry Lake, her actions surprised Selena. Juliet had never been cautious or held herself back like Bria, but she hadn't put herself out there as much as Selena. Nell, Missy, and Juliet had fallen between the two in various degrees. "It's Selena."

Two locks clicked before the door opened. Juliet greeted her with a smile, except it didn't reach her eyes—the same as last night. "I thought you were driving home today."

"I am." Selena hugged her. Juliet was so thin. Too thin. Something that wasn't noticeable with the clothes she wore. "I'll leave from here. I just... Do you mind if I come in?"

Juliet startled. "Oh, I'm sorry. I'm not used to having company. Please, come in."

No visitors?

That seemed odd, given Juliet had grown up here and been both homecoming queen and prom queen. The runner-up in both cases hadn't been close when the votes were tallied. Juliet had been the most beautiful girl at school, but her sweet personality made her a favorite and welcome in every clique from the most popular kids—a bunch of jerks in Selena's opinion—to the band geeks—Juliet played the flute. Not all those people still lived in Berry Lake, but enough did.

As Selena added that puzzle piece to her pile, she entered the house. A basket sat next to the door. "Do you want me to take off my shoes?"

"No, but thanks for offering."

The foyer was rounded and tall. Wood floors gleamed beneath her feet. The air was fresh and slightly scented with lemon.

"Your house is gorgeous." In the dining room on the left, a spectacular crystal chandelier hung over a table that seated eight. On the right, the very formal living room reminded Selena of a model home with nothing out of place, as if no one lived there. Still, it was home magazine-layout gorgeous. "Who did the interior design?"

"I did." Juliet bit her lip before staring at the floor.

This was worse than Selena thought. "Impressive."

Juliet shrugged. "I tried to give Ezra what he wanted."

What do you *want?* Selena bit her tongue to keep from asking that question. No need to push. Juliet had already provided information about her lack of self-confidence and self-worth. Both were common amongst her clients, but once upon a time, Juliet hadn't struggled with either. Rejection had made her work harder on her acting craft because she was determined to make it in show business. She hadn't cowered or lowered her voice in deference.

What caused her to do both now?

As far as Selena knew, Juliet had lived a charmed life. *What changed? What didn't she tell us last night?* "You have a keen eye for design."

Another shrug. "The internet has plenty of resources. The living room is a bit fussy for my tastes, but Ezra wanted it this way for entertaining. His company has accounts throughout the West Coast, and he enjoys inviting customers for dinner parties or brunch when they're in the area."

"Do you have the events catered?"

"It depends on who's coming and how much Ezra wants to impress them. I can manage brunch okay, but not all of the dinners. He doesn't want my cooking to mess up a deal or a relationship."

Grrr. Selena forced herself not to ball her hands. She'd never met Ezra. Probably a good thing because she wanted to strangle the man.

"I spend most of my time in the kitchen and family room. The open floor plan suits me better, I think." Juliet motioned toward an arched doorway. "Why don't we go in there?"

When Selena stepped through the doorway, she understood why Juliet said it suited her more. The warm and inviting space had floor-to-ceiling windows to let in natural light. Commercial-grade top-of-the-line appliances filled the gourmet kitchen with wood cabinets and a combination of butcher block and marble countertops with a farmhouse sink. A table with six chairs fit perfectly into a rounded nook. A huge TV above the fireplace was the centerpiece of the family room full of overstuffed furniture in soft leather and solid-colored fabrics. Floral and plaid throw pillows added more colors and texture. Framed photographs and artwork hung on the wall. A book and a cup on top of a coaster sat on the coffee table.

This part of the house looked lived-in. "Did you decorate this area, too?"

Juliet nodded. "I did the entire house."

"You have a gift."

She blushed. "I'll get us something to drink."

"Don't go to any trouble."

"It'll only take me a minute." She headed behind the massive island. "Have a seat at the table."

Selena sat where she could watch Juliet.

With the same ease as she set out the food last night, Juliet filled a teapot from an electric kettle, scooped tea leaves into an infuser, and dropped it into the pot. She pulled out a two-tier gold-rimmed tray and small bowls from an upper cabinet and then placed cookies and scones from plastic containers on it. Next came the clotted cream, butter, and jam that went into matching bowls.

"Can I help?" Selena offered.

"Thanks, but I've got it." Juliet placed items on the table, including teacups, saucers, and cloth napkins. She must have gotten those when Selena blinked.

Juliet carried over the teapot. "Do you take milk in your tea?"

"No milk or sugar."

Juliet sat across from her and placed a napkin on her lap. "Help yourself."

Selena stared at the charming tea table put together without any notice. There were even tiny gold spoons. "I can't believe you did this in less than five minutes."

Juliet shrugged—a gesture that bugged Selena. "My grand-mother serves afternoon tea at the Huckleberry Inn. She's done that for as long as I remember. I've always enjoyed that tradition, so I fit it in when I can. Though most days, I'm drinking alone."

"A good thing it's tea and not tequila shots."

Juliet laughed. "Right? Though I am addicted to chamomile."

Okay, that was the woman Selena remembered. Not all of Juliet had disappeared. "Nothing like a cup of Earl Grey to get me going in the morning."

"That's better than the sludge you used to drink when you worked the early shift at the cupcake shop." Juliet raised her teacup. "It's so good to see you again, but I'm not sure why you're here."

Selena sipped her tea. She didn't want to push her friend, but she needed to be honest. "We've known each other long enough, so I'll just say it. I'm worried about you."

What appeared to be panic flashed in Juliet's eyes. A smile spread across her face, but it seemed more plastic than real. "Look around. Look at me. I'm fine."

"Your home is lovely, and so are you." Selena took another sip. "But I got the sense last night that something was... wrong."

Juliet slowly raised her cup. Each movement was precise.

"I'm not trying to pry," Selena added.

Juliet half laughed. "Yes, you are."

"Okay, I am."

And if Juliet knew what Selena had done before coming over, her friend might not be happy. But it was for Juliet's good, even if she didn't want to admit life wasn't as perfect as it appeared.

"Life may have gotten in the way of us staying close all these years, but I care about you." Selena hoped her friend believed her. "I always will."

"It's the same for me with you. I appreciate your concern." Juliet set her teacup on the saucer and then blotted her mouth with a napkin. "But..."

As her words trailed off, she stared at the table. Her gaze was no longer clear, but her eyes brewed with something—trouble, or was it turmoil?

"You can still tell me anything, like old times." Selena hoped Juliet would trust her. "I won't tell a soul. I promise."

Juliet took another sip before eating a cookie.

This was the time for patience, so Selena ate one, too. "Delicious."

"My grandmother made them." Juliet picked up a small spoon and stirred her tea. "It's not like anything is wrong. It's just..."

Don't force it. Selena raised her teacup.

"I shouldn't complain." Juliet's lips narrowed into a thin line. "Look around. I have so much. A dream house, a wealthy husband, a fancy car, and whatever else I need."

Hmmm. A wealthy husband, not a husband who loves and adores me.

Selena liked Ezra less and less, but she sipped her tea. That made it impossible for her to interrupt Juliet.

"But it's not enough." Juliet's shoulders slumped. Her chin lowered to her chest. "Ezra tells me *I'm* not enough. No matter how hard I try, I'm not enough."

Selena's fingers tightened around the teacup. She set it on the saucer before she broke off the delicate handle. "It must hurt to hear him say that."

Nodding, Juliet stared into her cup. "It does. I don't know what to do about it."

Selena fought the urge to pull Juliet into a giant hug and tell her she would fix everything. But Juliet needed to do that for herself. "What do you think when he says things about you?"

She shrugged.

"I won't judge you, Juliet."

"I hate it." Her shoulders curled. "I do everything Ezra says, the way he wants, too, but the littlest thing has him exploding like Mount St. Helens. So, I've been learning how to do things better. From implementing a cleaning routine to cooking. If I work harder and do things better, he won't get upset that way."

Selena scooted her chair closer and touched Juliet's arm. "Or he might keep doing it. No one can say for sure."

"You're right." Juliet blew out a breath. "It won't change how he thinks of me."

"What do you mean?"

"I'm nothing more than a trophy wife and an appealing piece of arm candy to him." Juliet took a scone. "If I eat this, I'll need to spend enough time working off the calories this afternoon. He likes me a certain way and has me do weekly weigh-ins in front of him. You don't know how many times I've broken scales, only to have another one reappear in the bathroom."

Selena's blood boiled, but she kept her face neutral and didn't say anything. Juliet was a friend in need, and like Ezra or not, he was her husband. "That has to be frustrating."

"I'm so tired."

Stop trying and doing what he wants. He isn't worth it.

Selena wanted to scream those words. Instead, she pressed the balls of her shoes against the hardwood. She needed to ground herself before she packed a suitcase of clothes for Juliet and took her to Seattle. "It must be difficult to do your best and not be recognized for it."

Tears welled in Juliet's eyes. "I feel so stupid. This house is twice the size of our old one in LA, but Ezra wouldn't let me hire a housekeeper. He said I needed to contribute to the household. I didn't do a lot in LA since he likes me home when he gets off work, but here in Berry Lake, it's repressive. I feel more like a child or a paid staff member than his wife. And the more he tells me I can't do anything right, the more I start to believe it."

Selena squeezed her friend's hand. "Believe what's in your heart. Don't let Ezra or anyone tell you differently."

"I want my marriage to work, but I feel as if my husband is slipping away, and it's all my fault. I don't know what I can do to make things better. As soon as we moved here, he started working more hours. He's also become infatuated with art. I've wondered if he's having an affair or if he's bored with me. I'd be bored with me if I were him. All I do is take care of the house, grocery shop, spend time with my grandmother, and entertain his clients. No wonder I feel more like someone who works for him than his wife."

She rubbed Juliet's hand. This was worse than what Selena had thought, but her original idea would work. Her intuition had been on point once again. She would help her friend.

"Wow." Juliet grimaced before sitting back in her chair. "I'm sorry for unloading on you."

"I'm here to listen. Anytime." Selena let go of Juliet, took a scone, and added butter to it. "Have you considered doing something outside of the house?"

"I want to find a job." The words shot out. "I haven't mentioned it to Ezra because who would hire me? I guess Missy would, since I've worked at the cupcake shop before, but I don't think Ezra would approve of that."

Ezra wouldn't approve of anything that allowed Juliet to feel better about herself. "The cupcake shop is perfect for Missy, but you have other skills to offer."

Her cheeks reddened. "I have none."

"Look at this table. You created a lovely tea for us in a few minutes. Not everyone can do that."

Juliet rolled her eyes. "Mad skills. I have them."

"You do." Selena wouldn't let her friend think otherwise. "Last night, you made Italian takeout look like a spread from a five-star restaurant."

"Okay, I know how to do that. I also know how to host a dinner party and organize get-togethers." She went to touch her face but then lowered her hands. "I'm good at smiling and saying yes, even when I want to say no. But people don't pay for that."

"It's called customer service, and yes, they do." Selena's plan sharpened in her mind. "I happen to know someone who is looking for a person with your skills."

Juliet's mouth formed a perfect O. "Who?"

"Charlene Culpepper." Selena waited for Juliet to say anything, but she didn't. "She hires people for her events. I spoke with her this morning, and she's looking to hire."

"Really?" Juliet whispered.

Along with the word, Selena heard hope. That was an excellent first step. "Yes."

"I suppose I could call her and see."

"Please do. Charlene knows what she's looking for, and no one in Berry Lake or all of Washington state is more qualified than you. Trust me on this one." Okay, Selena was selling this a bit strong, but Juliet needed the push.

"I'll call her." Gratitude shone in Juliet's eyes. "If I get a job, Ezra might see me differently."

Or Juliet might see she didn't need him, but that was for her to decide. "You are beautiful and smart and kind. Don't let anyone tell you differently. One thing I've learned is some people will do whatever they can to hold you back if you let them."

Compassion filled Juliet's eyes. "Growing up here was hard for you."

Selena nodded. She wasn't used to talking about herself.

"Nope. You can't go quiet now." Juliet's voice was louder, more forceful. "I spilled my guts. It's your turn."

Selena laughed. "Not much to spill when you know I spent high school counting the days until graduation. I wanted to leave town, but I couldn't afford to. That's why I returned each summer during college. But after that, I never wanted to look or come back."

"You did for Missy's wedding."

"I would have for yours, too."

Juliet rubbed her chest. "Ezra didn't want a big wedding, so we got married on a beach in Maui. It was just the two of us and so romantic."

"I didn't know you had an intimate, destination wedding." That surprised Selena. Juliet had shared her dreams of a huge, fairytale-themed wedding the summer they worked together. "What did your grandmother say?"

"She was upset, but Ezra explained his reasons for wanting something so intimate, and she got over it. Though, I think it was a stumbling block in their relationship. Still, Ezra felt I needed to spend more time with her, so that's why we moved to Berry Lake."

"I'm sure Penelope loves having you nearby."

Juliet's face lit up, making her look younger and carefree. "She does, and so do I. Employees do most of the work at the inn, which gives her more free time to spend with me."

"That's great." Except... A weight pressed against Selena. Her throat thickened. "I'm so sorry I didn't stay in touch."

"You had your reasons. I'm sorry I didn't do better."

"You had your reasons, too."

She nodded. "So, enough of this heavy stuff. How are you and your hottie hockey player doing?"

"Logan is so hot." Selena fanned herself before laughing. "Things are great. He's in training camp right now. Once the season starts, we won't have much time together, but he loves me, and I love him, so we manage around hockey. My business is running smoothly, thanks to my awesome team. We had a hiccup yesterday, but things are better today. My life is as wonderful as I imagined it would be."

"You worked hard to make your dreams come true."

Selena had dreamed big and never given up, even when she'd begun with nothing. "I did at first, and it was so hard. I was on a never-ending roller coaster, but then it got easier."

"Why do you think that is?"

"Because I stopped waiting for someone else to help me or do it for me. I realized if I wanted to make everything I dreamed about in high school happen, I was the one who had to do it. I had to do it myself. And I had to believe in myself, that I *could* do it."

Juliet's face fell. "I used to believe in myself. But trying to make it in Hollywood was dream crushing. When I met Ezra, he wanted to do everything for me. It was wonderful. Until it wasn't."

"It's never too late to change. You can't go back and change the past or the decisions you made, but you can go forward from here toward whatever your heart desires."

Juliet listened intently before shaking her head. "You make it sound so easy."

"It is." Selena didn't want to go into too much now. "Your first step is calling Charlene, and then we'll talk about the rest. But you deserve all the happiness in the universe. You need to open yourself up and believe it will happen."

One side of Juliet's mouth slid upward in a lopsided grin. "Isn't part of that from one of your Instagram posts?"

"It could be. My team jots down whatever I say to use on social media posts."

"Thanks for saying it to me. I needed to hear it." Juliet touched Selena's shoulder. "I hope it's not years before we see each other again."

"It won't be. I want to support Bria and Missy with the cupcake shop. You and Nell, too. There's also the Cupcake Posse retreat that will be epic."

Juliet nodded. "The summer we worked together was epic. We all clicked."

"I think about you guys all the time."

Her eyes widened. "Why?"

"Because I saw how important it was having someone to talk to about boys and family and our futures. Remember Bria at the end of her senior year?"

Juliet cringed. "She was a mess."

"Thanks to that idiot Dalton Dwyer and his bully friends."

"All the Dwyers are like that. His mom has made a career out of marrying and divorcing rich men. It's so sad guys fall for it."

Selena had heard stories about the art gallery owner Sal DeMarco being her latest victim—er, husband. "Remember Bria before she headed off to college? She'd put herself back together and was stronger than before."

"We also stopped her unhealthy eating habits. She could have easily ended up with an eating disorder, but she didn't."

Selena nodded, thinking it ironic that Juliet brought that up, considering her husband forced her to weigh herself in front of him. "When I went back for my senior year of college, I didn't know what I wanted to do other than help people like we'd done with Bria. We'd told her how amazing she was and how much she deserved. I realized we all did. I mean, I knew that out here." She waved her hands in the air. "But I hadn't here." She pointed to her heart. "My parents assumed that even with a college degree, I would work at the cupcake shop or a café. They never saw beyond the limitations of their own lives. That summer with the Posse put me on the path to what I do now. It lit a fire under me and inside me. I can't thank you all enough, even if we haven't seen each other in over a decade."

"Thank you for sharing that. You need to tell the others." Juliet hugged her. "And come back to Berry Lake more often. And not because I need the awesome life coach Selena T. I also need my friend."

"She's right here." Selena needed Juliet, too. Nell, Bria, and Missy, too.

More than Selena realized.

She had her husband, team, and clients, but no close friends like the Posse had once been. "And I promise. I will be back."

chapter eleven

NELL SHOULD HAVE called in sick this morning. She sipped from her coffee cup, which was her fourth today. Usually, she only had one. But Nell was dragging. She hadn't drunk enough wine last night to be hungover, but seeing her friends left her keyed up. Falling asleep had been impossible, much to the chagrin of Mr. Teddy, a senior cat her stepmother, Sabine, convinced Nell to foster.

Cami sat at one of the computers. "You look tired."

"I am, but seeing my friends was worth it." Nell glanced at the clock. "Only two more hours to go, and I'm off for four glorious days." Twelve-hour days were long, but she enjoyed having three days off one week and four days off another.

"And then what?"

"I'll swing by the cupcake shop, go home, and then call it an early night."

"Oh, to have that freedom." Cami typed on the keyboard. "I'll leave here and go home. I'll have about twenty minutes to shower and throw something together for dinner. The kids have soccer tonight. Their teams practice at different times, so we'll eat in the car as we drive from one field to another."

"I don't know how you do it." Nell had pictured life as a mom so differently from Cami's as a single parent. "You have two full-time jobs. Here and at home."

"The kids are worth it. And I do get a break when their dad has them, but then I miss them and can't wait until they're home. It's weird."

"You love them. I want someone to love like that."

"You have Mr. Teddy."

Nell shrugged. "Once I feed him dinner, he ignores me until it's time for him to eat again."

"You love him."

He wasn't much trouble, other than him preferring her bed to his, but at least he didn't hog the covers. The cat needed daily meds and sub-Q fluids three times a week to manage his renal disease. Fortunately for her, he took the pills and needle pricks better than some of her human patients. And who didn't want a handsome fellow meeting her at the door when she got home? "I tolerate him."

"You're never getting rid of him."

"I'm his foster mom." Sabine kept saying Nell should adopt him, but she wasn't ready to do that yet. She had a vision of her future—first marriage, next a cat, followed by kids, and then a dog—that she hadn't been able to shake. Not that she'd tried. Though honestly, Mr. Teddy might remain with her anyway. Old cats with medical needs weren't at the top of the list for most adopters.

"You used the m-word. That means you will be a foster failure. Just wait and see. Hashtag cat mom will soon be yours."

Cami reached for the paper coming out of the printer. "Are your friends still around?"

"One is on her way home to Seattle. Another is here until Sunday. Two live in Berry Lake. I usually see one at the cupcake shop on my way home from work, and after last night, I hope I'll see more of the other."

"You're lucky to have any nearby, but I guess that's what small-town living is all about." Cami had moved to Berry Lake after her divorce. She could afford to buy a house there, and the town wasn't that far of a drive for her ex-husband when it was his turn with the kids. "I'm friends with a few people from high school and college on social media, but we don't see each other in real life. Though maybe it's a mom thing."

"Probably a season-of-life thing." Nell had been thinking about that last night. "None of us have kids, but we each went off to do our own thing—college, jobs, falling in love, marriage for two of us. Last night was the first time we made a conscious effort to get together in years. The last time was at a wedding, but that wasn't planned. If Elise hadn't died, we wouldn't have met up."

They were all to blame for that. Nell had tried to keep up with the other four after Missy's wedding. When she lived in Boston, she let the others know Rob Hanford had been killed in action and told them about Elise's cancer diagnosis. But no one, including her, had planned a get-together so they could see each other.

Not until last night.

Nell crossed her fingers, hoping to spend more time together in the future. She was fortunate to be close to her two sisters, Evie and Jojo, and her stepsister, Sheridan. Nell had friends at the hospital, around town, and from college. But she'd never experienced the same closeness with other friends as she shared with Bria, Juliet,

Missy, and Selena. It was a kinship—sisters of the heart. "We talked about a retreat or a girls' weekend, so I hope it happens."

"I've seen you advocate for patients. You can be relentless when you put your mind to it." Cami signed off the computer. "Don't let up if you want to see them again."

"I will." Nell had the most time. Once she left the hospital, she put work behind her. It was better than taking it home with her. "But relentless is how I describe Welles Riggs."

"How about diligent?"

"That works."

"Oh, sweet apple pie." Cami's mouth gaped. The papers in her hand floated to the floor. "Add a scoop of ice cream, and come to mama. What am I saying? Forget the ice cream. I'll take mine naked."

Only one thing would elicit that reaction.

Nell followed her coworker's sightline until she came to the backside of a man. He wore hiking boots, cargo shorts, and a T-shirt, but not a cotton one. The fitted fabric showed off his broad shoulders and muscular arms.

"Come to mama" was correct.

He would have no trouble carrying a woman—okay, *her*—over the threshold.

Sure, she had yet to see his face, but everything else from this viewpoint was on her perfect-partner list—something Selena had mentioned making on one of her podcasts a few years ago.

This guy was prime. Tall—he had to be over six feet with blond hair. He had that swimmer's build she found so appealing. As if on cue, he turned, giving a clear view of his profile as he raised his phone. A strong jawline. Soft-looking, full lips. High cheekbones. Ridiculously long eyelashes.

Flutters filled Nell's stomach. Her mouth watered, which usually only happened with desserts or a box of See's Victorian Toffee, her favorite candy. "Please save me a slice of that sweet apple pie."

Cami snickered. "I'd call dibs, but he belongs at the Academy Awards with a cover model or famous actress on his arm."

"True." Demigods like him didn't fall for nurses in their late thirties with sweet tooths that never went unsatisfied. Besides, for all they knew, he was married with a bunch of kids.

Not that his relationship status would change anything.

He was out of her league, which didn't bother Nell in the slightest. It was the way of the dating world, and nothing she would take personally. "At least we can appreciate his gorgeousness from afar."

"I'm in. Though if he were willing, I'd worship at his feet."

So would I.

She glanced at the board. The guy appeared to have use of both hands, so he wasn't the one with a broken arm. She also noticed the nurse assigned to that exam room. "We'll have to ask Lynette for the scoop."

Cami groaned. "Why does the one married nurse on duty get that assignment? It isn't fair. And they've been here for over an hour. Why didn't she tell us?"

"Lynette has seniority, and she probably didn't want to distract us."

"I'm totally distracted. The world could end, but if he's the last thing I see, I will go out smiling."

"Same." Nell glanced at the board to make sure she hadn't missed doing anything. "Thanks for going gaga over him, or I never would have noticed. That would have been a shame."

Cami hadn't looked away from the guy, not even to pick up the papers, so Nell did it for her. She stapled the discharge paperwork before handing it over.

The hottie smiled at something and then laughed.

Both Nell and Cami sighed.

"I have a new crush," Cami admitted. "I wonder if he likes kids. Though, you might have a better shot with him."

"In my dreams. But we're both catches. It'll happen for both of us." A call button from exam room three lit up. That was one of Nell's patients. "Enjoy the view."

"I intend to."

Nell entered the exam room. As Mrs. Vernon lay on the bed, knitting something with light-blue yarn, a talk show played on the TV. The woman came in at least once a week with some sort of ailment. Usually, the diagnosis was loneliness—her husband of fifty-five years had died six months ago, and none of her kids lived in Berry Lake—but not today. Her EKG had been abnormal and her blood pressure high. They were monitoring her while preparing to admit her after the doctor consulted with her cardiologist.

"Did you need something, Mrs. V?" Nell asked.

"I've stayed long enough today. I'm almost out of yarn, so I'm ready to go home." The woman showed off the cute baby cap she'd been knitting. "I got more done today than I planned. I'm so productive with people around me."

Nell's heart ached for the woman. "Is that for a family member?"

"I wish it were, but I have to wait for my grandchildren to have babies, and that'll be a few years from now." Mrs. Vernon placed the needles and cap into her bag. "There are a few charity groups that ask for caps and blankets. I make whatever they need."

"That's sweet of you."

"I love to knit, so it's no hardship. I also have an Etsy store. Sales from that cover my bingo money and cable TV bill." Mrs. Vernon glanced at the clock. "I need to go home. Lulu will wonder where I've been. It's almost time for me to cook her dinner. Tonight is her favorite—doggy stew."

Of course, Mrs. Vernon's dog received a homecooked, hot dinner each day. Nell knew how to cook, but she rarely did so, relying on meals she only needed to bake or microwave. But hearing about the dog raised a question. "Is Lulu staying with someone today?"

"There's no one to leave her with, dear." Mrs. Vernon sounded resigned. "Most of my friends are in the assisted living center or dead. Penelope Jones is still around, but she doesn't allow pets at the inn. Lulu doesn't mind. She has a doggy door, so she doesn't tinkle in the house."

A doggy door was great, but that was a daytime solution, not an overnight one. It wasn't Nell's place to tell Mrs. Vernon she wouldn't go home tonight. But Nell would make sure someone took care of the dog until her owner was home. They'd been through this before, unfortunately. "You can't leave yet. The doctor wants to speak with you."

"Oh, I've heard that speech before. Lower your salt intake. Stay upright after eating. Stop drinking so much coffee."

"The doctor only wants you to be in top health."

"I'm eighty-five. I gave birth to five children and don't need adult diapers. I can still do the New York Times crossword puzzle each day and walk a few miles without huffing and puffing. That's top health to me."

Nell hoped she was as feisty and fit as Mrs. Vernon in her eighties. "I agree with you."

Mrs. Vernon peered around Nell. "Come here."

She hurried to the bed. The monitor showed no change. "Is something wrong?"

"No. A handsome young man has walked by this room twice and glanced in both times." Mrs. Vernon's blue eyes twinkled. "I'm a little old for him, and my heart will always belong to my beloved Walter, God rest his soul, so you go out there and talk to him."

Nell had a feeling she knew who Mrs. Vernon meant. "Is it Welles Riggs?"

"Oh, Welles is a sweet boy. He mows my lawn each week. He's handsome, too, but the man I'm talking about isn't from here. He's dressed like a hiker, so maybe a tourist. But that face…"

"I know who you mean. He's handsome, but he wouldn't be interested in me. He's probably being nosy or is bored."

Mrs. Vernon tsked. "Don't talk about yourself like that. You, Nell Culpepper, are a catch. You're kind, nurturing, and pretty."

"Thanks." She patted her hips. "I'm also hippy and overweight."

Mrs. Vernon's assessing gaze ran the length of her. "You're not out of shape. You're bigger boned, like Sheila, my youngest. Men appreciate curves."

"Some do." And a good thing, since Nell wasn't about to give up cupcakes.

"Even if others don't say it aloud, they do, too. It's built into their DNA."

"DNA?" That wasn't something Nell thought she'd hear from a patient.

Mrs. Vernon nodded. "Preservation of their genetics. Their line. They want a woman who can birth their babies. It goes way back, so most don't even realize that's the reason they're attracted."

Nell grinned. Her patient was too cute. "Interesting, and I'd love if my ever-expanding hips were an asset, but if I go on a date, it's for coffee or a meal, not to procreate."

"You have to start somewhere, dear." Mrs. Vernon winked. "Now, go appease an old woman's curiosity and talk to the hot guy. Then report back with all the deets. Or is it the four-one-one that my grandchildren use?"

Nell bit back a laugh. "There won't be much to tell, but I'll go out there." That would give her a chance to contact the hospital's care coordinator about Lulu. She wanted to make sure the dog was safe until her owner returned home. "I'll be right back."

"I hope not."

Smiling, Nell opened the sliding glass door. Cami wasn't at the nurses' station. Neither was Lynette. She glanced to her right but saw no one.

"Hello," a man said on her left.

Nell jumped.

"Sorry if I scared you."

"It's fine." She turned in his direction. It was the hottie they'd been admiring before, only this time she had a view of his whole face. *Boy-oh-boy.* He was better looking up close. His eyes weren't blue—the color on her list of perfect-partner qualities—but green wasn't a deal breaker. "Hi."

"I'm Gage Adler," he said as if he hadn't turned her world upside down by speaking with her. "I noticed you when they brought us back here, but you were hard at work. You didn't look up."

He'd noticed me?

Nell's pulse accelerated. Okay, he was probably being friendly. Hanging out in the ER was boring if you didn't work here. Still, she needed to play it cool. "I'm Nell Culpepper, and they don't pay me to stand around looking pretty."

His gaze appeared to soak in all of her. He grinned wryly. "They should."

"Thanks." Nell sounded breathless. She shouldn't be flattered, but she was. She fought the urge to smooth her hair. Had she worn makeup today? She'd been running late and didn't remember putting it on this morning. "I hope whoever you came in with is doing okay."

"My friend broke his arm." Gage glanced at the exam room where she'd seen him earlier. "He'll be in a cast for a while, but it's a clean break. His wife spoils him rotten, and this will make that worse, but only after she tells him I told you so for going out with me. He'll agree, and they'll live happily ever after."

She noticed a hint of sarcasm in his tone. "Nice story."

"If you're into that sort of thing."

Nell was, but that was none of his business. She glimpsed at Gage's left hand. No ring or tan line, but he might not wear one, and if his friend was married… "Not a fan of relationships, or jealous?"

He laughed. "You don't hold back."

Not when she had nothing to lose with a guy like him. He was looking for a distraction. Nothing more. "Just going by what you said."

"Not jealous or anti-relationship." A sheepish expression formed. "I'm also not dating anyone, so I'm tired of being the third wheel with my best friend and his wife, who are deliriously in love. How about you?"

"Not jealous or anti-relationship, either."

His grin widened. "I like you, Nell. Would you want to go out sometime?"

As tingles raced through Nell, her nerve endings exploded like the Fourth of July fireworks. She wiggled her toes. "Sure."

That response was better than shimmying her shoulders, pumping her fist, and screaming, "Yes."

He pulled out his phone. "Are you from Berry Lake?"

"Born and raised. How about you?"

"Hood River."

That was a forty-minute drive across the Columbia River into Oregon. *Not that far.* "Nice place to live. Especially if you enjoy the outdoors."

He straightened. "Do you?"

His expensive boots and clothing suggested he was the outdoor type. If Nell admitted she preferred staying indoors, would that be a turnoff? *Probably.* All she wanted was one date with him. Mrs. Vernon would be thrilled, her mom might stop mentioning her lack of a relationship for a week or two, and Cami would have hope that something like this would happen to her, too.

Nell pictured the park where she took walks on her lunch break when the weather was nice. That was outdoors. "I enjoy flowers, sunshine, and blue sky."

"So do I."

She noticed the care coordinator and waved her hand to snag the man's attention. "I need to talk to someone about a patient."

"Before you go, put your number in here." Gage handed Nell his phone. "How does a hike or coffee sound?"

"Coffee is more my style when I first meet someone."

"It's also safer based on what happened to my friend today."

His charming grin made her breath catch. She sent herself a text from his phone before handing it back. "There you go."

"When are you off?"

"It depends on the week."

"I work from home, so my schedule is flexible. I'll be in touch."

"Sounds good." The care coordinator shot her a look. "I'll talk to you later."

"Count on it."

A thrill shot through her. Nell couldn't believe this had happened. She hoped Gage called her, but the fact a guy who looked like him—his name could be Thor, and no one would bat an eye—sought her out was enough.

Whether he called or not, she had a story to tell Mrs. Vernon and Cami. Not to mention the Posse, using their newly formed group chat. And of course, Mr. Teddy.

Nell couldn't wait to hear what they said.

* * *

After work, Nell made her way to the cupcake shop. Her feet barely touched the sidewalk. She was still riding the high from meeting Gage. Mrs. Vernon had appeared giddy, as if she'd been the one asked out. Cami admitted being a tad jealous, but she was happy for Nell and shared ideas for what she should wear for the coffee date.

It was fun. A way she hadn't felt about men or dating in far too long.

She entered the cupcake shop. No one was waiting in line, and all the tables were empty—the complete opposite of yesterday's birthday sale.

"Hey, Nell." Bentley, a high school senior who also volunteered at the hospital, greeted her with a big smile. "I'd ask if you want the usual, but you never order the same thing."

"Variety is the spice of life." She studied the menu board, even though she had it memorized. She had two chocolate cupcakes at home. She'd taken the others to work and left them in the breakroom. They'd disappeared by lunchtime. "I'll have a pumpkin spice cupcake and an iced tea."

"Great choice." He rang her up. "For here, right?"

Nell nodded and handed him a ten-dollar bill.

He returned her change. "I'll bring that over to you in a minute."

She stuck a dollar in the tip jar before sitting at her usual table. A favorite part of working there was when tips were divided at the end of a shift. No one ever knew how much they'd get, but any amount was a welcome surprise. A text notification sounded.

541-555-2313: *It's Gage. Wanted to see if you're free on Friday for coffee?*

He texted! Nell shimmied her shoulders. A ball of emotion formed in her core—a mix of anticipation, excitement, and surprise. She still couldn't believe this was happening.

She reread the message. Friday worked for her, but…

Should I reply immediately? It had been a while since she'd done this, and she felt out of practice. But did it matter? He hadn't waited to text her, and a woman would have to be dead not to be interested in him. She typed a reply.

Nell: *I'm off Friday, so whatever time works for you will be fine.*
541-555-2313: *10:30 a.m. at the coffee shop in Berry Lake?*
Nell: *I'll see you there.*
541-555-2313: *Great.*
Nell: *Enjoy the rest of your week.*
541-555-2313: *You, too. But you may hear from me before Friday.*
Nell: *Fine by me.*

Nell hit send. Was this really happening to her?

"One pumpkin spice cupcake and iced tea." Bentley placed the plate with a single cupcake on it and glass on the table. He pulled a fork rolled in a paper napkin from his apron pocket. "I didn't bring sugar or sweetener since you never ask for it, but if you need it, yell."

"Thanks." As he returned to the front counter, she arranged the cupcake, drink, and napkin, so the cupcake shop's logo showed before taking a photo of it. The cinnamon sugar sprinkled over the cream cheese frosting was new.

She bit into it.

Her tastebuds did a happy dance. Missy had outdone herself by adding the sugary topping to the recipe. Nell took another photo and then uploaded both to Instagram with a Berry Lake cupcake hashtag. Something she did whenever she visited.

Nell ate another bite of cupcake. Delicious and perfect for September.

"Who was the man you spoke to at the hospital?"

She was so distracted, she didn't notice someone walk up to her table. When she glanced up, she cringed, seeing her mom. "I speak to a lot of people at work."

Her mother sat at the table, disturbing Nell's routine of winding down before she got home and making her glad she had those chocolate cupcakes waiting for her.

"He's gorgeous and seemed into you." Her mother's intense gaze zeroed in on Nell. "Especially since he wanted your digits."

Digits? Nell nearly groaned. "How do you know about that?"

Her mother's lips curved into a smug smile. "I saw a photo of you handing him a phone. You don't carry yours when you're working, so it must have been his."

"Seriously, Mom? You've got people spying on me at work?"

"They thought I'd want to know."

"Know what?"

"That you're not completely hopeless when it comes to men." Her mom clucked her tongue. "I joined one of those dating apps to see if I should make you a profile. Though I still can't figure out if I'm supposed to swipe right or left if I see someone promising."

"Swipe right, but don't you dare set up anything for me." Anger spiraled, but Nell knew better than to try to take on her mother in public. Still, she had to say something to stop the madness. "I'm far from hopeless. I have a great job and an apartment. I'm happy with my life. Stop making me feel as if something is missing."

"I love you."

"I love you, too, but I don't need you to keep introducing me to men. I'm doing fine on my own."

"You're thirty-seven and single." She spoke as if those were the two worst things her daughter could be. "If I don't help you, who will?"

"I don't need help." Her exasperated tone matched the way she felt inside. "Did you not hear what I said about being happy?"

Her mom raised her chin. "Mothers know what their daughters need."

Not about this. Nell ate another bite of her cupcake, but it wasn't as enjoyable as it had been before her mother arrived.

Her mom studied her. "Given you're not wearing much makeup, need a haircut, and could lose weight, I'm surprised he wanted your number. I know your shifts are long, but you should make sure to look your best. Otherwise, you'll end up with Welles Riggs."

Nell was used to not living up to her mother's expectations—trying out for the cheer team in high school and marrying a doctor to name two them. Though in her defense, the second one hadn't been Nell's choice. And she had no interest in dating whatever single breathing man Charlene Culpepper deemed worthy. But Nell wouldn't let her mother speak badly about Welles. She might not want to date the guy, but she considered him a friend.

"Welles is a sweet guy. Whoever ends up with him won't be stuck. She'll be a lucky woman. And if I never marry, who cares? Elise was single, and you didn't harp on her the way you do on me."

"Elise was different."

"So am I. And may I point out, you're single, too."

"I was married for over thirty years. That's long enough."

"So, you want me to be miserable like you were?"

"Some people aren't cut out for marriage, but you'll be happier with a husband. When the new vet starts…"

"I'm having coffee with that guy from the hospital on Friday," Nell blurted.

Her mother's mouth gaped. "What?"

Ugh. Nell hadn't meant to tell her mom about the date, but she had to stop her mother's matchmaking. The vet was a big N-O. "Coffee date on Friday."

Her mom clapped her hands together. "Oh, sweet Nell. That's fantastic news. We must make you an appointment at the salon for a cut and color. Waxing, too. I don't have time to get to Portland to buy new clothes for you—"

"Stop." Nell wouldn't enable her mother's meddling. "I don't need my hair cut. You know I've never colored my hair, and I have plenty of clothes. We're having coffee. A casual, get-to-know-you meeting. No big deal."

"But—"

"Nope." She sipped her iced tea. "And if you want to hear about the coffee date, you'll butt out. Or I'll cancel."

Her mother gasped. "You wouldn't."

Nell hoped she didn't have to make that decision. She stared down her nose. "Try me."

🧁 chapter twelve 🧁

THE NEXT MORNING, Bria entered the Huckleberry Inn. She hadn't been inside the old Victorian in years. The dark, plum-painted walls were now a soothing mauve, making the space brighter and more welcoming, but the floral potpourri scent was the same.

It wasn't overpowering, but the smell was a distinctive one she associated with the inn and Penelope Jones. Juliet's grandmother was nice, but she used to intimidate Bria with her perfect posture and mannerisms. The etiquette lessons at the cupcake shop had struck terror into her. She hadn't wanted to mess up and earn a disapproving glare, even though the woman was more known for passing out full-size candy bars at Halloween than criticism.

No one stood behind the front desk, so Bria went into the dining room. Striped wallpaper in mauve tones covered the walls. The potpourri scent wasn't as strong.

A man and woman sat at a round table to the left of the entrance, having an animated conversation. Her father was seated at a table for four next to a large window, overlooking the side garden. He must have wanted the view because they didn't need a big table.

His gray pinstriped suit, white dress shirt, and pink tie coordinated with the décor. Anyone looking at Brian Landon would see a successful businessman. Few knew appearances were everything to him. He was nothing more than smoke and mirrors.

It had been a hard truth to learn about her father, but the older she got, the more she understood why her mom had left him. She only wanted to know why Annie Landon hadn't taken Bria with her.

She removed the laptop bag strap from her shoulder and sat on the opposite side of the table. Her water glass was full—no ice. The way she preferred. Had her dad remembered or had the ice already melted? She would go with the latter.

A menu lay on her plate, but her coffee cup was empty. She reached for the carafe, but her dad beat her to it.

"Coffee?" he asked.

"Please." Her insides were in knots and her heart hurt. She hadn't slept well once again and needed a boost from the caffeine.

As her dad filled her cup, the scent wafted between them.

He pushed the sugar bowl toward her. "Did you file with the court?"

"Yesterday afternoon." She'd driven to the county superior courthouse. "I'm officially Aunt Elise's personal representative, and the necessary paperwork to open probate was filed."

The one-hour drive each way had given her time to think about what Charlene had told Bria and Missy. Her aunt wanted father and daughter to reconcile, and Bria would be open to that, as long as her dad was reasonable about their shared inheritance. Elise wouldn't have wanted the cupcake shop to get dragged into his next get-rich-quick scheme.

Her dad sipped his coffee. "How long will probate take?"

"Six months to a year."

His face dropped. "That's ridiculous."

His reaction didn't surprise her. Patience had never been his strong point, but he had no choice this time. "That's the normal length. I'm doing what I can to shorten it. The local paper will publish Elise's death notice for three weeks. That gives creditors four months to file a claim against the estate. Otherwise, they get two years."

His face snarled. "Talk about a scam."

She nearly snorted, given what he'd pulled with his sister.

"Creditors need to be paid before beneficiaries receive their part." Beneficiaries sounded more official than saying him and her. She wanted to put distance between the estate and her father for as long as possible.

"But you can sell assets, right? I can't be stuck in limbo for the entire six months."

Bria fought the urge to remind him that he wasn't the sole beneficiary of the cupcake shop and that it could take up to a year. She sipped her coffee so she wouldn't say the wrong thing.

"Marc is helping me understand all the ins and outs of my duties to the estate." Elise's savings and checking accounts and life insurance payout would transfer directly to Bria. The house and business would go into probate. "It's been less than twenty-four hours since I filed. Paying creditors and bills and keeping the cupcake shop running are my priorities."

"But you can make decisions about the bakery."

It wasn't a question.

"Yes." She wouldn't lie, but she wouldn't tell him how much power she had as Elise's personal representative. Not until Bria found out his intentions because she didn't trust him. He shouldn't show up thinking the past, especially his lack of participation in her life, would be brushed aside that easily. "I went through the books. I want to show you a few things."

Several, actually.

Last night, she'd reviewed the cupcake shop's financials, analyzing the shop's profit for the past five years, calculating projections for the future, and itemizing capital expenditures that had been put off for too long. She'd organized the data into easily digestible spreadsheets for her father.

"After we order. I'm hungry." He picked up his menu. "They've updated their offerings since the last time I was here with Elise. Does anything look good to you?"

Bria hadn't touched the menu yet. A glance told her what to get. "The stuffed French toast."

"That sounds good, but I'm having the big breakfast and the Danish aebleskivers." He lowered his menu. "So many breakfast foods have nationalities as part of their names, but I can't think of anything called American except cheese."

A young woman wearing a Victorian-inspired apron took their order and checked the coffee level in the carafe. "The breakfast crowd is light today, so your food won't take too long."

"Thank you." Bria would have preferred unzipping her bag and pulling out her printouts so they could get the discussion over with, but they had all morning. "I examined the cupcake shop's numbers over the past five years. There'd been a slight decrease in profits when Elise relapsed, but things have improved with the change of management three months ago."

Her father raised his cup. "Does Missy Hanford want to stay on as manager?"

His question allowed hope to blossom. Bria wanted to cling to that with both hands. "Yes. Missy gave up another part-time job to manage the cupcake shop full time. The two made plans together, so Missy would know what Elise wanted for the bakery."

As he sipped his coffee, his eyes betrayed nothing.

"The employees have wonderful things to say about Missy." Bria had to protect her friend's job. No matter what it took.

"Elise never delegated well. I hope Missy will."

What her father said was true. Aunt Elise had been a control freak, but cancer had made her realize she couldn't do it all herself. "Elise handed off a lot to Missy, even before she stopped working, and taught her all she needed to know about running the bakery. Missy delegates and has put her own touches on things, including some recipes. The birthday sale sold the most cupcakes ever. That had a lot to do with her passing being so fresh in people's minds, but it wasn't the only thing driving sales. Missy played a big part in the success, too."

The server set their breakfasts in front of them. "If you need anything, please let me know."

"Everything looks delicious." Her dad picked up his fork. "Thank you."

Bria waited for the server to walk away so that she could continue. "There's room for growth, but I'm not sure how much you expect the cupcake shop to bring in."

"The Danes need kudos for creating pancake balls." He dipped one of the aebleskivers in jam before popping it into his mouth. "Want one?"

"No, thanks." Bria doubted she would eat much of what she'd ordered. "Dad—"

"You're thinking too small, baby doll." He wiped his mouth with a napkin. "Just like Elise did."

Warning bells rang in Bria's head, but she wouldn't panic. Her father was wired to chase pots of gold. Nothing would happen without her approval. No matter what he said or wanted, she had the power.

Still, she had no idea what he meant. A bakery didn't have that many variables to play with. Though, she realized a bigger one. "Customers accept the current prices, but the volume doesn't come close to the annual birthday sale. I'm sure places in Portland and Seattle charge more, but I doubt that would work in Berry Lake except for special, limited-time products."

He finished what was in his mouth and took a sip of coffee. "I'm not talking about pricing or volume."

Her fingers gripped her fork, so she didn't drop it. "Then, I have no idea what you mean."

Her dad checked his watch. "Let's finish our breakfast. I have someone joining us who will explain this better than I can."

"Who?"

"A consultant from Portland. He works with small businesses, though real estate is his specialty, and he's originally from Berry Lake. He'll help us recognize opportunities we can't see and weigh our options."

There is only one option.

Her dad would recognize that after he went over the data.

She stabbed a piece of French toast with her fork and ate it. "We don't need help."

Especially a real estate consultant who was merely her father's yes man.

"You need to return to San Diego, and I have other things going on. He'll make our lives easier."

Only if the consultant agreed with Bria. "The estate won't pay unnecessary expenses. I'm not taking payment for being the personal representative."

"I'm covering the cost. His services will pay for themselves." He pushed up his sleeve and checked his watch before glancing toward the dining room's entrance and waving. "Right on time."

Bria wanted to see who was foolish enough to work with her father. Most likely another fortune seeker. She turned to her right.

A six-foot-one man with brown wavy hair and warm hazel eyes she used to dream about strode toward the table with a leather briefcase in hand.

No.

Oh, no.

Her blood turned ice cold. Her muscles tensed into tight balls. Nerve endings shrieked before snapping to attention like soldiers preparing to storm the battlefield.

She clutched the fork so hard it would leave an impression against her palm. "What have you done?"

"I found the perfect person to help us." Her father spoke as if he'd forgotten what happened during her senior year of high school. He must have, or he would've never hired the one person she hated in this world—*her* worst enemy. "You remember Dalton Dwyer, right?"

He'd been her first boyfriend, her first kiss, her first love.

She'd tried to forget Dalton, but he'd remained a warning that hearing "I love you" from a man meant nothing. How could it, when he'd dumped her a week before their senior prom in the hallway outside the cafeteria. He let everyone hear his reasons for breaking up—not good enough or thin enough for him. He'd struck at her weak points with bullseye precision. He'd never used the word "fat" but implied it.

The result?

Fat shaming from his friends for the rest of the school year.

Remembering the taunts and bullying sent her to a deep, dark place inside her that she'd hoped never to go to again.

Snort, snort.

Here, piggy, piggy.

You must eat cupcakes for breakfast, lunch, and dinner.

I hear meth will help you lose weight.

Do you have to lie down to zip up your jeans?

Dalton had never said those things, but he hadn't spoken up when his friends did. The humiliation and the heartbreak had sent her spiraling.

Bile rose into her throat. She shivered.

It had taken every ounce of power to finish the final month of school and graduate. If not for her job at the cupcake shop and her friends there, she might not have survived in one piece. The Posse had helped her in ways she would never be able to repay. By the end of the summer, she was doing better—therapy helped—but all she'd wanted was to put Dalton Dwyer and Berry Lake behind her.

She'd succeeded until her aunt got sick.

And then, she regretted allowing him and his jerk friends to keep her away for so long. Aunt Elise had visited San Diego, but Bria had lost so much time with her.

If only Bria had been stronger.

Dalton stood next to the table. "Hello, Brian. It's nice to see you again, Bria."

She didn't—couldn't—look at him. Instead, she raised her coffee cup, forcing her hand not to shake, and took a sip. She barely tasted the coffee, but the action gave her time to pull herself together. She wasn't eighteen but thirty-three. That mousey girl she'd been was nothing more than a shadow of the woman she was now, especially after her aunt's illness and death.

He sat in the chair next to her dad. "I've lived in Portland for over five years, and the morning traffic keeps getting worse. I should have stayed here last night instead of driving over today."

"I thought the same thing yesterday." Her father filled Dalton's coffee cup. "But you're right on time, as usual."

As usual?

The two appeared familiar with one another, and that burned as if she'd swallowed a glowing red charcoal briquette. Bria took another sip. Part of her wanted to make a scene and storm out, but the whole reason she was there was the cupcake shop. That had to be her priority, nothing else.

Dalton added cream to his coffee. "My condolences. Elise was a wonderful woman. This must be a difficult time for both of you."

"Thank you. It is," her father said. "But life goes on, and decisions must be made before Bria returns to San Diego."

She appreciated him answering so she wouldn't have to, but his flippant tone bristled.

"Is that where you live?" Dalton asked.

There was no way of avoiding him now. She placed her cup on the table and met his gaze.

A lightning bolt didn't strike, and nothing exploded. More surprisingly, her heart continued to beat. But couldn't the guy have not aged so well? He was more attractive now than he'd been as a teenager.

147

"Yes," she said finally.

"Bria is a CPA with a top accounting firm." Her father motioned to the server and then gestured to his plate. "She doesn't mind the nine-to-five grind and even bought a place. Not the life for me, but she enjoys it."

"I love it." She would take the stability of a secure job and a thirty-year mortgage over the nomad lifestyle she'd lived with him before her aunt stepped in.

"An accountant, huh?" Dalton half laughed. "That doesn't surprise me. You always had a thing for numbers."

She had no idea what he meant, nor did she care.

"Are you finished, ma'am?" the server asked.

Bria had only picked at her food until Dalton arrived. No way would she be able to eat more now. With her stomach churning so much, Bria felt physically ill. She pushed her plate toward the server. "I am."

As soon as the server picked up the plates, Dalton removed two glossy folders.

Not to be outdone, Bria pulled out her analysis and gave it to her dad. "I didn't know my father had hired anyone, so I only made one copy."

Her dad laughed. "You both came prepared."

She placed her hand on top of her knee to keep it from bouncing. "That's what this meeting is about."

"I put together the options we discussed to bring Bria up to date." He handed her a folder. "See what you think."

Bria opened it and nearly gasped at the table of contents. This information wasn't something thrown together after a quick phone call with her dad yesterday. She closed the cover. "How long have you been working on this?"

"Almost two months."

She'd had no reason to doubt what Charlene had said, but Dalton's answer was proof. The fact her father had hired a guy before mentioning anything to her was an added betrayal.

Oh, Aunt Elise, he's played you and me.

As Bria's temper shot into the red zone, she took a breath and then stared at her father. "Why did you act surprised when Marc read the will? You knew Aunt Elise left you half of the cupcake shop, yet pretended as if you didn't."

Her father shrugged. "I realized you didn't know, or you would have reached out before."

"Before?"

"Before Elise died."

Bria balled her fists. "I would have never discussed that before Aunt Elise was gone. I only talked about the cupcake shop with Missy after Elise went into hospice. It would have been inappropriate."

Her father's face went blank. "Someone needs to be reasonable about the cupcake shop."

"Reasonable?" She lowered her voice and opened the folder. "Franchise opportunities. Building sale assessment. Nowhere do I see anything that says continue running the cupcake shop as Aunt Elise wanted."

"Elise didn't want to sell the shop?" Dalton asked, sounding surprised.

"No," Bria said sharply. "She wanted Missy Hanford to manage and upgrade the shop. If you look at my analysis, you'll see a breakdown of the costs as well as projected profits. It's doable, and we'd both receive a decent monthly income after expenses."

Dalton skimmed the pages she'd provided, but his face remained neutral. "You never mentioned keeping the cupcake shop, Brian."

Her dad's face flushed. "Elise is dead. Bria and I don't live in Berry Lake. We can't keep the cupcake shop operating as it is today. Besides, the value is in the building."

Bria wanted to know her father's intentions. Well, he'd laid them out as clear as the water in Berry Lake come springtime. It was as she feared—he didn't care about the shop and her aunt's legacy—but that didn't stop her stomach from sinking and her aching heart to feel as if it had been used as a punching bag.

Dalton stared over her report. "Your father told me keeping the shop wasn't an option."

Of course, he did. "It's the only option for me."

Her dad rolled his eyes. "Be reasonable, Bria."

"I am one hundred percent reasonable." She kept her voice even. "You're almost sixty. Social security payments will only go so far. You don't have a 401K, but do you have a Roth IRA or a SEP? We can structure profit payments any way you want. Monthly or weekly, even."

"I'd rather have my proceeds from selling the building, invest it, and double my money."

So typical. "You could lose it all."

His chin jutted forward. "That's a chance I'm willing to take."

Bria sat back in her chair. "I wonder what Elise would say."

Her father did a double take. "Excuse me?"

"According to Charlene Culpepper, the only reason Elise left you fifty percent was to bring us closer."

"She may have mentioned that."

"You're the one who called her and suggested she do this. It was you. Not her."

Fear flashed in her father's eyes, but a second later, he was back in control, sipping his coffee.

Bria had to get this out. "How can you talk about selling and investing and being okay with losing what she spent her life creating? Do you think she would have rewritten her will if she thought you would sell the building or franchise the bakery?"

A vein ticced at his jaw.

Bria didn't expect him to answer. "You've ignored everything Elise wanted you to do. Instead of reaching out to me two months ago, you hired the one person I never wanted to see again. You act as if you're doing this for me when it's only about you."

Dalton shifted, appearing uncomfortable. "Bria—"

"I'm sorry my father dragged you into this." She looked at her father. "Aunt Elise wanted Missy to keep the cupcake shop going, and that's what I will make sure happens with or without you."

Her father's face hardened. "Fifty percent of the cupcake shop belongs to me."

"It will, but it doesn't yet," she countered.

"I have an idea." Dalton flashed a tight smile. "Why don't I review your numbers with your dad? In the meantime, gather up any blueprints or proposals you have on the upgrades Elise intended to make. We can meet tomorrow to discuss everything. Say at two o'clock at the cupcake shop?"

Bria had no idea where the plans were, but maybe Missy knew. "Fine."

"Read what Dalton gave you." Tight lines formed around her father's mouth.

Her father handed her his report. Now she had two of them.

"It's only polite after the work he put into this," her father added.

A waste of time, too, but... "I can do that."

"We'll see you tomorrow," her dad said.

Bria shoved the shiny folder into her laptop bag, left the other one for her dad, removed a twenty from her purse, and tossed it onto the table. She had no idea what kind of game her father was playing or what Dalton's role in this was, but she didn't trust either of them. No matter what it took, she would protect her aunt's legacy from both men.

🧁 🧁 🧁

Dalton stared at Bria as she stood. Even though gold flames flickered in her eyes, her frustration and disappointment was palpable. She'd been blindsided multiple ways today.

By her father. And by him.

She didn't storm out, but she left the dining room without a glance back.

Brian scrubbed his face with his hands. "That didn't go the way I expected."

Dalton, either.

The girl he remembered would've never stood up to her father the way Bria had. The only thing the woman he'd met this morning and the mousy smart girl from high school had in common was their devotion to Elise Landon.

Dalton glanced at her analysis. "You left out a few details when you mentioned selling the building."

The man had aged ten years in the last few minutes. "Bria will come around once she sees the money involved."

He didn't understand Brian's desperation. Nor did Dalton appreciate the way the man hadn't been open with his daughter. "Whether or not Bria wants to sell is secondary. She doesn't want to work with me. I'll ask Tanner to replace me with someone else."

His boss wanted that building, and Dalton wouldn't be an obstacle to that happening.

Brian shook his head. "No one else knows Berry Lake as well as you do."

"I haven't been here in fifteen years." He spoke to his mother a couple of times a year but only when she needed him. He'd given up on Remy and Owen, and Dalton feared Ian would be next to take advantage of people to increase their net worth.

The worst part?

His mother did it by marrying and divorcing the wealthier men and business owners in the area. Those men lost everything over his mom's fake affections.

"It has to be you." Brian lifted his coffee cup and stared over the lip. "Besides, you owe me."

"My father owed you." Dalton had no idea what that debt entailed, but as his father lay on his death bed, he'd told a seventeen-year-old Dalton to do whatever Brian Landon needed if he ever asked for help or a favor. Dalton, who thought of his father every day, had promised he would.

He had no idea why his dad, who'd been an honorable and kind man, had been friends with Brian Landon. The man went from shady to charming in the blink of an eye. Even at his best, he gave off a scam artist vibe. But a promise was a promise.

Melissa McClone

"I'll help you, but Bria might refuse to work with me."

"Perhaps." Brian tapped his chin. "Or we use this in our favor."

"Use what?"

"The way she feels about you."

Dalton shook his head. "We were kids back then."

"You saw the way she reacted when you came in."

"Yeah, she hates me." He'd hurt her. Breakups were never pleasant, whether as an adult or teenager. But her feelings about seeing him had been clear. She'd even mentioned it to her dad. Dalton had ended things with her during their lunch period. He couldn't remember what he'd said, but she'd cried, and others had laughed. He'd tried to play it cool, but that had only upset Bria more. "I should have broken up with her in a better way."

"Sometimes, there is no good way." Brian tilted his chin. "I don't blame you for dumping Bria and taking Heather Young to the prom. My daughter wasn't about to put out. She clung to her virginity like a badge of honor, which is surprising given how much Elise slept around. I'm sure you had more fun with that cheerleader."

Dalton couldn't believe Brian. It wasn't as if he'd been around when Bria was in high school. No wonder they weren't close. The guy was a jerk.

"Prom wasn't my only reason for breaking up with her." His dad would have been disappointed in him, but Dalton had found himself trapped in a box canyon with no way out. His mom went crazy dating every guy she could after his dad died, if only to have leftovers to bring home for them to eat. The twins had rebelled and acted out. And Dalton was the one left to take care of Ian. Bria had been the calm, the eye of the hurricane in his turbulent world, but he'd needed his friends and a way to help his family more than he needed her.

"Whatever your reason, it doesn't matter now, but you should apologize to Bria."

Dalton nearly laughed. "A little late, don't you think?"

"Not at all." Brian's eyes brightened. "You were the first boy she fell in love with, and she still has feelings for you. A father knows these things. If you apologize and ask her out, compliment her, romance her, she'll be on our side before she leaves town."

"That's…"

"Brilliant."

"Wrong."

"How is it wrong? Your boss believes Berry Lake is prime for redevelopment. Tanner wants to start with the cupcake shop's building. If you get it for him, you'll end up with a hefty commission and his gratitude, possibly a raise. All you're doing is helping Bria to see other options. Selling the building will set her up for the future. That's why I'm pushing so hard."

"You'd be set up, too."

"Never said I wouldn't."

"It's not ethical."

Brian shrugged. "I'd say it's more a gray area."

"Not to me. I don't work that way."

He held up his hands. "I wasn't implying anything about you."

Yeah, right. Dalton didn't know what Brian was trying to pull. He hated being dragged into this mess. But thanks to Tanner and a promise made to his late father, Dalton couldn't say no.

"It doesn't matter what either of us wants." Dalton had seen the determined set of her jaw. "If Bria wants to sell, it'll be because she's convinced it's the best option for her aunt's estate. Nothing else will sway her."

The lines on Brian's forehead deepened. "Why do you say that?"

"She's a CPA. She'll go by the numbers."

Brian dragged his hand through his hair. "That's true, so we need to show her that selling is the best option."

"She has the info, but..." Dalton couldn't shake the expression on her face when she first saw him. "I do need to apologize to her. That's something I should have done years ago."

He would have, except he didn't want to look bad in front of his friends. Back then, that had mattered, especially when dating Bria had almost made him an outcast, when he could least afford to be.

Literally.

Brian wagged his eyebrows. "Flowers wouldn't hurt."

"I'll do this my way. But if she doesn't want anything to do with me after that, I'll talk to Tanner. I won't be the reason this deal falls apart."

"That's reasonable." Brian studied him. "You remind me of your father. Paul Dwyer was a good man."

"Thanks." Dalton's chest swelled with pride. His dad had been a great man, better than his mom deserved and nothing at all like Brian Landon.

But taking flowers to Bria might not be such a bad idea.

chapter thirteen

INSIDE THE CUPCAKE shop, Juliet sat at a table by herself. The place wasn't as crowded as on Monday, but she would have preferred to have more people around to distract her. She clasped her hands on her lap, but that might make her appear to be trying too hard. She shook out her fingers.

Why can't I get comfortable?

This bakery and the Huckleberry Inn were her two favorite places in town. But all she could think was how she looked out of place in her blush pink skirt and matching short-sleeve jacket when everyone else wore shorts because of the late-summer weather. At least she'd left off the pearl necklace. The stud earrings were plenty for this afternoon meeting.

Well, interview.

Which was why she'd dressed more like a European royal than a stay-at-home housewife from the Pacific Northwest.

Charlene had shocked her by wanting to meet today, only hours after they'd spoken on the phone this morning.

You have nothing to lose.

Juliet kept telling herself that. Whether or not she got hired, making that phone call was a huge step. One she wouldn't discount. If Juliet had called one person for a job, she could do it again. And again. No matter how many times it took until she was hired.

Juliet rubbed her palms over her skirt. She wasn't sweating yet, and she hoped that continued. She hadn't looked for a job since college, but she'd lucked out with the first application she'd submitted to the theme park. There'd been hundreds of women who showed up, but they'd chosen her to be one of the princesses.

It had been so easy.

Too easy?

Maybe that was why questions and doubt plagued her now.

Juliet clasped her hands again and rested them on the tabletop. The last time she'd been this nervous had been...

Her first date with Ezra.

Ezra.

Juliet hadn't wanted to tell him face-to-face about her interview because he would tear down the confidence boost Selena had given her, but Juliet had been too afraid *not* to say something to him, so she'd texted him after phoning Charlene. Cowardly, yes, but Juliet hadn't wanted to give him more ammunition to make her feel bad about herself.

Of course, he'd managed to do that via text, anyway.

Thank goodness she'd already spoken to Charlene or Juliet might not have called her.

Still, she had her husband's permission to accept a job if she found one. And that was a big *if*—an impossible one—according to him. She reread the text exchange.

Juliet: *Charlene Culpepper is hiring. I want to apply for a job with her.*

Ezra: *She would never hire someone unskilled like you.*

Juliet: *I'd still like to apply, if only for the experience.*

Ezra: *If you want to waste your time, go ahead.*

Juliet: *On the off chance I got the job, can I take it?*

Ezra: *You have nothing to offer Charlene or any employer. You won't get it.*

Juliet: *Maybe if it was entry level.*

Ezra: *No, but if someone out there takes pity on you, go ahead and accept. It's past time you contributed to our household income.*

Juliet: *Thank you so much.*

Ezra: *But don't you dare cry when you don't get the job. You know I hate tears.*

Juliet: *I promise I won't.*

Missy came out of the kitchen, caught Juliet's eye, and did a double take. "Hey. Look at you, all pretty in pink. What can I get you?"

"I'm not sure."

She wiped her hands on her apron streaked with chocolate. "That's a first for you."

"Yes, but…" Despite Selena's assurances, Juliet had told no one about her job hunt. This interview was her first attempt to find work in more than a decade. The odds of being hired were slim, so she hadn't mentioned anything on the new Posse group chat. Her four friends wouldn't laugh at her, but she wasn't used to putting herself out there. The last time had been when she'd baked sweet potatoes instead of russets, and Ezra had thrown a fit.

Missy isn't him.

And she would find out soon enough when Charlene arrived.

Juliet took a steadying breath. "I'm meeting Charlene. We're, um, discussing a job she wants to fill, so this is like an interview."

"Sounds like it *is* an interview. And that's wonderful." Missy clapped her hands together. "Charlene would be a fool not to hire you. You were born to be an event planner. A shoo-in."

Heat rushed up Juliet's neck. "Thanks. I hope that's true. I'm nervous."

Missy glanced at her hands. "I'd hug you, but you don't need chocolate on your clothes. But I will say this. Being nervous is a natural reaction. I felt the same way when Elise wanted to discuss the future of the cupcake shop, even though I've worked here forever."

"That makes me feel better."

"Good." Missy's smile brightened her face. "Now, since your interview is with Nell's mom, you're allowed a minor freak-out. The woman makes her daughters nervous."

"That's true." Juliet laughed. "Thanks."

"You're welcome. What you need is a cupcake or something to drink." Missy thought for a moment. "Charlene has a cupcake tasting here, too, so food might be too much, but I'll get two coffees. If you don't want any, you can at least hold the cup. That'll give you something to do with your hands. That's a problem for me when nerves get the best of me."

Leave it to Missy to not only understand but offer a solution. "Thank you."

"It's my pleasure." She cleaned a nearby table. "The Posse helps each other. That's what we said the other night."

160

"We did." If not for that dinner and Selena coming over the next day, Juliet wouldn't be here today. "Nell setting up the group chat was a good step."

"We should have done that long ago." Missy cradled dirty dishes. "Bria's upstairs in the office. She burst in like a woman on a mission. I'll let her know you're here but tell her not to disturb you during your interview. Good luck."

"Thanks, I need it." Juliet wanted this to go well, more than she'd wanted anything in a long time.

The bell on the door jingled. Juliet glanced at the shop's entrance to see Charlene Culpepper. She wore an orange dress and stylish pumps, and a matching handbag.

Customers parted like the Red Sea to get out of the woman's way. If Charlene noticed, she didn't acknowledge them. Instead, she made a beeline to where Juliet sat. A floral fragrance floated in the air as if announcing the arrival of its wearer. "Good afternoon, Juliet."

"Lovely shoes."

Charlene tittered. "Oh, these old things. Thank you. They're comfortable and classic, so they never go out of style."

"Those are the best."

As Charlene sat at the table, a high school kid brought over two coffees and napkins. "Courtesy of the Berry Lake Cupcake Shop. Enjoy."

Leave it to Missy. Juliet smiled at the teenager and took a cup. The heat warmed her cold hands. "Thank you."

Charlene placed her purse on an empty chair. "How are you today?"

"Good." Juliet moistened her lips, hoping she hadn't bit off her lipstick. "Thanks for meeting with me."

"I'm delighted you called. Selena gave me a heads-up when we had coffee yesterday, so thank you for following through."

Juliet had no idea what to say other than, "You're welcome."

Charlene studied her. "You're ready to work outside the home?"

"Yes." Juliet waited to see if a one-word answer was enough, but no reply came, so she tried to think of more to add. "We've lived in Berry Lake for almost a year. I have my household routine dialed in. With Ezra's work hours, I have plenty of free time on my hands."

"Does your husband support you taking on the job?"

"We haven't discussed this particular job." Or any, but Charlene didn't need to know that. "But he's mentioned wanting me to contribute more."

"It's good to have your spouse on board when you do something new."

"Yes, and Ezra is the reason I feel qualified to work as an event planner." Juliet's voice sounded stronger than she felt, but she dug deep to keep from hunching her shoulders and giving up. She focused on what Selena had told her—that Charlene needed Juliet. "I have no formal training, but I've organized dinners, brunches, and parties for Ezra's clients for years. I worked with caterers in Los Angeles and locally, but I've done some of my own cooking here. I also did the interior design on our home. As I mentioned in my resume, my job at the theme park provided me with plenty of interaction to hone my customer service skills and patience."

That summed up her limited skills. Juliet hoped it was enough.

"You also helped your grandmother at the Huckleberry Inn, correct?"

"Yes." Juliet's parents had traveled so much the inn became her second home. But that hadn't been a job per se, so she hadn't listed it on her resume. "My favorite thing was to assist her with the afternoon tea service."

Charlene took a sip of coffee, so Juliet did the same.

"Events by Charlene is a niche business. Many don't expect to find our level of service in a small town." Charlene's voice was animated. "People wonder how we stay in business, but our reputation extends beyond Berry Lake, and we've organized events around the state and in Oregon."

As Juliet gripped the cup, it almost crumpled. She set her coffee on the table and placed her hands on her lap. "I had no idea."

That didn't bode well for a newbie to the industry. Her fingernails dug into her palms.

"I'm known as the town's busybody, and you're friends with my eldest daughter, so I'm sure she's said plenty about me." Charlene didn't appear upset about that. If anything, her chest puffed, and laughter gleamed in her eyes. "But my business speaks for itself, so I don't have to. Word of mouth brings in more clients than we can handle at the moment, which is why I'm hiring more staff."

Please, oh please. Pick me.

Juliet forced herself from saying that or leaning forward or offering to work for free during a trial period. Instead, she took a slow sip from her coffee cup. "What are you looking for?"

Charlene's lips curved into a predatorial smile as if she'd been hunting and snared her prey. "Someone exactly like you."

Juliet's mouth fell open. "Wow. I don't know what to say."

"Say yes to being my assistant. I want to train you to handle events without me being there. That would keep me from having to turn down clients," Charlene said without missing a beat. "The work is hard and the hours long. There are times I've put on an apron to serve when the caterers ran short of staff while trying to keep a wedding on track. But the key is to let the clients think everything's happening as planned."

Juliet tapped her toes. She couldn't believe this was happening. "Yes."

"I do a sixty-day trial period with new employees. That's usually enough time to give people a taste of the events we do and determine if this is the job for them. I'll pay twenty dollars an hour, and then we'll readdress the rate after two months."

That was more than the minimum wage. She forced herself to breathe. "Thank you for such a wonderful opportunity."

"You might not thank me after a client yells at you for something out of your control."

"It can't be worse than some of the parents I dealt with at the theme park."

The bell jingled. Charlene glanced at the door. "The couple who just entered is engaged. We're doing their wedding in December. I won't throw you into the fire and make you stay for the cupcake tasting, but I'd like to introduce you."

"Sure." Juliet glanced that way.

The couple was tall and striking with brown hair and big smiles. Juliet recognized the woman. "I know Sheridan DeMarco."

"I thought you might, even though she's younger than you and Nell."

Sheridan's father, Sal, owned the gallery. Last Thanksgiving, he'd fired her to hire his stepdaughter, Remy Dwyer. It turned out Sal had evicted his daughter, too, so Remy could have the apartment above the gallery. Juliet hadn't seen Sheridan since she'd worked at the cupcake shop in December.

"Juliet." As Sheridan made her way to the table, she had a bounce to her step. "How are you?"

"Good." Juliet stood to hug Sheridan. "I hear congratulations are in order."

Sheridan held out her left hand, showing off a three-carat diamond engagement ring. Guess the rumors about her marrying well were true. If so, she deserved it, given what her father and stepmother had put her through.

Juliet peered closer. "It's stunning."

And so was Sheridan. She glowed.

"This is my fiancé, Michael Patterson." Sheridan touched the man's arm. "This is Juliet Monroe. She worked at the cupcake shop a long time ago, moved away, and returned last year."

Michael was handsome with blue eyes, a beard, and an athletic build. He shook Juliet's hand. His grip was firm. "It's nice to meet you."

The two made a cute couple. She'd forgotten how all-consuming love looked. "You, too."

"I'm happy you know each other." Charlene greeted the couple. "Juliet will be working with me."

"Wonderful." Sheridan leaned into Michael. "We want cupcakes at the reception, which is why we're here."

"Thanks for postponing the tasting, Charlene." Michael wrapped his arm around Sheridan. "I'm glad Buddy Riggs could fit us in. The Bigfoot overnight search was on my bucket list."

Sheridan nodded. "It wasn't on mine, but I had fun seeing what all the fuss was about. And the s'mores we ate were to die for."

"You can special order s'mores cupcakes." Juliet remembered how Elise kept the same sixteen flavors on the menu, but she did custom ones for events. Only it wouldn't be Elise making them any longer.

Juliet's throat tightened.

"I forgot the shop sold them." Sheridan glanced at Michael.

His gaze softened. "You only worked here for three weeks in December."

Sheridan nodded. "And I've been distracted since then in the best possible way."

Juliet remembered being like that when she'd first met Ezra. If only things hadn't changed…

"If those aren't included in today's sample, I'll talk to Missy about getting a couple for you to try." Charlene typed on her phone. "I'm making a note to myself, so I don't forget."

"Thanks," Sheridan and Michael said at the same time. They looked at each other and then brought their foreheads together.

So adorable. Juliet ignored the pang of jealousy. "It's great seeing you again, Sheridan, and meeting you, Michael. I'm sure you're eager to taste cupcakes."

Both nodded.

She placed her purse strap on her shoulder before grabbing the coffee cups and napkins from the table. "I'll take these, so you have a clean table."

"Thanks, Juliet. I'll be in touch soon." Charlene motioned to the couple. "Why don't we sit so we can get started?"

"I'll let Missy know you're ready." Juliet carried the cups into the kitchen and threw them away. "Charlene is ready for the tasting."

Missy stopped frosting cupcakes. "Thanks, how did it go?"

"Hired on the spot." Juliet pumped her fists in the air. "I can't believe it."

"Woo-hoo," Missy cheered. "And believe it because the job is perfect for you."

"There's a sixty-day probation period."

"Which you will nail."

"I'm crossing my fingers." Juliet did.

Missy laughed. "Just wait. You'll see I'm right. Bria's still upstairs if you want to tell her."

"Thanks." Juliet climbed the stairs. She hadn't been up this way in fifteen years. At some point, the walls had been painted, but they could use a new coat.

The lockers and bench were in the same place. She remembered sitting there as they changed out of uniforms and into their regular clothes—the chatting, the laughing, and sometimes the tears.

Good times.

She peered into the office.

Bria was hunched over the desk, going through the filing drawer. She appeared oblivious to everything.

Juliet knocked. "Hey."

Bria glanced up. "Juliet, is everything okay?"

"You're looking at the newest employee at Events by Charlene."

"Oh, wonderful." The words lacked Bria's usual enthusiasm.

Juliet took a closer look. Her friend's eyes were red and puffy.

Oh, no. She tossed her purse onto the daybed—that was new—and went to Bria. "Missing Elise?"

"Always, but today"—Bria sniffled—"my dad upset me. He'll inherit fifty percent of the cupcake shop, but he's not interested in the bakery. He wants to sell the building. He hired Dalton Dwyer to help him."

Juliet's jaw dropped. "Dalton Dwyer?"

Bria nodded. "*The* Dalton Dwyer, who I never wanted to see again as long as I lived."

Juliet touched Bria's shoulder. "Are you okay?"

"I have no idea. My world has spun off its axis, and I fear it'll never go back to the way it should be."

Bria's ex-boyfriend had done a number on her. She'd started binging or not eating at all, but thankfully, enough of them had found out what she was doing and gone to Elise before it erupted into an eating disorder. That had been too big an issue for them to handle themselves when Bria would be away at college soon.

"What can I do to help?" Juliet asked.

"I'm looking for the cupcake shop's remodeling plans. They were done three years ago. I want to bring them with me to a meeting I have with Dad and Dalton tomorrow." She slammed the file drawer closed. "I remember looking at a binder and the floorplans. They weren't blueprints but that same size and rolled up, so not easy to hide."

The office was large, but there wasn't much storage. "Did you ask Missy?"

Bria nodded. "She said they were here at one point, but she doesn't remember where they went."

"Could they be at Elise's house?"

"Possibly. I don't remember seeing them anywhere, which is why I came here."

And had torn apart the office, searching for them.

Poor Bria. She was a neat freak. To make a mess showed her frustration.

Or panic.

Juliet thought for a moment. "If they aren't here, the house seems like the most logical place."

"You're right. It's the only place they would be." Bria rubbed the back of her neck. "I don't think my aunt would have thrown them away, but she'd gotten rid of a lot of stuff between my visits."

"Why don't we see if we can find them?" Juliet offered.

Bria perked up. "Do you have time?"

"Yes." Ezra's dinner was in the slow cooker, so Juliet only had to be home before him. "But let's clean up first."

"Oh, boy. This is a disaster. Missy doesn't need to deal with this."

Juliet smiled, hoping to reassure Bria. "Then let's work fast, so she doesn't see it."

chapter fourteen

A FTER CLOSING THE cupcake shop, Missy went to Elise's house and rang the doorbell. She didn't know if Bria was grieving or worried about the cupcake shop. Based on her question about the remodeling plans, probably the latter, but whichever it was, they would get through this. The alternative was... unacceptable.

Nell opened the door. "You made it."

Missy nodded, surprised to see her friend. "Hey, what are you doing here?"

"Juliet texted me. Bria needed help, and I was catching up on laundry and cleaning, so I came over." Nell wore shorts, a T-shirt, and flip-flops. She stepped back to give Missy room to enter the house. "We had Selena on FaceTime with us for a bit. Juliet was here, but she had to leave. Not quite a second Posse reunion, but two nights in a row of some of us being together bodes well for the future."

"I hope so." Missy had her sister-in-law, who was her best friend, but Jenny was busier than ever with a skyrocketing writing career, a husband, and a baby. They ate dinner together a few nights a week, but that was about it.

Time moved forward.

Missy had decided to do the same after Briley's birth, but making progress had been difficult. She loved the guest cottage in Jenny's backyard where Missy and her two fur babies lived, but she didn't want to be a burden to the growing family. That was how she felt when Dare's mom or one of his sisters visited. Jenny's house had a guest room, but between her writing schedule and Briley's sleep habits (or rather, lack of them lately), the cottage was a better option.

A few weeks ago, Missy had submitted an application to become pre-qualified for a mortgage, but with things up in the air with the cupcake shop, she would have to put buying a place on hold.

One step forward, another back.

She might see if there were any pet-friendly apartments available. Her dream place would be similar to Elise's. Extra touches and details added charm to the Craftsman-style home's classic design. If only the other things she'd loved about the house remained. The living room had once been cluttered with overflowing bookcases and cooking magazines—some years old—sitting in piles on the floor and end tables. Now, it was nearly empty. And...

The entire vibe in the house had changed. Not only from when Elise had been alive, but also since Saturday, when Missy brought Bria home after the funeral reception. A cloud of grief from the death of a loved one had hung over the house then. Today was different.

Darker. Suffocating. Hopeless.

Nell closed the door. "Bria... Missy's here."

Missy swallowed. "What's going on?"

"I'll let Bria explain."

Bria came into the living room. Strands of her hair went every which way. The streaks of dirt on her leggings and T-shirt suggested she'd been cleaning or doing yard work.

"I'm so glad you're here." Bria hugged Missy. "I didn't want to tell you what happened with my dad while you were working."

A weight as heavy as one of Rob's kettlebells settled in the bottom of her stomach, making her feel heavy all over. She'd hoped things would work out as Elise wanted, but that no longer appeared likely. Still, she smiled for her friend's sake. "I'm here now."

Bria rubbed her forehead with the back of her hand. "We've been searching the house for the remodeling plans and found nothing."

"Selena is contacting the designer who worked with Elise to see if she has a copy. That's plan B if we can't find them here." Nell handed Bria a bottle of water. "Hydrate. You've had a rough day."

"Thanks." Bria removed the lid and drank. "It's been a bad day, but things will get better."

"They will. I'll keep looking while you speak to Missy." Nell headed toward the hallway.

"Let's sit." Bria led her to the love seat. Only that, a coffee table, a TV, and Elise's recliner remained in the living room. Everything else had been donated or taken to the dump. "I had breakfast with my dad this morning. Unfortunately, it's what I thought. He doesn't care about the cupcake shop. He's all about selling the building. The sooner, the better."

Air squeezed from Missy's lungs. This was her second-worst nightmare. She'd lived through the first when Rob died.

Don't cry.

But that didn't stop the prickling behind her eyelids. "That would make for a bad day."

"My dad hired a consultant to help him. Dalton Dwyer."

Missy's mouth dropped. "Not the jerk Dalton Dwyer from high school."

"The jerk is now working for my father." Bria half laughed. "I guess it can't get any worse, right?"

"I sure hope not." Missy covered Bria's hand with her own. "I'm so sorry. Does your dad have the right to sell the building?"

"No, but at some point, he'll own fifty percent of the business. There's a mediation clause in the will if we can't agree, and I don't know on what grounds they would settle a situation like this."

Missy had no idea how mediation worked, but Bria's concerned expression quadrupled her worry. Bria had a job and a life somewhere else. Missy only had the cupcake shop. "Why do you need the renovation plans?"

As Bria explained what happened earlier, Missy's heart ached for her friend. To face her dad and Dalton together, when both wanted to sell Elise's legacy, had to have been impossibly difficult.

"The good thing that came out of the meeting is I know my dad's intention. I read through Dalton's proposal. Their plan includes more than the cupcake shop. They want to turn Berry Lake into a travel destination."

"It already is one during the summer."

"As the quaint small town we know and love, but investors want to make it year-round with higher-end shops and cafés on Main Street and a resort on Berry Lake."

"So, a fancy bakery instead of a cute cupcake shop with character."

"Exactly. And the investors see this for all the businesses in town. The cupcake shop is first on their list. I fear if they get ahold of one, they'll make a play for all the others."

"I'd love to be a fly on the wall when they approach Penelope Jones about the Huckleberry Inn."

"Oh, me, too. I imagine Penelope will grab them by the ear, give a twist, and toss them out the door before they know what hit them."

"I can picture her doing that." Missy laughed. "But seriously, whatever you need from me, I'm all in."

"I knew you would be. You're the one who has the most to lose, so I want you at the meeting tomorrow at two o'clock. It's at the cupcake shop. Be sure whatever you have going on in the kitchen is finished by then."

Missy sat taller. "I will. Thank you."

"I'm sorry this happened. Here's Dalton's proposal." Bria handed over a shiny folder. "I know you mentioned a notebook, but most of the plans we've discussed are a mix of texts and emails and notes. We need to formalize the details so others understand, namely my dad and Dalton, what we want to do."

"Tonight?"

"Before tomorrow's meeting. I know you have to wake up early."

"I can do a few things still tonight." Missy would do whatever it took, including losing sleep, to save the cupcake shop.

"I know you have more ideas than you shared with me. If you could please put everything in one place and email it to me tonight, that would be a huge help."

"The notebook Elise and I put together is in the office. I'll grab it on my way home."

"Thanks. I'm working on a proposal for the meeting. That's why I want the remodel plans. To convince my dad of the potential. Dalton works for a real estate development company, so he already sees it."

"And then?"

"We wait for creditors to file against the estate. They have four months. In the meantime, I'll pay the bills, and you'll keep the cupcake shop running."

Missy released the breath she'd been holding. "So, we don't have to close?"

"That's not an option."

"Are you going back to San Diego?"

"On Sunday, so I want everything settled by then. We need to get my dad and Dalton to give up on the crazy idea to sell. If we can't, Nell and Juliet are here, and Selena can be here in a few hours if you need her. You won't be on your own."

"Even if I'm by myself, I can handle it."

And them.

"I know you can, but I'd rather you not because you also have the cupcake shop to manage."

Yes, Missy did, and she would do her best for as long as that job was hers. "I don't have to go right home. Do you want me to help with the search?"

"The bedrooms are almost finished. How about the garage?"

Missy stood. "I'm on it."

An hour later, Missy carried a box containing photo albums and other memorabilia into the living room. A floral-fabric-covered journal with handwritten recipes sat on top. Nell and Bria relaxed on the couch with water bottles in hand.

"No plans or notebook, but I found this box." Missy set it on the hardwood floor. "You should go through it to see if there's anything you want to keep."

"Thanks." Bria took a sip from the bottle. "No plans in here, either."

"Selena will come through for us," Nell said without missing a beat.

Missy nodded before picking up the journal. "This has recipes in it. Do you mind if I take it home to read? I want to see if there are any new ones we could add to the menu."

"You're the baker." Bria yawned, stretching her arms over her head. "And something like that belongs at the shop, not in a box in San Diego."

"I'll put it in the office when I finish with it." Both Bria and Nell looked tired. "Do you want me to order you guys a pizza?"

"Thanks, but I have a fridge full of casseroles people dropped off. You're more than welcome to stay."

"I need to feed Mario and Peach. They don't mind me being gone all day as long as they get dinner on time."

"Spoiled kitties."

Missy laughed. "Both are divas. But what can I say? I love them."

She and Rob had adopted the two kittens before he deployed. The cats had been the leftovers from two different litters after an adoption event. He'd fallen in love with them at first glance. When they'd Skyped, Rob always had to see his babies as he called them, and before he blew them a goodbye kiss, he would tell them to take care of Mommy.

The two had. On the days when Missy wanted to stay in bed, Mario and Peach made her get up and feed them. They stayed by her side, morning and night, and their over-the-top antics helped her remember to smile and laugh.

Bria smiled at her. "Thanks for the help tonight."

"I'll email you the list before I go to bed." Missy tucked the journal into her purse. "And don't stay up all night. You don't have to finish until the meeting."

"You sound more and more like Nell." Bria winked.

"Well, someone has to look after all of you." Nell jumped up from the couch and hugged Missy. "Drive safe."

Ten minutes later, Missy parked in the driveway. The lights were on in the main house, but she didn't want to disturb Jenny and Dare. Missy went around to the side gate to let herself into the backyard. A few minutes later, she unlocked the front door to the sound of meows.

"I'm coming." The cats cried louder. "I promise you won't starve to death."

As Missy walked into the house, she blew a kiss at Rob's photo on the mantel and then dropped her keys in a bowl on the kitchen counter. That was the only way she remembered where they were.

The cats circled her legs. "One of these days, you'll make me fall, then who would feed you?"

They ignored her, as usual.

She opened a can of cat food and scooped the turkey into two bowls. The crying continued. "It's coming."

Not that it mattered what she said. They reacted this way at each mealtime, even though they had a small bowl of low-calorie dry cat food if they got hungry during the day. But both preferred the wet stuff.

Missy glanced at the mantel. "I should have known everything was too good to be true. But Bria and I will take care of everything. Fight if we have to."

Her heart ached. No, the new plan for her life—managing the cupcake shop, turning it into what Elise dreamed it could be, and buying a small house—wasn't over, but moving forward wasn't as easy—as simple—as she imagined it to be.

Her vision blurred, but no tears fell. Strange, given she'd been crying over Elise for days. Maybe she had no tears left.

"Heaven knows I've cried enough over you, babe." She reached under her shirt and felt Rob's dog tags and their wedding rings. They hadn't been able to afford anything more than plain gold bands, but it had been enough. "But I know you're watching over us. Me, the cats, Jenny, and her family. If you can put in a good word about Bria and the cupcake shop, I would appreciate it. I need things to work out the way we planned."

Otherwise, what will I do?

A knock sounded on the door.

That could only be one person. "Come in, Jenny."

Her sister-in-law entered, with her caramel-blond hair piled in a messy bun. She wore flannel pajama pants, a sweatshirt that had spit-up on the left sleeve, and fuzzy slippers—her usual writing attire. "I noticed you got home late. Were you at the rescue shelter?"

"No, I was helping Bria."

Jenny sat on the sofa. "You haven't been by this week. Briley misses Aunt Missy."

"It's been crazy with the birthday sale, the Posse reunion, and now the plans Bria and I made for the cupcake shop are up in the air because her dad inherited fifty percent of the business."

Jenny's forehead creased. "I thought it was all hers."

"Elise hadn't said for sure, but we assumed that. Now, Bria's dad wants to sell the building."

"I'm so sorry." Jenny hugged her. "I know how excited you've been."

"Thanks." Missy had hit the jackpot when she married Rob and got Jenny as a sister-in-law. "It's unexpected, but it's just a roadblock. Bria and I know what Elise wanted, and we're committed to making that happen. Otherwise, I have no idea what I'll do or where I'll end up."

"No matter how this turns out, you know we'll support you." Jenny held Missy's hand. "You always have a place here."

"Thanks, but you have your own family now. I can't live in your backyard cottage forever."

"Yes, you can. You're a part of the family, Missy. It's not only because I never would have survived losing my brother and parents without you but you also belong here. Like it or not, you're stuck with me."

Adrenaline shot through her, followed by a rush of warmth. Logically, Missy knew this, but hearing it helped her remember it. "Thanks and the same with you."

"I'm sure you and Bria will work out the issues with the cupcake shop, but if you ever need another job, you should start your own virtual assistant business. I know authors who would love someone like you."

Jenny would give her a glowing testimonial, so that was a possibility Missy hadn't considered, but she wanted to manage the cupcake shop. "I'll keep that in mind."

It was a good backup plan if she needed one. What had Nell called it? Plan B.

"Do," Jenny encouraged. "Dare would hire you to do all the stuff he hates."

"Ads." Those hadn't been Missy's favorite to do, either.

"Yep." A mischievous grin spread across Jenny's face. "He's also not pleased with the Ashton Thorpe fangirling in my reader group."

Missy laughed. "Tell your husband not to be jealous of the fictional character his wife writes. Ashton can only ever be the ultimate book boyfriend. Dare is all things."

"I have, but I like the way you put it." Jenny glanced at Rob's photo. "He would be proud of you."

"I haven't done much since he died."

"You've kept going, and I know there were times you didn't want to. I felt the same way. Elise and the cupcake shop helped you, too. Working there isn't just a job for you. So, no matter what roadblock you face, don't lose hope. You're a survivor. You and Bria will find a way to go around or over it. Maybe right through it. Your friends will help you. Me and Dare, too."

"Aw." Missy hugged Jenny. "I needed to hear this."

"Everything I said is true."

"Thank you." And Missy stared at Rob. *Thank you, too.*

chapter fifteen

A S THE PRINTER spewed out pages of the final proposal, Bria sat on the living room floor with the box of
memorabilia from the garage in front of her. A cup of
coffee and a half-eaten blueberry muffin were within arm's reach
on the coffee table. Her aunt's favorite music played—this playlist
included Duran Duran, Wham, Elton John, Queen, Culture
Club, Bon Jovi, Madonna, Kool and the Gang, and The Bangles.

A typical morning in some ways. A chaotic mess in others.

You finished the proposal. Everything is fine.

True.

The meeting with her father and Dalton wasn't for hours, so
she was ahead of schedule. A nap would be her smartest move—
she hadn't slept well again—but sleep wasn't happening. Still,
she needed something to keep her mind from running over the
what-ifs and possible outcomes. Otherwise, she would end up
feeling queasier than she did now.

Maybe whatever was inside the box would do it.

The box was non-descript, plain cardboard with flaps on the top. A faint musty smell lingered, suggesting some of the stuff, if not most of it, hadn't been touched in years. Weird, because Aunt Elise had enjoyed sifting through photographs and scrapbooks she'd put together. Similar boxes sat in her aunt's closet—ones Bria planned to ship to San Diego before she left.

She reached in and pulled out an old photo album with stained edges. She opened it. The plastic overlay was crinkled. A few photographs had slipped out of place based on the whiter squares on the page, but she recognized her aunt and dad.

They were so young.

Bria laughed at Aunt Elise's toothless grin and her father standing on Berry Lake's shore with a fishing pole in one hand and a trout in the other. She flipped through the pages, seeing a chronicle of the brother and sister as they grew up. Her dad appeared to be a happy kid. In no photo was he not smiling. Elise varied from being outrageously gregarious in some to thoughtful in others. They'd seemed to be close in the pictures. Something that surprised Bria because they'd not always been warm to each other, especially where she was concerned. The final photograph was from her aunt's high school graduation. She wore a cap and gown and held a diploma. So young and beautiful with her life ahead of her and so many dreams.

Like the Berry Lake Cupcake Shop.

"You made that one come true, Auntie."

Bria hoped other dreams had, too, but Aunt Elise hadn't spoken much about anything other than the bakery. She always wanted to know about Bria's life when they spoke or visited. Even after the cancer, her aunt had wanted to focus on her niece and not her illness.

"I hope I made you happy. Proud."

She set the photo album to the side and reached inside again: bandana, ticket stubs, knit scarf, varsity high school letter, county and state fair ribbons, school activities programs, photos of Elise and Charlene through their childhood and into their teens, and old greeting cards from birthdays and Christmases. A high school ASB card was in there, too.

Bria laughed. "It's a time capsule, but then again, you enjoyed hanging on to things."

Which was why not finding the floorplans and notebook was so strange. *They should be here.*

As she pulled out the cards, a notecard-sized envelope fell out.

Bria picked it up. No name or address was written on the front, and the flap hadn't been sealed. She opened it, pulled out a folded piece of paper with yellow edges, and read.

My love,

I wish with my whole heart that things could be differ-ent. I know you want to do the right thing, but I also see and hear how much you don't want to lose me. It's a tough spot to find yourself in. I know because I feel the same. And it sucks.

I'll be honest. This whole "be honorable" cloak you're wearing isn't helping heal my broken heart. Quite the opposite. But it proves the kind of man you are—caring and kind—and why I wanted to grow old with you at my side.

But I can't smile and pretend to be happy with how things turned out. I'm not like you. I'm not that big of a person. And I hate myself because I know what this means for us. Well, what's left of us because that must end, too.

From this day on, we must stop all contact. I don't want you to acknowledge me, not even with a wave. I can't go back to being just friends, and your new family deserves your full attention. There is no other way.

We find ourselves in an unexpected situation. The future we planned is no longer possible, but the stakes are too high to ignore to put this off any longer. Doing this is the right decision. I feel that in my heart. And I also know in my heart it is one you would have made yourself eventually.

So, I'm saving you the effort of having to decide this and saying goodbye now. It'll be easier for both of us. I stole my photo from your wallet. Don't be mad because it's not something you need any longer.

Forget me. Don't look back at what might have been. Start fresh. Give your heart away with no regrets. You'll always have a piece of my heart, and I'll remember enough of what we shared for both of us. I love you. I will always love you.

The heartfelt words brought tears to Bria's eyes. She flipped over the paper, but it was blank. The handwriting looked feminine, but it wasn't Aunt Elise's distinctive scrawl. But if it wasn't hers, why did she have this letter? And who wrote it?

Questions popped into Bria's mind like the bang snaps kids threw on the Fourth of July.

The printer stopped.

Bria glanced from the letter to the pages waiting for her. She was intrigued, but she didn't have time to ponder an anonymous letter. Maybe after she put together the folders for the meeting. She placed everything back into the box and slid it under the coffee table.

She collated the printouts and placed them in manila folders she'd found in her aunt's home office. They didn't look fancy, but they would do. The only thing that was missing—the remodeling plans. Selena was trying to track down the designer who'd worked on them. If the mighty Selena T, Queen of the Internet, couldn't get her hands on them, the stuff no longer existed.

A knock sounded.

It had become a familiar sound, with people wanting to drop off food. She hadn't realized it would keep going after the funeral. She'd been overwhelmed by the generosity.

She rose and padded her way to the front door in her bare feet.

Roasted chicken, casserole, or zucchini bread would be her guesses. She would gladly accept anything. No way would she eat it all before she flew home, so Bria would share with friends, and if she had leftovers, she would ask the church if they knew of anyone who might want them.

Bria opened the door.

Dalton stood on the front porch with his hands behind his back. "Hi."

What next? An emergency broadcast saying an asteroid would hit Berry Lake today?

At this point, it was as likely as anything else happening.

Tension simmered in the air. Not the I-want-to-kiss-you-until-we-need-to-breathe tension, but the need-a-knife-to-slice-through-it-because-I-hate-you tension. She clutched the doorknob. "Why are you here?"

"I upset you yesterday."

Did he want a gold star? The guy had some nerve to show up unannounced. Not that he had her number, and Bria had disconnected the landline.

She eyed him warily. "That appears to be a skill of yours."

He flinched. "I deserve that."

"And so much more."

Dalton pulled his arm from behind his back. He held a bouquet of wildflowers—her favorite, but she might need to rethink that now. "I owe you an apology."

Unbelievable. "Do you think a few nice words and flowers will make a difference for what happened yesterday?"

"These are for everything."

She crossed her arms in front of her chest. "Then, you're fifteen and a half years too late."

"More like fifteen years and four months."

"If we're counting."

"You did."

Heat pooled in her cheeks. She had. *What is wrong with me?*

"Fine. You apologized. Go. Give the flowers to someone else. A random act of kindness. I'm sure you've heard of that, or maybe not."

Uh-oh. She was rambling.

Bria tried to shut the door, but Dalton stuck his foot in the way so she couldn't.

"I want…" He glanced around as if to see if any neighbors were spying on them. "Can we please not do this out here?"

"You apologized. What else—"

"Five minutes. Give me five minutes," he interrupted. "Please."

He didn't appear ready to surrender, and she didn't want to stand there all day. "You have five minutes." That might be the easiest way to get him to leave.

Dalton hurried inside as if he feared she might change her mind. "Thanks."

She closed the door behind him, ignoring the woodsy scent of his cologne. The last thing she should notice about him was how he smelled.

"Thanks." He handed her the bouquet. "You can give them away if you want."

Trimmed roses with the thorns and guard petals removed and the stems cut at the perfect angle were more her style now, but once upon a time, Bria had loved wildflowers. She'd never understood why those called to her back then, but she did now.

The pretty blossoms growing along the roadside or in a field with no rhyme or reason were like her life with her father. He'd dragged her from place to place, and she'd learned to carve out a small space of her own, only to leave it behind when something better pinged on his radar. She'd loved the stability of her aunt's house. But part of her had missed the adventure and newness. The wildflowers had been a reminder that she could blossom anywhere and under any circumstances.

Something she'd forgotten until now. "Thank you."

The floral scent tickled her nose, but Bria forced herself not to sniff the bouquet. Dalton hadn't picked these because he remembered something special to her. He'd gotten lucky with his purchase; that was all.

Bria side-eyed him. "Ticktock."

"Right." Dalton flexed his fingers. "Do you want to sit down?"

And be at an even lesser height advantage? No way. "I prefer standing."

"So, yesterday…" He rubbed his lips together. "Your dad knew information about your aunt's will that you didn't. I assumed he'd mentioned hiring me, but it was obvious he blindsided you with everything."

The sincerity in his voice surprised her. "You mean, you."

A vein pulsed at his jaw. "Yes. Brian told me the past was in the past, so I walked into the dining room thinking it was true. But your reaction told me how much it wasn't."

Part of her believed him. "My dad appears to have misled both of us."

"Yes. And I'm sorry for my part in that." His apologetic tone matched the regret on his face.

"I forgive you."

Relief—or perhaps, gratitude—reflected in his eyes. "Thank you."

"The clock's still ticking." Bria didn't want him to think anything had changed.

"Your father may have different… ideas about what to do with the cupcake shop, but he wants to work with you. He mentioned that, saying a neutral third party would help when he hired me, given you haven't been close for many years. He feels, since I'm from Berry Lake and know you, I'm the person who is best suited to work with you guys."

Her jaw dropped. It might have hit the floor had she not been standing. "You seriously expect me to believe that after what happened in…"

Dalton nodded. "I'm sorry about that, too. But face it, we were young. Kids do and say stupid stuff."

Laughter burst out. Or it might have been a scoff or maybe a cackle. "That's what you're going with? Being young and stupid?"

He raised his chin. "It's true."

"Except it wasn't 'kids.'" She tried to keep her voice steady. "It was you being stupid and mean. A bully."

Dalton's nostrils flared. "All I did was break up with you. I never bullied you."

"Let me refresh your memory." She took a breath. Part of her wanted to sit, but she forced herself to remain standing. "A week before senior prom, you told me you couldn't wait to see me in the dress I bought in Portland. You said, 'I love you.' Those were your exact words. But the next day, on our way into the cafeteria, you stopped me. People were all around us, watching and listening. You told me you wanted to break up, that you decided to take Heather Young to the dance because she was thin enough to wear a sleeveless dress. You said I wasn't good enough to date. You also admitted going out with me to get help in Calculus, so you could play baseball, and to have sex, only I wouldn't."

Thank goodness.

Dalton hung his head. "I don't remember that part."

"Guess you don't remember your friends taunting and bullying me, making oinking sounds and rude comments about my weight and virginity while you stood next to them without saying a word. Not one word."

"I had my reasons," he muttered, his eyes focused on the floor.

"I hope they were good ones because words have the power to hurt and damage people."

"I never meant… I was stupid." Dalton blew out a breath. "My dad had taken a loan against his life insurance, so that had to be repaid after he died. There wasn't much left. My mom had

189

no idea how to support us. She didn't want me dating you because Heather's dad owned the bank. My mom thought he might not foreclose on the house if I was his daughter's boyfriend. We relied on my friends' families for food and help. But they didn't want me dating you, either. So I broke up with you. I needed to stay part of the crowd, so I didn't speak up because my family's weekly veggie box and milk or my rides to practice might go away. I had to do what was best for my family."

Bria let what he said sink in. The Dwyers had been one of the wealthier families in Berry Lake. "You could have told me."

His gaze shot up to meet hers. His eyes gleamed. "Would it have made a difference?"

"I don't know, but…" It might have made a difference with how she reacted. Bria hugged herself.

"It was a long time ago." He gave a shake to his head. "I'm sorry for hurting your feelings, but we need to move on."

"Hurting my feelings?" Her voice rose an octave. She took a step forward, her hands balling into fists. "The breakup devastated me. I would have gotten over it, except your friends kept on me until I spiraled downward into a dark place. I barely graduated, but I kept on going because I knew it was my way out of this town. I didn't want to be stuck here with the jerks and bullies who thought nothing of tearing someone down because they didn't like how she looked or dressed. But knowing that didn't stop me from finding myself on the verge of an eating disorder because I believed no one would love me, let alone like me. After all, I was fat and not good enough. Thankfully, my friends and aunt stepped in. Therapy helped, too. So you did more than hurt my feelings, Dalton. A lot more."

"I—I didn't know. I'm not that same boy."

"But you *were* him." Dalton Dwyer was handsome and appeared to be successful, but that wasn't all she saw. "That's still who I see when I look at you. I don't know what it'll take for that to change."

He reached for her. "Bria—"

She jerked away. "I'm not that same quiet, shy girl I was. I forgave you a long time ago because I needed to do that to heal and get healthy. But I haven't forgotten. I'm not sure I ever will."

As he lowered his arm to his side, his jaw tensed. "Can you work with me?"

"Do I have a choice?"

"Your dad wants me." Dalton spoke confidently, but there may have been a touch of arrogance, too.

"And you want to work with him." She didn't need him to answer to know it was true. "That makes me believe you're the same person you were in high school because my father has made chasing get-rich-quick schemes his life's work. He's out to make a fast buck without caring what he has to do or who he hurts in the process."

Dalton stiffened. "I'm not like that."

"Yesterday, you saw what he did to me, his equal partner in the cupcake shop and his daughter. That's who my dad is, who he's always been."

He scraped his hand through his hair. "I'm trying to do my job."

"So am I." She stared down her nose. "My loyalty lies with my aunt, and I will do everything in my power to save the cupcake shop from my father and make sure Berry Lake isn't turned into a small-town theme park for the rich."

His eyes bulged. He started to speak but then stopped himself.

"It was in the proposal. Which, based on your reaction, was supposed to be my father's copy." She shouldn't enjoy watching Dalton squirm as much as she did. "Did the one you intended for me leave a few things out?"

A beat passed, and then he straightened. "The plans in that proposal are the best option for long-range profitability and viability for Berry Lake and its residents."

"And my aunt's cupcakes have zero calories." She glanced at her phone, but the screen was dark. "We've gone past five minutes. Do you have anything else to say to me?"

Dalton's gaze ran the length of her. "You've changed."

"Not really." She raised her chin. "I just learned to stop hiding parts of myself."

"Me, too." The words flew out. "I won't lie or try to scam you. You have my word."

It would take more than Dalton saying that for her to believe him. "Actions speak louder than words, considering you had two different proposals."

"I'll see you at two." He didn't wait for her to reply but turned and walked to the door.

Bria wasn't looking forward to the meeting, but fifteen years ago, she'd run away. She would never do that again, even if it meant postponing her return to San Diego for a few more days.

chapter sixteen

O N WEDNESDAY AT twelve fifteen, Juliet headed up the walkway to the Huckleberry Inn. She'd spent the morning across the street at Events by Charlene, filling out paperwork and making seventy-five favors for a fiftieth wedding anniversary celebration.

She flexed her fingers. Her hands were tired from gift wrapping seventy-five gold-framed photos of the couple from Hood River and filling gold organza pouches with Hershey's Kisses with Almonds. But it had been a great first day.

She would post on the Posse chat eventually, but Bria's big meeting was in less than two hours, and she didn't want to distract her. Juliet wanted to call Ezra, and she almost had, except he didn't know she'd been hired.

She'd tried to tell him, but he hadn't wanted to listen. She'd bought a bottle of champagne to celebrate her new job, but during dinner, he hadn't asked about her interview. He hadn't mentioned the texts about her working. Nothing. Instead, he'd discussed the amount of starch she used on his dress shirt. If she put in more effort, he was confident she would do a better job.

Grrrrrr.

Part of Juliet had wanted to tell him where to stuff his shirts, but she hadn't. She'd nodded demurely and promised to do better, even though she'd changed nothing in how she washed, starched, and ironed his shirts. But agreeing with him would make her life easier. Even if she changed nothing in how she did his shirt, he would notice a change.

He must think I'm an idiot.

Not that she blamed him.

She rarely said what was on her mind. It hadn't mattered when she saw her grandmother a couple of times a week. But now that the Posse was back in touch, and she had Charlene for a boss, Juliet needed to do better.

A bird flew overhead and landed on a branch of the inn's maple tree.

When she was younger, she'd dreamed of finding her Prince Charming—white horse optional, a brown one would do—and engraving their initials on the tree trunk and surrounding them with a heart. When she'd moved back to Berry Lake, she hadn't been tempted to do that. The tree deserved better.

So do you.

Juliet needed to quiet that voice in her head. She was working on improving their marriage. She deserved a husband who loved and adored her, didn't she?

As for telling Ezra about the job, a text with her hours might suffice. Juliet needed to say something because she was working this weekend, so he would know she was gone.

She entered the inn.

The familiar scent of vanilla, rose petals, and sandalwood greeted her like an old friend. Her grandmother knew she was coming—only customers dropped in on Penelope Jones unannounced—but no one was at the front desk. "Grandma?"

"In the parlor, dear."

Juliet's heels clicked against the hardwood floor until her shoes sank into the plush carpet.

Her grandmother was five-seven but appeared taller because of her ramrod-straight posture. Her long gray hair was in a bun. Sometimes, she wore a braid, but her hair was either pulled back or worn up, making her features look sterner than they were. She wore frilly aprons around the inn because Juliet's grandfather had liked them. And even though Harold Jones had left this earth four years ago, not once had grief—or anything else—slowed her grandmother down. Not even after she'd fallen a year and a half ago. Her accident had led to Ezra suggesting they move closer.

As her grandmother bent over the coffee table, she arranged the makings of a tea service—tiered serving platters filled with finger sandwiches, scones, Madeline cakes, chocolate-dipped strawberries, and cookies.

Juliet's heart split wide open. "We're having tea?"

"A celebration tea with a few extra sandwiches since you've been working."

Tears stung her eyes. At least someone loved her.

"Thank you, Grandma. I haven't eaten lunch yet." She glanced up before blinking. "Everything is lovely."

"Then, I made the right call." Her grandma beamed brighter than her set of heirloom sterling silver. "I know how much you enjoy tea, so I thought this would be nice."

"It's perfect. Exactly what I need."

"I'm so excited about your new job." Her grandmother rubbed her hands together. "Though you can always work here, you know."

"Thanks, I know." Ezra, however, would never stop with the nepotism jabs if Juliet worked for her grandmother. "But Charlene had an opening, so I gave it a try."

"And you got the job." Her grandmother applauded.

Juliet raised her shoulders. "I did."

"Have a seat." Grandma pointed to the antique love seat that had been reupholstered many times over the years. "What did Ezra say?"

Juliet sat, swallowing around the sugar cube-sized lump in her throat. "He, um, doesn't know yet. We didn't have a chance to talk last night, but we will. He told me it was fine to accept a job if I was offered one. I need to give him my hours."

Her grandmother's eyes darkened. "Is everything okay with Ezra, dear?"

Skin itching, Juliet nodded emphatically. Her grandmother didn't need to know anything about their marriage—time to change the subject.

"Do you need help?" Juliet asked, even though she knew the answer. It was always the same.

"No, thank you. I'll be right back with our teas."

As her grandma went into the kitchen, Juliet smoothed her skirt and waited. Her palms were clammy, but she fought the urge to wipe them. Nothing like being thirty-five and nervous because she didn't want her grandmother to know her marriage might be in trouble.

Might.

Juliet half laughed. Sometimes, it felt as if she lived in a different dimension from Ezra. But this had to be a phase.

Things would get better between them. *Face it. They couldn't get any worse.* Her working for Charlene would show Ezra she was more than a woman who looked good on his arm and kept his house in order.

"I know you love chamomile, so I made a pot of that." Grandma carried a tray with two teapots, small plates, cups, and saucers. She skillfully placed everything on the table in what appeared to be predetermined spots. "I also have a pot of Rose Congou. It's a blend of black tea with rose petals I've wanted to try."

"It sounds delicious." Juliet took another sniff. "You spoil me."

"You deserve to be spoiled. That's what grandchildren are for." Her grandmother sat before motioning to the teapots. "Would you like chamomile?"

Juliet usually drank that flavor, but if there was a day to try something new, it was today. "I'd like the rose one, please."

"I'll have the same." Grandma poured the tea. "So, your first day went well?"

"It was fun." Juliet told her about the favors she'd made. "Charlene is a stickler for details, but she was so complimentary of my work. I'm not used to that."

"You haven't had a boss since you were a princess."

Juliet froze, realizing what she'd said. Thankfully, her grandmother hadn't picked up on it. "It's been a long time since then."

Her grandmother raised a gold-rimmed floral teacup. "I know it's none of my business…"

"That's never stopped you before."

"True." She took a sip. "Oh, this new blend is scrumptious."

Juliet tasted hers. "Delicious. You should add this to the tea menu." She took a cucumber sandwich and bit into it.

"I will." Her grandmother took another sip before setting her cup on the saucer. "Now, where was I? Oh, yes. I remember. Are you and Ezra planning to have children?"

Juliet choked. Her eyes watered, and she couldn't breathe, but somehow she managed to swallow what was in her mouth. "I'm sorry. You caught me off guard."

The ticking of the grandfather clock in the corner barely drowned out the beating of her heart and breathing.

"Are you?" Grandma asked with furrowed brows.

"Ezra doesn't want children." He'd been clear about that from the beginning of their relationship. "With his work schedule, he's barely around. Especially since we moved to Berry Lake. It wouldn't be fair to our kids to have a father who is never there."

Or one who didn't want "snotty-nosed, germ-spreading progeny." But Juliet would keep that to herself.

"A child can't always have two parents, but that makes it easier for the family," her grandmother said. "Your grandfather always made time for our children. But that doesn't always happen."

As Juliet thought about Bria and her dad, her chest hurt. What a mess.

"You always wanted children, though," her grandmother reminded her.

"I did, and if circumstances change in the future, maybe we'll add to our family." Though, that was the last thing they needed right now. "I'm only thirty-five. Women have babies in their forties. Some in their early fifties."

Her grandmother touched her lower back. "Just thinking about that hurts, but more power to those women who take that on. I wouldn't have been able to handle it."

Juliet did a double take. "Where is my grandmother? What have you done with her? She would never admit to not being able to handle something."

"Mark this occasion in your calendar," Grandma joked. "I'm not always right. More like ninety-nine percent of the time, but that other one percent shows I'm human."

"Good to know." Juliet was wrong most of the time, which was why she was trying so hard to do better.

"Now your grandfather—God rest his soul—didn't get as much right as me, but when he did, it was so right the choirs of angels in heaven sang."

"I must take more after him." Minus the singing angels.

Grandma laughed. "You do, which is why you've always been the light of my life, Juliet. And always will be."

"Thank you." She smiled, but inside her, pressure built.

No matter how much Juliet might want to ignore it or pretend things with her husband weren't going downhill, she no longer could. She needed to talk to Ezra, not only about her new job but also about their marriage.

For herself and her grandmother.

Juliet was trying to fix things on her own, but they might need to do this together. Counseling or a romantic getaway or a once-a-week date night. Perhaps all three and more.

It was worth a shot.

Unless he said no.

Her heart slammed against her chest. Then what would she do?

After visiting her grandmother, Juliet wasn't ready to go home. She had finished the housework before going to work. A walk would burn off some calories from the sweets she'd indulged in at lunch.

She strolled along Main Street at a pleasant pace. She wasn't dressed to sweat or make her muscles burn. But she enjoyed the exercise and the fresh air.

The sidewalks weren't as crowded as they'd been a month ago at the height of tourist season, but the weather was nice and warm like it had been in August. A boon for the permanent residents. Still, fall wasn't that far away, and she loved to watch the trees turn colors and see the pumpkins and straw bales appear as entryway decorations to usher in the new season.

Up ahead, the Berry Lake Art Gallery sign caught her attention. She still wanted to see Hope Ryan Cooper's painting, and the *Open* sign was out. Tonight's salmon dinner was quick and easy to make.

Why not?

Besides, Juliet deserved another treat on her first day of work.

As she opened the door, the bell over it jingled. She stepped inside.

No one sat behind the counter, but all the lights were on. Soothing instrumental music played.

Juliet knew little about art, but she preferred actual settings or subjects to anything abstract. If she learned more, she might change her mind, but Ezra hadn't shared his art knowledge with her.

Sculptures weren't her thing because if they bought one, she'd knock it over with the vacuum or dust it too hard. But the large Squatchy figurine in a nearby alcove caught her eye.

She moved closer.

Fingerprints shone in Bigfoot's eyes. Food and drinks had been spilled on him, congealing in the lines of his fur. The layer of dust suggested no one had cleaned the sculpture in days, maybe weeks. If this kept up, no one would want their picture with Squatchy, who had been deemed one of the top photo ops in Berry Lake.

A large artwork on the side wall caught her attention. The wintertime landscape was large.

She walked toward it. The painting was Berry Lake in the wintertime, and the placard next to it listed Hope's name.

This must be the painting people had mentioned.

Beautiful.

Too bad Ezra hadn't purchased this one to go with the others. The size and colors would work perfectly in the house. She searched for a price tag, but all she saw was a small red sold sign. *Bummer.* But she would keep her eye out for more paintings by the talented artist.

Laughter sounded. A man and a woman.

She glanced at the doorway that led to the part of the gallery not open to the public. Remy walked out, followed by…

"Ezra?" Juliet squinted. Yes, that was him. An icky sensation flowed through her, settling like a pool of slime in her stomach. "What are you doing here?"

"I was about to ask you the same question." He came over to her and kissed her on the cheek. "Why aren't you at home cleaning?"

Remy hovered in the background, adjusting a placard on a print.

"The housework is all done. I had lunch with my grandmother at the inn." Juliet didn't like how Remy kept glancing at Ezra as if trying to send him a secret message. "I decided to walk afterward and remembered I hadn't seen Hope's painting. I wish the piece hadn't sold. It would be perfect for the house."

Ezra started to speak, then stopped himself when Remy moved toward him. He stepped back. "You didn't mention coming to town today."

"I had to fill out paperwork for work, and then Charlene asked me to help prepare for an upcoming event."

His face paled. "Work?"

"I told you about my interview. I got the job."

"You did?" He sounded incredulous.

Juliet nodded, waiting for him to answer her question. "Charlene said I was exactly what she was looking for."

His face scrunched. "I suppose there aren't many people who accept minimum wage."

"I'm making twenty dollars an hour. After sixty days, that will go up."

He tilted his head as if seeing her for the first time. "Charlene Culpepper hired you?"

"Yes." Juliet raised her chin. "Now, tell me why *you're* here?"

He smoothed his suit jacket. "Remy wanted to show me a painting that arrived."

Remy nodded fast enough to give herself whiplash. She wore a short red dress that clung to her and black ankle boots.

"It just arrived, and Mr. M needed to see this one right away." Remy held out her arms. "It's like huge with colors. Primary ones, I mean. Though it looks like someone painted it when they were drunk or high, but people buy them for outrageous amounts, so who am I to call it trash? Even if it is."

Juliet had to check that her mouth wasn't gaping. She remembered Sal DeMarco giving tours of the gallery. Even his daughter, Sheridan, had been well-spoken in her teens. But Remy Dwyer…

The high school kids who worked at the cupcake shop counter would be more professional than this young woman.

Ezra cleared his throat. "Thanks for showing me the painting."

"You're welcome, Mr. M."

He touched Juliet's forearm. "Let me walk you out."

That was fine with her. She would rather not have this discussion in front of Remy.

Juliet stepped into the sunshine and faced her husband. "What are you really doing here?"

"Looking at art."

His tone was even. His tie wasn't askew like last time he'd been in the back of the gallery. All his shirt buttons were fastened, and his wedding ring was on his finger. But none of those things quieted the warning bells sounding in her head.

She pursed her lips. "Or were you looking at Remy?"

"Of course not." He laughed. Only it wasn't natural. "Why would I look at her when I'm married to the most beautiful woman in Berry Lake?"

"I don't believe you," she blurted, even though she hadn't meant to do that.

Someone waved from across the street. Juliet returned the gesture, even though she didn't recognize them. But doing that was better than doing nothing while she waited for her husband to admit he'd lied to her.

So not how I'd planned to spend this afternoon.

But she didn't want to stand there while he figured out what he wanted to say. She recognized his concentration face. "Ezra—"

"Fine, you're correct."

Her heart dropped. Splat. Right on the sidewalk.

Why had she asked? What if…

"I wasn't here just looking at that artwork Remy described. Though she did show it to me."

Juliet's heart pounded so loudly she was sure everyone in Berry Lake would hear it. Fear slithered through her. She didn't want to ask, but she needed to know. "What were you doing, then?"

"It's supposed to be a surprise, but it won't be if I tell you now."

He held her hand, and it took all her strength not to jerk her arm away.

"I bought that painting you mentioned. As a surprise. An early anniversary gift for you. Us."

That was unexpected.

"Thank you?" Juliet hadn't meant to make it a question, but she wasn't sure what to say. "It's an amazing piece."

"I knew you'd love the painting." He squeezed her hand. "I was in the back of the gallery, looking at gift-wrapping options."

"They wrap huge paintings?"

He rolled his eyes. "The crates. That's how they're transported to clients."

"Oh, that's a nice touch."

Ezra let go of her hand and touched her cheek, cupping one half of her face with his large hand.

"Anything for you, Princess." Except Juliet wasn't sure she believed him. It all sounded too… convenient. "Am I allowed to hang the painting in the house?"

Unlike all the others in your office you call investments.

"Of course. It's yours." He tucked a stray strand of hair behind her ear. "But you need to curb your jealousy over Remy Dwyer. It's not becoming, Juliet."

"I know." But something fed her feeling that way. Whether it was an overactive imagination or her hinky meter sensing something was up, it needed to stop. Only one way to do that came to mind. "I want us to go to marriage counseling."

chapter seventeen

D ALTON ARRIVED AT the cupcake shop at a quarter
to two. He preferred preparing for meetings where they
happened. He wanted to be comfortable and ready to
do business when it was time. Only today, that seemed more
important. It didn't help being torn over the outcome he wanted
to happen regarding the cupcake shop.

Don't think about Bria.

Except that was all he'd done since seeing her this morning.

As he stood in line, Dalton studied the menu board on the
wall behind the counter. Familiar ones were still there with a few
flavors he didn't remember. But sixteen choices weren't enough.
Savvy customers preferred a greater selection, and only a handful
of the offerings were gourmet enough. That might work now, as
in every other mom-and-pop bakery in America, but not if Berry
Lake 2.0, as Tanner called it, rolled out.

Dalton glanced around.

Not much had changed since he'd been there last. A new coat of paint in a different color covered the walls. A new display case and counter. New tables and chairs. But those things appeared worn.

The man in front of him moved out of the way with a box of cupcakes in his hands.

Dalton stepped forward. He didn't recognize the woman wearing the apron and hairnet. She didn't wear a name tag. The employees used to. At least, Bria had. He didn't remember anyone else except her aunt. She used to give him free cupcakes. "The boyfriend discount," she had called it.

"Welcome to the Berry Lake Cupcake Shop." The woman's cheerful voice matched her bright eyes. "Can I take your order?"

"A coffee with a dash of cream and a chocolate cupcake with sprinkles." That flavor had been his favorite growing up, and he hadn't had one in forever. After the breakup, he'd stayed away from the cupcake shop. He might have been a stupid kid, but he hadn't been a complete idiot to think he'd be welcome here by Elise Landon or the staff.

However, what Bria had said this morning made him rethink not being an idiot and everything else.

You want to work with him. That makes me believe you're the same person you were in high school because Brian Landon has made chasing get-rich-quick schemes his life's work. He's out to make a fast buck without caring what he has to do or who he hurts in the process.

I'm not like that.

Yesterday, you saw what he did to me, his equal partner in the cupcake shop and his daughter. That's who my dad is, who he's always been.

Bria might be correct about her father, and he planned to find out more about Brian Landon, but she was wrong about Dalton.

He'd changed from the frightened teen, struggling to fit in with friends and doing his best for his family, even though it meant hurting the girl he'd loved. And he had loved her, as much as an eighteen-year-old who was in love for the first time knew how to love.

Yes, his job mattered to him. Yes, he wanted to be successful. Yes, his ambitions ran high. Perhaps higher than most. But he wouldn't apologize for having goals and earning a good salary. Until people lacked basic necessities like food and a roof over their heads, they didn't understand the value of money.

The importance of it.

Without money, people found themselves at the mercy of others.

It was a horrible position to be in.

That was where he and his family had been his senior year of high school.

Only a few had known because… appearances. The Dwyer family was wealthy and would never struggle, or so the myth went. The truth was something far darker, with a steady stream of foreclosure notices and constant hunger pains.

He may not have liked what his mother did after his dad died, but Dalton understood why. She'd been a single mother of four—ages eighteen to two—with no college degree and no job experience, living in a town that relied on summer tourists to survive the rest of the year. She hadn't been able to relocate them to a bigger city—no money for that—so she'd done what she could to provide for her family.

Namely, marry rich.

It had given his mom a way to get what she needed for herself and her kids.

Her second husband had paid for Dalton's college. If that hadn't happened, joining the military would have been the only way to further his education. Not a bad option, but his life would be different. Thanks to his first stepfather, it turned out better than he'd hoped. The guy loved Mom so much he gave anything she wanted, including a generous divorce settlement when she decided it was time to trade up for a richer husband.

Dalton only wished his mom would stop using men now that her situation had improved. But she saw nothing wrong with what she did, even though she'd left her husbands' former wives, children from their previous marriages, and the men themselves in her wake.

After watching her in action, he'd vowed never to lie or scam others to succeed. It wasn't necessary. If Brian was like that, as Bria had told him, Dalton would stop working with him.

Favor owed or not.

Besides, Tanner would never deal with that kind of guy. Dalton respected much about his boss, but Tanner's business ethics ranked high on the list. Anything shady, and he was out of there.

For now, Dalton was stuck working with Bria's father, but he would watch Brian and see for himself if what she said was true. If so, he would do something about it. Dalton owed Bria that much.

Probably more, but he didn't want to think about that.

After paying, he picked up the plate with his cupcake, a napkin, and coffee. As he stepped into the table area, someone waved from the far corner.

Brian sat at a table. "Over here."

So much for having time to prep, but the guy was paying for Dalton to be there. He wove around the other tables and sat with Brian. "You're early."

"I had nothing else to do." The guy held a cup of coffee. Not from the cupcake shop, but Brew and Steep. "And you never know who you'll see here."

"Like your daughter?"

"Among others." He eyed the chocolate cupcake like a dog wanting a bone. "Did you speak to Bria?"

Dalton's muscles tensed. "I did."

"And?"

"It could have gone better." That was putting it mildly, but he wasn't ready to discuss Bria. He peeled the paper liner away and bit into the cupcake. *So good.* It tasted like… home. "Time will tell if we can work together."

"She's only in town until Sunday."

That wasn't long, but they wouldn't need to meet in person once they decided on a path. The realization bothered him.

Dalton respected Bria for following her aunt's wishes, but this wasn't an all-or-nothing proposition. Tanner had been clear about wanting the cupcake shop, but his boss understood probate sales, so he wasn't as impatient as Brian. Until this morning, Dalton was Team Tanner. The guy signed his paycheck. But now, Dalton hoped to find a compromise that satisfied everyone. Bria could keep the shop. Brian received the payout he wanted. And Tanner would make the first inroads to his redevelopment of the town.

That would happen with or without the cupcake shop building. If Tanner didn't buy it, he would purchase another. He'd made a fortune turning small towns into gold mines for investors. Nothing would stop him from doing the same in Berry Lake.

"Did you stay in town last night?" Brian asked.

"At an Airbnb." The place had strong Wi-Fi and a color printer. Dalton removed the proposals from his briefcase and handed one to Brian. "I had work to do."

"Why do you have four of them?"

"For you, me, Bria, and Missy. She's the current manager, so she has a vested interest in the outcome."

As Brian paged through the document, he huffed. "You've added additional franchise opportunities in this new one."

That was interesting. Brian hadn't appeared to care about the proposal yesterday. Still, he didn't seem happy. "Yes."

After a call with Tanner, Dalton revised his proposal to include that and Bria's option of keeping the business as is. Tanner understood what Dalton did. As the personal representative to Elise's estate, Bria had the power, including the authority to keep the cupcake shop running. And she wasn't being unreasonable about what she wanted. The same couldn't be said for her father.

Brian turned the pages. The lines around his mouth deepened. "I don't want to franchise. I want to sell my interest for the highest amount possible."

"You've made that clear."

"I have a reason." He sounded more like a preschooler than an adult. "I've been presented a once-in-a-lifetime investment opportunity. It's a sure thing, but I'm low on capital."

What Brian said matched what Bria had told Dalton. "No investment is a sure thing."

"True, but this is close." Those familiar dollar signs flashed in Brian's eyes. "I need to get my hands on some money, but Bria said probate isn't a fast process, and the creditors are paid first."

"That's true."

Brian leaned forward. The stench of desperation was familiar and off-putting. "But she can still sell the cupcake shop, right?"

"Yes." The personal representative of an estate had a lot of leeway. "Depending on the creditors who file a claim against the estate, selling assets might be the only way to pay them."

Brian set his cup on the table. "I don't know what Elise owed. Do you think Bria knows?"

"She might, but that's why creditors have four months to two years to contact estates. Not all debts or loans may be known to others."

Brian rubbed his forehead. "Once the creditors are paid, the remainder distributes to the beneficiaries, right?"

Dalton thought Elise's attorney would have reviewed how the process worked. "I'm not a lawyer. If you have specific questions, you should talk to one."

"Would Tanner buy my interest in the cupcake shop?"

The question caught Dalton off guard, but he knew the answer—in a heartbeat. The one-and-a-half-million-dollar value of the business and building matched Bria's analysis yesterday. However, Tanner would go higher if need be, but Dalton wouldn't disclose that to Brian. With a probate sale, they would deal with the estate. "Once it's available, possibly."

"So, not immediately?"

"Again, probate doesn't work that way."

Brian scoffed before swearing under his breath.

The guy needed to suck it up. A person didn't always get their way, but one thing didn't make sense to Dalton. "Doesn't selling the shop defeat your reason for wanting half of the bakery?"

A sheepish expression crossed Brian's face.

As Dalton's chest tightened, Bria's words repeated in his head. "It was never about you and Bria becoming closer, was it?"

Brian shrugged. "Elise planned on leaving everything to Bria. She'd mentioned that years ago, but I knew a deal was on the horizon."

"The sure thing?"

Brian nodded. "I didn't know how long probate took. The government has everything messed up. Or the courts. I suppose they are one and the same. Bloodsucking criminals. All of them."

Dalton drank his coffee so he didn't have to reply. His opinion of Brian Landon was falling lower by the minute.

"Until I called, Elise was worried about Bria being on her own. I made my sister happy." Pride filled his voice. "I don't regret that."

Dalton needed to talk to Tanner. This wasn't a client they wanted or needed. "You lied to your sister, who was dying of cancer."

Another shrug. "I withheld some information."

Talk about a jerk, which raised another question weighing on Dalton's mind. "Why did my dad owe you a favor?"

Brian leaned back in his chair. "Your dad needed help. I offered to do something for him. It worked out better than he imagined, and he said he owed me. Anytime. Anyplace."

"It must have been important."

"Your dad thought so." A thoughtful expression formed—one that was unexpected given Brian's normal reactions. "Look, your dad was the best guy. I didn't deserve to have Paul Dwyer call me a friend. But he did the entire time we were growing up. I wasn't around Berry Lake much after high school, but he told me you, your brothers, and sister meant everything to him. He would do anything for you kids. Anything."

Hearing that almost made up for everything else Brian had said and done. Emphasis on *almost*. Still, Dalton was happy to know that. "That's what my mom always says."

"It's true, and your mother is smart."

Smart and cunning, a dangerous combination for a woman in her fifties who still caught men's attention. But his mom wasn't someone he wanted to discuss with Brian. "You should take advantage of having Bria around and spend time with her. That's what your sister would have wanted."

And what you told Elise you would do.

Brian stared into his coffee cup. "Bria loved her more than she loved me."

"Elise was there for her."

"I tried… Not that hard. I wanted to be there. But what can you do?" He spoke as if he were talking about a pet, not his child. "Work kept getting in the way."

"It's not too late."

He wouldn't look at Dalton. "That's what Elise told me."

"You might enjoy getting to know Bria."

Brian shrugged before returning to the proposal. He inhaled sharply. "Why did you put Bria's analysis in here? The numbers are pathetic."

"Elise had a strong profit margin. It helped that she didn't pay rent, only property taxes. But those are excellent numbers."

"Hello." Missy stood next to Bria. Both women had serious expressions on their faces. They weren't there to talk but to negotiate or fight.

Dalton wasn't surprised. He stood. "Hi."

Bria's mouth slanted, but her eyes didn't tell him anything she felt. She wore different clothes from earlier. Her brown dress pants and blue button-up shirt were more professional. She'd also pulled her hair into a ponytail. "You remember Missy Hanford."

"Of course. Nice to see you again." Dalton shook her hand and gave her a folder. "I made a packet for you."

Missy shared a look with Bria. "Thanks."

Dalton gave Bria one, too. "This is yours."

She handed manila folders to him and Brian. "This is what I have for you two."

Bria and Missy sat. Dalton, did too.

No one spoke, so he decided to take the lead. "I updated my proposal with expanded info and added your analysis, Bria. That was thorough, so I'm curious what's in the folder."

She didn't glance at the report. "A recap of my analysis and projections and plans for the cupcake shop, including the remodeling plans."

Brian stiffened. "Where did you find those?"

"The designer in Seattle had a copy, so she emailed them to me. I couldn't find the originals." Bria pinned her father with a stare. "Do you have them?"

"Of course not. Elise lost them." Brian touched his mouth, a telltale sign of lying.

"It doesn't matter now, since we have copies." Dalton would play peacekeeper if that kept them moving toward a decision. He was curious to see what Bria had put together. "Why don't we read through everything, and then we can discuss the various options?"

Everyone agreed.

He had a funny feeling that was all anyone would agree upon today.

Bria read Dalton's updated proposal—professional. She would give him that. The colorful and easy-to-read charts suggested the guy must be a spreadsheet expert or have an assistant who was. A specific section had been expanded more than the others.

"You put a lot of work into this, Dalton, but I'm not interested in the franchise opportunities." She bristled. No way would she allow Dalton and her father to turn this place into a soulless franchise. "The cupcake shop is doing well on its own. Franchising under a new branding isn't necessary."

Both that option and selling the business—a polite way of saying the building—weren't happening. Not on her watch.

"There are expenses involved with the franchise fees but benefits, too. You can get loans to remodel the space. Some with low interest," Dalton explained. "The bakery might do better under a larger umbrella."

"No," Bria and Missy said at the same time.

"I say no to your option of keeping this place as is." Red-faced, her father waved the folder she'd given him. "You honestly think you can build this bakery to a million-dollar-a-year business?"

Bria pushed back her shoulders. "Yes. There are costs involved, but Elise had planned to use her savings and take out a small business loan."

Her dad rolled his eyes. "Borrowing affects profit."

"You have to spend money to make money, Mr. Landon." A V formed above Missy's nose. "I'm committed to managing the cupcake shop. If that includes overseeing a remodel or whatever else is needed, so be it, because that's what Elise wanted."

He cursed under his breath. "Elise was dying. She wasn't in the right—"

"Stop." Bria held out her hand, palm facing her father. He'd gone too far, and she hoped Dalton saw this. "If you believe Aunt Elise wasn't of sound mind, I'll challenge the will because she was telling Missy this at the same time she gave you half of her business."

"That's not what I meant." Her father pressed his lips together and leaned back in his chair. "Why do you have to be so dramatic about everything?"

Bria nearly laughed. She wasn't a drama princess at all.

"Your report is impressive." Dalton sounded excited. "Elise had big plans."

Missy sighed. "She did, and I'm grateful she shared them with me."

Bria patted Missy's hand. "Major items like the physical remodel would have to wait until after probate. But others are so cheap to implement, they'll pay for themselves."

Dalton turned the page. "Which are you considering doing now?"

"An updated menu," Missy answered. "I made the old board. I can make a new one. Elise and I tested recipes for months, and we found more recipes of hers we haven't tried yet, so lots of possibilities."

Bria was so excited to see how the newly discovered cupcake recipes inside the old cloth journal tasted. These weren't like any of the regular cupcake recipes they currently sold.

Dalton leaned forward. "That sounds interesting."

Missy's eyes twinkled with anticipation. "Just you wait."

"There's so much potential." Bria glanced around the shop until her gaze came to the wall of photos. "My aunt created something special. It needs to continue. Not only in her memory but as a legacy to the town."

"Are you kidding me?" Her father's lips curled. "Cupcakes aren't a legacy. They're food. Sugary mini cakes. Nothing special. For all we know, there are enough creditors that selling is the only option."

Her father's harsh words sliced Bria's heart, but he was wrong. Her aunt didn't believe in debt unless necessary. Still, the estate needed to follow the requirements. "We'll have to wait and see."

"Why wait?" Her father scooted to the edge of his chair. "If we sell now, we'll get a better offer than when we're desperate."

Dalton shook his head. "No one is desperate."

"Maybe not you," her dad mumbled.

Her dad was acting like a child. Bria would spell it out for him again. "I'm not selling unless that's the only way to pay creditors."

"We're back where we started." Her father threw up his arms. "I want one thing. Bria wants another."

She knew this would happen. "Trying to decide anything right now is premature."

"What do you mean?" Dalton asked.

Her dad eyed her warily.

"I hoped to have this resolved before I left, and I know my father wanted that, too, but I don't think we can. My dad and I disagree on what we should do, but we won't know what's owed to creditors for four months. Until then, Missy should keep running the bakery. Once we see what's owed, we can decide which direction we go."

Dalton stared at her. "That sounds sensible."

Bria was happy he hadn't shot her down. Dalton was a wild-card in all this, but she needed one other person to agree besides Missy. "What do you think, Dad?"

"I hate waiting, but…" He tilted his head as if thinking about it, and then a wide grin lit up his face. "It's a brilliant idea."

Whoa. Her dad's turnaround felt off after all his earlier complaints. She should be happy, but his reaction worried her. Unless he realized this was what Aunt Elise wanted. Could that be it?

"We have an agreement." Dalton sounded pleased.

Not that Bria cared. *Okay, maybe a little.*

But she was relieved. Missy had four months to implement their plans. If the cupcake shop increased profits as Bria suspected—and calculated—it would, her dad would change his mind about selling.

And once that happened, the cupcake shop's future would be in Missy's hands, just as Aunt Elise wanted.

chapter eighteen

THURSDAY AFTERNOON, DALTON entered the cupcake shop. He should have driven to Portland yesterday after Bria and Brian had decided to wait four months to meet again, but Dalton hadn't wanted to leave Berry Lake.

Not the town.

Bria.

Flutters filled his stomach. Something he wasn't used to feeling and hadn't felt in years. But he needed to ignore them. She'd gone from not tolerating him to minor acceptance. He wouldn't push for more.

Except here he was.

Not a conflict of interest.

He'd been running that through his mind, too.

At their meeting, Bria had gotten what she wanted. Not the shop forever, but four months was better than nothing. Missy was pleased. And he was happy for both of them. Surprisingly, Brian acted satisfied, if not resigned to wait. That shocked Dalton, but maybe this would bring father and daughter closer together. He hoped so for Bria's sake. They were each other's family. Bria needed her dad. And even if Dalton stayed away from his mom, she was still family. His dad used to say family ruled, even if not all members were likeable.

Which was why Dalton hadn't told his mom he was in town. He'd dropped by the high school earlier to watch Ian's football practice and say hello, but that was enough family time to last until the new year.

A teenager who looked to be around his brother's age stood behind the counter and smiled. "Welcome to the Berry Lake Cupcake Shop. How can I help you?"

"Is Bria Landon here?"

The boy nodded. "She's in the kitchen with Missy. Want me to get her?"

"Please."

He stuck his head through the doorway. "She'll be right out."

"Thanks." Dalton moved off to the side so he wouldn't be in the way. But he kept shifting his weight between his feet. It wasn't weird for him to be there. They were becoming closer. Not best buds, they were… acquaintances.

Bria appeared, wearing an apron over her clothes and a hairnet.

"Dalton?" She sounded surprised to see him. So was he for being there. But he was glad he'd come.

A decade and a half had passed since the last time he'd seen her dressed like this. Her face and body had changed over the years, but the kindness in her gaze still remained. Back in school, she took notes and created study guides for those she tutored and were in her classes. She'd had a pure heart, and she still might.

Something inside his chest shifted.

"Dalton?" Bria repeated.

Oh, right. He was the one who'd come to see her. He straightened.

"Hey." Not the smoothest of openings, but Dalton had trouble thinking straight.

That wasn't like him. He had female friends. This was no different. He rubbed below his collarbone. It didn't help.

Her gaze narrowed. "Do you need something?"

He nodded. *Use words, Dwyer.* "I wanted to see you before I left."

"You're seeing me."

He rocked back on his heels. "How are things going?"

She shrugged. "Missy's working on new recipes today. I had to order more death certificates. And my dad may have left town without saying goodbye."

Really, Brian? The guy seemed to be vying for the *worst father of the year* award.

Bria glanced out the front window and smiled. "But it's a beautiful day, and I'm alive, so I shouldn't complain."

"Great attitude." And it sounded familiar.

"Something similar was on Selena T's podcast earlier." Laughter lit Bria's eyes. "I realized I have a lot to be grateful for, but I don't always recognize it."

Wonder what Bria would think if she knew I listened to her friend, too. "I'm guilty of the same."

"Missy and I didn't run away from the meeting yesterday afternoon. We had to get back to work. I wanted to tell you how much I appreciated your support with my father. I... I wasn't expecting that."

Dalton stood taller. "I told you I've changed."

"I saw a glimpse yesterday."

"Only a glimpse?"

She shrugged. "It's more than I thought I'd see."

"I don't blame you for being cautious. Given…"

"The past."

He nodded. "We're both leaving Berry Lake soon."

"Sunday."

"What?"

"I'm leaving for San Diego on Sunday."

Brian had mentioned that, but Dalton nodded again. Sweat beaded at his hairline. "Anyway, I was wondering."

Her gaze met his. "What?"

"Would you…" He had a feeling whatever he said would sound pathetic or apologetic or desperate. But this might be his last chance to spend time with Bria—to make amends. Except the beating of his heart suggested that wasn't the only reason he'd come to see her. "Would you want to grab a cup of coffee or dinner, depending on your schedule? I know you're busy, but I thought I'd ask."

Ugh. Just shoot me now.

Her eyebrows drew together. "With you?"

"Yes." He rubbed the back of his neck. "With me. You and me."

She glanced around as if searching for what to say.

He would give her more if she needed it. "I just… I want to spend time with you where it's not all about the cupcake shop."

"We did that yesterday morning."

Dalton wanted to pretend that hadn't happened.

"And where it's not about the past." He hesitated. "That's not exactly true because I want to show you I'm not that same guy who broke your heart so badly. Please." He must be caught in a time warp and was now twelve again. That was the only explanation for the way he acted.

"Why not?" she answered finally.

Not a yes, but it wasn't a no. "Coffee or dinner?"

"I still need to help Missy, and I'd rather not have caffeine that late, so dinner?"

Score. "That works. Where do you want to go?"

"Honestly, I have more food than I can eat. There's a broccoli and chicken casserole I haven't touched and was planning to have tonight. Will that work?"

To spend time with her, he would agree to anything, except liver and onions. "Yes. That sounds great."

"Say six?"

"I'll be there. Should I bring anything?"

"Nothing unless you want soda, wine, or beer to drink. I've got juice, milk, and water."

A bottle of white wine would go with the chicken. No flowers this time, but Bria used to love peanut clusters. He would look for some of those, too. "See you at six."

🧁 🧁 🧁

Cupcake Posse Group Chat...

> **Bria:** *Guess who's coming for dinner?*
> **Nell:** *Your dad.*
> **Selena:** *The new vet.*
> **Nell:** *He hasn't moved to Berry Lake yet.*
> **Juliet:** *Missy and Nell?*
> **Nell:** *I wish.*

Missy: *I wish, too.*
Selena: *So, who?*
Juliet: *Yes, please spill.*
Bria: *Dalton Dwyer.*
Nell: *Whoa!*
Missy: *Don't we hate him?*
Nell: *Yes, we hate him.*
Selena: *Public enemy #1*
Juliet: *I have so many questions.*
Bria: *I'll answer everything tomorrow.*
Missy: *Frenemies are still a thing.*
Nell: *Are you sure you're okay with this?*
Bria: *No, but we talked about what happened, and I want to do this.*
Juliet: *Just know we're here for you.*
Selena: *Always.*
Missy: *BFFs forever.*
Nell: *I don't have to work tomorrow. If you need me to come over, let me know.*
Selena: *We'll be waiting for a full report.*
Bria: *If there's anything to tell.*
Juliet: *I'm not sure what to hope for.*
Selena: *No drama.*
Juliet: *Have fun.*
Nell: *Take care.*
Missy: *Watch yourself.*
Bria: *Thanks. xoxox*

At her aunt's dining table, Bria sat across from Dalton. He wore khakis and a polo shirt that intensified the green in his hazel eyes, but she hadn't quite meshed the teenager she'd once loved with the man with her tonight.

Still, the dinner was going better than she expected. Oh, tension existed, and uncomfortable gaps in conversation occurred, but things should have been weirder given their past. Bria didn't understand why it wasn't.

She eyed the bag from the candy store he'd brought her. "Peanut clusters?"

"You used to love them."

Bria couldn't believe he remembered. "I still do."

"You loved wildflowers, peanut clusters, and caramel apple cider from Brew and Steep."

"Excellent memory." Impressive, actually, but she wondered why he hadn't forgotten those things given he'd forgotten her. She refilled their wineglasses with the Chardonnay he'd brought. "I suppose that means I must share."

He laughed. "It doesn't sound like you want to."

"I'll see how many are in there first."

Dalton raised his glass. "To a delicious dinner and getting reacquainted."

She tapped her wineglass against his. As a chime hung in the air, she sipped. "I'm glad you suggested this."

He leaned against the back of the chair. "Tell me about your life in San Diego."

"Not much to tell." She sipped her wine. "I work for a large accounting firm, own a condo, and I love the area. There's so much to do, and the weather isn't anything like the Pacific Northwest."

"Do you have a boyfriend?"

That was an unexpected question. "Not at the moment. I did. We met at work, but then Elise got sick. It was a mutual breakup. We've stayed friends."

"That's good." Dalton drank more wine.

Was it? If Fritz had pushed all her buttons and her his, would things have been different even though they were so similar she often felt as if she were dating herself? Bria remembered how opposite she and Dalton had been, yet they'd clicked in so many ways.

But that was the past, and they weren't discussing it. Not really. "Tell me about Portland."

"I work for a real estate development firm and love my job. We have projects in three states, so I get to travel. I have a condo in Goose Hollow. I'm used to the rain. We get occasional snow, but it's nothing like here, and I'm okay with that."

"Berry Lake has had a couple of bad winters." Bria swirled her wine in the glass. She wanted to ask him the same question he'd asked her, but she didn't want him to take it the wrong way. "Are you dating anyone?"

He shrugged, which wasn't the reaction she'd expected to see. "I see people off and on. No one special right now."

That suggested there had been someone, but it was none of her business. Except she wanted to know more about the last person, and the others, including Heather Young from senior year.

Bria placed her glass on the table before reaching for the candy. She opened the bag and held it out to him. "I've decided to share."

"I'm honored." He took a piece. "This one looks good."

It was her turn. She grabbed the one nearest the top without even looking at it. Her friends would be mortified—that was so not her. Dalton seemed to bring that out in her. And she didn't mind as much as she should.

"Chocolate and nuts are my favorite combination." She bit into the candy and then swallowed. "It's so good."

He ate his. "I agree."

The silence wasn't as awkward as earlier. *Progress.* Though, it might be the chocolate.

"Do you plan on coming back to Berry Lake?" he asked.

"I wasn't going to, but now I will. There are a few things I can't do long distance, but I'm not sure I can get it all finished before I leave. I thought selling this house would be easy, but now I start crying when I think of never being able to come back here."

"There's no rush to do anything."

She nodded. "The house is almost paid off, and the payment is ridiculously low, so there's no reason not to hold on to it for now."

"It gives you a place to stay when you visit."

"That's a good point. I have to return in four months to meet with my dad." She dragged her teeth over her lower lip. "Will you be there?"

"Depends on what projects I'm assigned, but I hope so." He gazed into her eyes, making her heart bump. "It's nice getting to know you again."

Goose bumps covered her arms. Her muscles bunched. "Dalton."

He covered her hand with his. "Relax, Bri."

No one else had ever called her that. And forget about relaxing when her pulse shot off the charts. "I'm not sure I can."

"Try." Dalton lifted his hand, and a chill rushed up her arm as if missing his touch. "Tonight is dinner with an old friend. Nothing more."

"Friend?" Bria tried out the word, but she wasn't sure she liked it to describe him. Yes, they'd been friends up to junior year. But something had changed, and he stopped feeling like a friend and more like a boyfriend. They'd never transitioned back because they'd never talked until this week. "Is that what we are?"

"Not yet, but I'd like to be." He scooted closer to her. "What about you?"

A mix of emotions swirled, but that only heightened her apprehension. "Maybe."

That was as much as she felt comfortable saying.

Dalton laughed. "I'll take your maybe and another peanut cluster, please."

"What if you can only have one?"

He reached out again. This time, he squeezed her hand. "Then I'll take the maybe."

Bria only wished she felt as confident as he sounded with that choice.

How could it be after midnight? Music kept the office from being too quiet, but Missy had lost track of time, focusing on menu ideas. This was the fun part. It also felt so good to sit after taking everything out of the storage room after dinner. A delivery of supplies had prompted the reorganization. Now, the dining area was full of neatly organized stacks or piles, depending on the items. Her muscles hurt, but the hard part was over. *Tomorrow.* She would put everything back where it belonged and check off a big item on her to-do list.

Missy wanted to finish a few more things tonight.

As she stared at her notes on the desk, satisfaction filled her. Her ideas, combined with Elise's, were gelling into something amazing for the cupcake shop's future.

Missy picked up the journal full of a treasure trove of recipes. Not all were for cupcakes, either. She flipped through the pages: muffins, coffeecakes, and small layered cakes that served one or two people.

She had no idea why her boss had never used it. Given they'd been in a box with other old stuff, Elise might have forgotten about them. Whatever the reason, finding the journal had been a blessing and the timing perfect. These next four months were critical to convincing Mr. Landon the bakery was worth keeping.

Four months.

Not forever.

But that was better than no time at all.

She would make the most of it.

First up was the new menu board. She studied the rough sketch.

The sixteen original flavors would stay. She would add daily, weekly, and monthly flavors to keep the inventory fresh and exciting.

She shimmied her shoulders to the music, eager to hear what customers thought about the new additions.

Her cell phone buzzed.

Jenny: *Where are you?*
Missy: *Cupcake shop.*
Jenny: *Did you feed Mario and Peach?*
Missy: *Yes. I ran home for a few minutes.*
Jenny: *I would have fed them.*
Missy: *I know, but I wanted to eat and change clothes.*

Missy yawned. The daybed was behind her, ready if she needed it. She'd spent the night there a few times. Staying overnight would allow her to get everything in the storage room before she started the morning baking. Otherwise, she would have to get up earlier than usual.

Nope.

She woke up early enough as it was.

Missy typed another text.

> **Missy:** *I'm sleeping here.*
> **Missy:** *But never fear, I'll be home tomorrow to watch Briley. Can you feed the cats in the morning?*
> **Jenny:** *Will do. I wasn't worried, because you enjoy Friday date night more than we do.*
> **Missy:** *Guilty. I need my Briley time.*
> **Jenny:** *She needs her aunt. Don't work too late.*
> **Missy:** *I won't.*

Missy, however, needed to be more tired or her mind would keep running after she lay down. She knew just the thing to work on.

She opened the journal to make a list of ingredients needed to test more recipes.

First up, the Sasquatch one. She would call these Squatchy's Cupcake. Buddy Riggs might want to buy them to take on his Bigfoot tours. She wrote a note to ask him.

The cupcakes didn't have a Bigfoot made of chocolate or a Sasquatch figure stuck on the top. These were specially flavored and decorated to be like Bigfoot, at least the recipe character's idea of him or her. The cake batter ingredients resembled the s'mores flavor but with a touch of rocky road influence. The ingredients, however, were different.

231

She wrote *mini marshmallows, walnuts, chocolate, coconut* on her list. Shaved chocolate and toasted coconut would top the frosting. Malted milk balls might be something to try, so she wrote those down, too.

The huckleberry cupcake required a visit to the general store. Missy needed to see if they had any preserves or jam in stock. It was currently huckleberry season, so they might have fresh berries for sale. She would love to find all of the above to experiment, including picking some herself, so she would have a better idea of what they needed next year.

Four months.

Nothing wrong with making plans.

The Berry Lake cupcake's blue icing and gummy fish toppings would be a hit with the younger crowd. Elise had listed two bases—graham cracker and gingerbread. Missy would try both, but she leaned more toward gingerbread.

As she sang along to a song, Missy lost herself, imagining new toppings and variations to the recipes she'd found.

She sniffed.

That smells like smoke.

Oh, no. Had she left an oven on?

She ran down the stairs, but the ovens were off.

Good.

A forest fire in the area hadn't been contained yet, so it could be that. Or allergies or a cold playing tricks on her. She'd heard about phantom smells before, too. If she were hallucinating, she should call it a night. No reason to overdo after she'd worked plenty today.

Missy returned upstairs to the office. After a quick trip to the bathroom, she kicked off her shoes, pulled back the covers on the daybed, and slid in. She had a feeling sleep would come easy.

Something blared.

Missy bolted upright. She blinked in the darkness, disoriented from being awoken.

The noise continued.

It wasn't a sound she recognized.

And then she remembered the smell of smoke.

That had to be the smoke detector.

As Missy grabbed her phone, adrenaline rushed through her.

She ran down the stairs, nearly stumbling.

Smoke was in the kitchen, but no fire.

Thank goodness.

Missy turned on the light. The brightness made her blink. Smoke drifted from the shop side of the kitchen doorway.

Her heart slammed against her chest.

She peered into the front. The smoke was heavier, and flames burned in the seating area, where she'd sorted and organized the items from the storage room. The fire hadn't reached the ceiling yet.

As Missy glanced at the fire extinguisher, she thought better of it.

Time to get out of here.

On her way to the back door, she called 911.

"This is nine-one-one, what's your emergency?"

"The Berry Lake Cupcake Shop on Main Street. The dining area is on fire. Please hurry."

"Is anyone in the structure?"

"Just me. I'm Missy Hanford, the manager."

"I'm dispatching units. Are you out of the building?"

"Almost."

She pushed open the back door to the alley and inhaled the fresh air. "I'm outside."

Sirens wailed. The fire station wasn't far. "I hear the fire trucks."

"They will be there shortly."

Missy hoped so. "Thank you."

The asphalt was rough beneath her bare feet. She hadn't thought to put on shoes or even grab her purse. Those things could be replaced. And then she remembered...

Elise's journal.

Missy's heart dropped. It was sitting on the desk. "I have to go back in."

"Please stay where you are."

She hadn't realized 911 was still on the line.

"I'll be fast."

"Stop," a voice called her.

Missy ran inside. They needed those recipes. The smoke was thicker, but the light she'd turned on helped. "I'm almost at the stairs."

"Get outside. Now."

The floor was hot beneath the soles of her feet. She took the stairs two at a time.

Tomorrow, she would take photos of every page, so they would have a copy of the recipes.

Upstairs, she grabbed the journal. Thank goodness the notebook and her and Elise's plans were at home.

"Got it. On my way out."

Blinding smoke, however, now filled the stairwell. She tucked her phone inside her pocket, so she didn't drop anything. Her eyes watered.

Missy coughed.

It was getting hotter.

She shoved the journal under her shirt. That would keep the smoke away from it.

Missy stumbled down the stairs into the darkness.

She found herself on her stomach in the kitchen.

Her head pounded.

What happened? Where was the light?

There was so much smoke now. Way more than before.

She coughed. It hurt to breathe.

Missy tried to get up, but she couldn't. She was too dizzy.

And her head...

But she needed to get to the door.

It should be to her left.

At least that was where she thought it would be.

Except she wasn't sure where she was.

Fear pounded through her. Her head ached.

The smoke kept getting thicker.

Oh, man. Missy coughed again. Tried to inhale. But she couldn't suck in air.

Something crackled, a sickening sound. She glanced over her shoulder.

Flames covered the doorway, coming into the kitchen.

Out.

I have to get out.

Missy tried to crawl.

Hot, so hot.

Need air.

She dropped as low as she could, until her chest hit the floor, slithering like a snake, gasping for air.

Help.

Rob.

chapter nineteen

THE SHRILL RING of Bria's phone woke her. Right in the middle of what she assumed to be a good dream because she wanted to close her eyes and return to wherever she'd been. Another ring made her reach for the nightstand. She patted around in the darkness until she found it.

A number illuminated the screen without an associated name. She doubted robo-callers phoned this late at night, so she answered. "Hello?"

"Bria?" a woman asked in a rushed voice.

This person knew her. She sat up. "Yes. Who is this?"

"Penelope Jones from the Huckleberry Inn. There's no easy way to say this."

Bria's breath seized. She gripped the phone. "Is Juliet okay?"

"She's fine, dear. But the cupcake shop is on fire."

Fire? Bria must be half-asleep. She shook her head. "Can you please repeat that?"

"The cupcake shop is on fire. A fire truck is parked on Main Street. I thought you should know."

Oh, no. Bria scrambled out of bed. "Thank you, Mrs. Jones. I'll be right there."

As Bria threw on a pair of leggings, bra, and shirt, she called Missy.

"I can't take your call," Missy's message played. "Leave a message, and I'll be in touch as soon as I can." A beep followed.

"It's Bria. Penelope Jones called. She said the cupcake shop is on fire. The fire department is there, and I'm heading over now." Bria shoved her feet into sneakers. "I'll let you know what I find out."

She hoped it was nothing major. A kitchen fire had occurred a month after the shop first opened. A faulty oven, according to Elise, but that had been over twenty years ago.

If a fire truck was there, the sheriff probably had people there, too.

Going on foot might be faster.

With her cell phone on flashlight mode, Bria ran to the cupcake shop. She slowed when her legs burned. That was what she got for not running in… well, since PE in high school.

As her feet pounded against the asphalt, various scenarios played in her mind.

Smoke damage.

Interior damage.

A gutted kitchen.

Not what they needed, but whatever was wrong, they would repair and keep moving forward.

Her phone rang. The name on her screen showed Jenny O'Rourke. "Hey, Jenny, did Missy tell you about the fire?"

"Have you talked to Missy?" The words tumbled out one after another with no breaks in between.

"I left her a voice mail."

"She texted me around midnight." Jenny's voice cracked. "Missy's at the cupcake shop. She's spending the night."

The rising panic in Jenny's voice made Bria run faster. "I'm on my way."

"I'm getting dressed and coming down there."

As Bria turned the corner, flashing red lights lit up Main Street. She skidded to a stop. "No!"

"Bria?" Jenny asked.

Halfway down the block, firefighters aimed a hose at the flames engulfing the front of the cupcake shop.

Her heart raced so fast she thought it would explode. Jenny had lost her brother and parents. If Missy…

Bria's limbs were shaky, nearly making her double over so she didn't fall flat on her face.

"Are you there?" Jenny's voice was more frantic. "Bria?"

"I'm here." Bria stood frozen, staring in disbelief. The sounds and lights, everything stopped. Her heart hadn't stopped beating, but she thought it might have. If Missy were still inside… "I need to tell them about Missy."

Two firefighters held a hose, but a third stood between them and the truck. She took a closer look at the tall man dressed in bunker gear and a helmet who spoke into his jacket.

The fire chief.

She sprinted to him. Her breathing was ragged, but she tried to control it so she could speak. "The shop's manager, Missy Hanford, was inside earlier tonight. I don't know if she still is."

The flashing lights and shadows didn't hide the grim expression on his face, causing Bria's heart to drop. "She was in there and called nine-one-one. She made it out, but then she went back inside."

Bria wrapped her arms around her chest and stared in horror, gulping breaths of air. Everyone knew not to go back into a fire when you were out. Things were replaceable. People weren't. Missy wasn't.

The chief glanced back at the fire. "Paramedics found her. She's on her way to the hospital."

Thank goodness. Tears blurred Bria's vision. She struggled to get words out. "Is she… okay?"

"I don't know her condition. We're trying to get this under control so we can save the second floor and the structures on either side. We've got this engine in the front and a crew from another parked at the entrance to the alley. Whatever this was spread faster than it should."

I have to go to the hospital. "Do you need anything from me?"

"Not right now."

That was all she needed to hear. As she ran home, she called Jenny.

"Is Missy okay?" Jenny sounded shaky.

"She's on the way to the hospital."

A cry ripped from Jenny. "No, no, no."

"The fire chief said Missy called nine-one-one. She got out but then went back inside."

"Why?"

The pain in Jenny's voice squeezed Bria's heart. "I wish I knew."

Jenny sniffled. "Dare put the baby into her car seat. We'll head to the hospital now."

"I'm on my way, too."

The line disconnected. Bria grabbed her purse and then climbed into her aunt's car, which she'd been using. Her hands trembled. "Get it together."

But her mind was a minefield. And her heart was in a million pieces.

Missy had kept a to-do list. Nothing seemed to be a safety issue or a fire hazard. Bria's stomach turned to stone. "What if…"

…it's my fault.

Bria fastened her seat belt, trying to calm herself enough so she could drive. Before she started the engine, she texted the Posse's group chat with trembling fingers.

> **Bria:** *Fire at the cupcake shop.*
> **Bria:** *Missy was inside.*
> **Bria:** *No idea on her condition.*
> **Bria:** *She's on the way to the hospital.*
> **Bria:** *I'm headed there now.*
> **Bria:** *Will update you when I know more.*
> **Bria:** *But Missy needs prayers.*

No one would be awake at this hour, but by the time everyone woke in the morning, Bria hoped she had good news about Missy.

Please let that be the case.

She had one more person to call. If she ever wished for a father, one who loved her and wanted to be there for her, it was now.

He picked up on the second ring. "Bria?"

"Dad." Her voice cracked.

"What's wrong?"

"The cupcake shop is on fire." Saying those words seemed unreal, even though she'd seen the flames destroy what her aunt had built. "It's bad. They're hoping to save the second floor, but everything else is…"

"What?" Silence filled the line. "Do you know what happened?"

"No. I'm on the way to the hospital."

"The hospital? Are you hurt?" He actually sounded concerned.

Part of her heart softened. "Missy was spending the night in the office. Paramedics found her, but we don't know her condition."

"Oh, Bria." His anguished tone was genuine. No one could fake that. "I'm so sorry."

"All I want is for Missy to be okay." Bria choked on a sob. Images flashed of the burning building and how scared Missy must have been. "She has to be okay. Is there any way you can meet me at the hospital, Dad?"

In the waiting area, Bria sat with Dare and Jenny. Hope and Josh Cooper had picked up Briley and exchanged car keys with Dare since they didn't have a base for the baby's car seat. Jenny gave them instructions about frozen breast milk and Missy's cats, who would want to be fed in the morning.

Other patients came into the ER, were called back, and later left. This repeated until Bria wanted to scream. She was raw, and each sound around her seemed magnified, hurting her ears and grating on her frazzled nerves. She had no sense of time, but they'd been waiting forever. Okay, hours, but it felt like an eternity.

Jenny stared at the double doors leading to the exam area. "Why is this taking so long? They must know something."

Bria nodded. "I was thinking the same thing."

"The doctors take their time to make sure they don't miss anything. They're probably running tests. That's what they did with me after the helicopter crash." Dare had been an Army Ranger, a sergeant, but he'd been medically discharged after that accident. "I don't remember, but Yang… You know him as Lee… told me. He was conscious, unlike the rest of us."

Jenny leaned against her husband, nearly curling up on his lap. "I don't know what I would do if you weren't here."

"You would get through it because you're strong. But I'm happy if being here helps you." He kissed her forehead. "I won't tell you to sleep because I know you won't, but stop your writer brain from going to the worst-case scenarios, okay?"

She hunched. "I'm trying not to do that."

From the way her voice quivered, Jenny didn't appear to be succeeding. But Bria understood. "If it's any consolation, I'm not a writer, but my mind keeps going there, too."

"I've got two arms." Dare patted the seat next to him. "Come over here, Bria."

She didn't hesitate.

Still, Bria wished someone were here for her. Her dad had never said he would come. He also hadn't said he wouldn't, but he wasn't there.

Even though she'd asked.

That had been the first thing she'd asked of him since her college graduation.

He hadn't shown up for that, either.

And that hurt. Again.

A little while later, Nell rushed into the waiting area. "Sabine called, and then I saw your text. Any news?"

"No," all three said at the same time.

Nell put on a lanyard with her badge on it. "I'll see what I can find out."

"Thank you." Jenny rubbed her hands together. "The waiting is killing me."

She wasn't the only one.

The hospital's doors opened, but Bria was too worn out to glance over. Another person with the flu had probably arrived. That seemed to be the ailment of the day. If only Missy had that and not—

"Bria?"

She turned toward the familiar voice. "Dalton."

He hurried toward her, wrapped his arms around her, and pulled her close.

Bria sank against him. A hug had never felt so good, and she didn't want to let go, but she did. "Thank you for coming."

"Your dad called me about the fire and Missy. I'm so sorry." Dalton's gaze locked on Bria's. "Any word?"

"Nell's finding out information." Bria had to ask. "Is my dad coming?"

"He didn't say."

Of course, not. Bria pushed away her disappointment. "At least he called you, and now you're here. Thank you."

"Do you need anything?" Dalton asked. "Any of you?"

Everyone shook their heads.

Her legs were still shaky. "I need to sit."

"Of course." Dalton sat next to her on the couch and put his arm around her shoulders. "I drove by the cupcake shop. Well, as close as I could get. They have part of Main Street blocked. Fire trucks were still there, but no flames."

"That's good," she said automatically, but she didn't ask about the damage. She didn't want to know. The business wasn't the priority. Her friend was. Aunt Elise would have been the same way.

Her breathing hitched, and her throat clogged.

She blinked.

Dalton pulled her against him. Held her. And for now, even though it was him, that was enough.

A minute might have passed or three hours. Time ceased to have meaning or matter.

Nell came out from the exam area. "Missy is stable and getting the best possible care. I'm sorry, but that's all I can say."

"Thank you." Jenny reached out and squeezed Nell's hands. "At least we know Missy's alive."

Nell nodded, but the worry clouding her gaze and her pale face suggested Missy wasn't out of the woods. Suddenly, not knowing anything wasn't the worst thing in the world.

Eventually, a doctor dressed in scrubs came out. The woman glanced around the waiting area. "Jenny O'Rourke?"

Dare stood.

Jenny jumped to her feet. "That's me. But these people are Missy's family, too. Whatever you have to say to me, you can say it to all of us."

The doctor nodded. "I'm Dr. Anna Gomez. Missy is stable but unconscious. She has severe smoke inhalation and second-degree burns on her left foot. She's currently receiving oxygen. We see no evidence of thermal burns in the oral airway. We will continue to monitor her lungs and airway. She also has a closed head injury and superficial cuts and bruises."

"Thank you." Jenny's lips trembled. Her eyes blinked rapidly. She crumpled against Dare as if her legs had given out.

Bria's stomach roiled. As she buried her face against Dalton, she inhaled, allowing his scent and his strength to surround her. She was grateful he'd shown up.

"I wish I had more information for you." The doctor's tone was compassionate. "But we need to watch and wait."

"We understand." Dare patted Jenny's back. "Thank you for the update."

"I'll let you know if anything changes." With that, the doctor headed back into the exam area.

Jenny's face was tight, and her eyes haunted.

Bria wanted to be strong for her, but she held on to Dalton, afraid if she let go, she would collapse on the floor in a heap and sob. "Missy has to be okay."

She waited for him to tell her everything would be okay, and Missy would be fine, but he said nothing. Instead, he kissed the top of Bria's head and tightened his arms around her.

And she remembered what he'd told her.

I won't lie or try to scam you. You have my word.

That was when she cried.

chapter twenty

N ELL WAS RUNNING on fumes and coffee.
Coffee!
She glanced at her cell phone—nine o'clock. She was supposed to meet Gage at ten, but no way was she leaving the hospital. If Missy woke up or if Bria or Jenny needed anything, Nell needed to be there.

She pulled out her phone and typed.

> **Nell:** *A friend was injured in a fire. I'm at the hospital. Can we reschedule?*

She hit send and waited to see if he was online, but the three little dots didn't show up. She hoped it didn't sound like she was blowing him off, but her mind—and her heart—were on her friends. Nell tucked her phone into her pocket before walking into Exam Room Two.

Welles and Jordan stood next to the empty bed. Their expressions reminded her of young boys who'd done something wrong and were hoping not to get caught.

However, everyone knew what they'd done. Nell wanted to hug them for being heroes and yell at them for being so reckless with their lives.

Jordan pointed to Welles and back to himself. "Before you say a word, we're both fine."

As Welles rubbed his arm, he nodded.

She side-eyed him. "Jordan may be fine, but you're hurting."

"A bruise, Nurse Nell." Welles wouldn't meet her eyes, which was a first. "X-rays don't show a fracture, but if you want to come over later and make me feel better, you're welcome to."

"I need to be here, Paramedic Welles." She tilted her chin. "Or should I call you Hero Welles?"

Jordan snickered.

Welles grimaced. "No."

"What I will do is order you a pizza, so you don't have to worry about dinner. You, too, Jordan." A lump formed in Nell's throat. Without these two men… "Thank you for saving Missy."

Jordan motioned to his partner. "It was this guy who charged in there like an action-movie hero before I knew what was happening and carried her out seconds before the kitchen lit up."

Nell shivered. "That was so brave. And stupid. S-T-U-P-I-D! You could have been killed."

Welles half laughed. "You sound like the chief."

Jordan nodded. "Except Nell won't bust your… Uh, she can't punish you the way Chief will."

"It wasn't reckless." Welles's jaw hardened. "We had a water can and a thermal imager that led us right to Missy."

"And if you'd been thirty seconds later getting her out the door—"

"Not now, Pierce." Welles sent a silent message to his partner, followed by a glare filled with at least a thousand daggers.

There must be more to the rescue, but Nell didn't want to hear those details. No matter how much Welles denied it, he'd risked his life for one of her best friends. Nell didn't know the full extent of Missy's injuries, but being hurt was better than dead. "You did the right thing, but don't ever run into a burning building again. Or a burning barn. Or any kind of structure that catches fire. Do you hear me?"

"Loud and clear." Welles thrust his chest out. "See, Pierce? I told you she cared. That twenty is going to be mine, mine, mine."

Jordan snickered. "Only in your dreams."

Ugh. These two were too much.

Lynette, one of the nurses on duty, entered. "Both of you have been cleared. If you have any difficulty breathing, get back here ASAP. This place would be boring without you, and who would bug Nell?"

Welles winked at Lynette. "No worries. We're not going anywhere."

"Oh, Nell." Lynette glanced her way. "That hottie from earlier this week asked to see you. He's out in the waiting room."

Nell's lips parted. "Gage is here?"

Welles frowned. "Who's Gage?"

"Weren't you paying attention? Gage is a hottie." Jordan laughed.

"See you later." Nell hurried out of the exam room and into the waiting room. Gage stood with two coffees in a tray in one hand and a bag from Brew and Steep and flowers in the other. "Since you couldn't make it to coffee, I thought I'd bring coffee to you."

Her heart melted. "Thanks. I'm sorry for the late notice, but—"

"You had a lot on your mind."

She nodded.

Someone cleared her throat. Nell glanced over to see Selena had joined them in the waiting room. She wasn't the only one. Sheridan, Michael, and Sabine were there, too. They all stared with curiosity written on their faces.

Wait, is that...

Nell's insides twisted. "Mom? What are you doing here?"

"I came to see how Missy was doing." Charlene focused her attention on Gage. "I'm Charlene Culpepper, Nell's mom, and you are?"

"Nice to meet you. I'm Gage Adler." He raised his arms. "I'd shake your hand, but I don't have a free one."

"What do you do, Gage?" her mom asked.

"I'm a copywriter." He didn't hesitate to answer, as if the nosy moms of women he invited to coffee interrogated him regularly. "I've worked for several advertising agencies in New York, but I'm currently freelancing."

Nell hadn't known that.

Her mom's gaze traveled the length of him before returning to Nell. "Why don't you two go someplace quiet? Nell's not even supposed to be here today, but she's one of Missy's closest friends, so of course she won't leave."

Gage glanced at Nell.

"Missy is the friend who was injured in a fire last night," Nell explained.

"The cupcake shop?"

Nell nodded.

"I saw it this morning." He shook his head. "The place has been gutted. Missy's lucky to have gotten out."

The doors to the exam area opened. Welles stormed out, followed by Jordan.

Everyone rushed to thank the paramedics for saving Missy, but Welles sized up Gage. The guy might be a hero, but he was taking his bet too far.

She took the tray from Gage. "I know a quieter place where we can have coffee. Follow me."

Gage's smile lit up his face and crinkled the corners. "I'll follow you anywhere."

A grin tugged at her lips. For such a horrible day, there was at least one bright spot.

* * *

Selena knew marrying Logan Tremblay had been the best decision she'd ever made, but this morning proved it once again. When her husband heard about Missy being in the hospital, he'd kissed Selena and then found the fastest way for her to get to Berry Lake. Not even her team had responded that quickly. He had training camp but told her if she needed him there, to say the word, and he would come.

Her husband was a prince among men.

And though she would love to be with him now, she only left Seattle because her friends needed her more.

Bria hadn't said much over the past hour, but she clung to Dalton Dwyer as if afraid to let go. Selena worried if the guy was taking advantage of Bria's emotional state. Whether or not he was, Bria seemed to appreciate him being there. Maybe frenemies was the way to describe them.

Selena touched Bria's shoulder. "Do you need anything?"

"No, thanks." Her voice was quieter than a mouse.

Selena wouldn't push her friend. Not yet, anyway. But if ever Bria needed her dad, it was now. Except he wasn't there. Bria had wondered if he was still in town. If he'd left without saying goodbye to Bria, Brian Landon was an even bigger loser than Selena thought. And not that smart because this morning would have been the perfect opportunity for him to repair some of the hurt he'd caused his daughter… if he had shown up.

Selena's mom and dad had been far from ideal parental role models, but they'd done the best they could and shown up when she needed them. They saw her living a similar life to theirs because they didn't know any better. When she moved out, they wished her luck and gave her a hundred-dollar VISA gift card, more than they'd ever given her and most likely all they had at the time. Which was why as soon as she could afford to pay for it herself, even though Logan offered, she moved them out of that double-wide trailer to a beautiful retirement home in Palm Springs. They would never want for anything.

Her phone rang, but Selena had ignored it. She'd left numbers for her team if anyone needed help today. Otherwise, people could wait until she was free again.

Priorities.

Hers were there in the hospital.

"Nell hasn't come back." Selena glanced in the direction she'd walked with Mr. Hottie. "I'm going to make sure she's okay."

As Bria nodded, Dalton rubbed her shoulders. "I'll be here with Bria."

Selena went toward the atrium. That seemed the best place for a hospital date.

She rounded the corner and stopped. Nell and Gage sat on a bench, surrounded by lush green plants and quiet music. Only, Nell was asleep against his side, looking comfy and cozy with a serene smile on her lips.

Selena came closer. "What—"

Gage held his finger to his mouth. "Shhh," he whispered. "She sat down, took a bite of her muffin, closed her eyes for a minute, and was out. She must need the rest."

"Are you comfortable?" Selena whispered.

He stared down at Nell. "She is, so that's all that matters."

His words sounded like a pet owner who wouldn't move for fear of waking his cat or dog. He was already acting more like a decent guy than that loser Andrew, who strung her along for ten years. But time would tell. Selena would reserve judgment for now.

Gage smiled. "I'll admit, I've never had a first date like this."

Nell snored softly.

Oh, boy. Selena bit back a laugh. Nell would be so embarrassed. Charlene would go apoplectic when she found out. "I hope you understand what a difficult night it's been, emotionally and physically."

"It's why I showed up. I figured Nell needed a break or a distraction."

"Or a nap." Selena wasn't about to leave it at that. "But if you ghost her after this, I'll hurt you. Bad."

Gage chuckled. "I won't."

Selena returned to the waiting area where Juliet, red-eyed and sniffling, hugged her.

"This is so awful." Juliet carefully dabbed a tissue beneath her eyes. "I feel like I should do something, but I don't know what."

Before Selena could say anything, a man approached. He wore a designer suit and polished leather shoes. He was handsome—she would give him that—and in his fifties, old enough to be called debonair and a cradle robber.

The man must be Ezra, and Selena liked him even less in person. He hadn't spoken, but he gave off a weird vibe. One that made her wish for an iron shield and cloves of garlic.

He cupped the side of Juliet's head, not with a caring touch but a possessive one. "You care so much about your friend, but Missy wouldn't want you so upset."

Juliet said nothing but gave a slight nod.

"That's my princess." He kissed her forehead. "When you want to go home, call me. You're too upset to be behind the wheel. I wouldn't want anything to happen to you."

Not unless he had a huge life insurance policy on her.

Selena saw through the nice suit and expensive haircut to the controlling jerk he was. There was a word for men like him—bully.

"Goodbye," Ezra said to no one in particular. "I'm praying for Missy."

Yeah, Selena wasn't impressed. She wouldn't call the guy charming. He was too smooth and polished, which suggested it was all for show, a façade to the monster who treated his wife so badly. Juliet must have seen something in him when they met, but Selena had no idea what. He reminded her of a snake in the grass, calculating and conniving, ready to attack the innocent and unsuspecting.

One step at a time.

Juliet had a job. She hadn't told Selena yet, but Charlene had.

That was a big first step for Juliet, but Selena had many more in mind. It would take… time.

Sheridan DeMarco, who was all grown from the middle schooler with braces Selena remembered, paced across the waiting room. Her fiancé was no longer around.

"Want company?" Selena offered. "Between the two of us, we can wear a path in the carpet faster."

Sheridan glanced down as if to check. "I thought you were serious."

"It took your mind off Missy for a second."

Sheridan nodded. "She has to be okay."

"Missy will be." Selena would only think of Missy as okay and fully recovered. Nothing else was possible. "Where's Michael?"

Sheridan stared at the carpet again, but that didn't stop her face from flushing.

"I won't tell anyone." Selena carried thousands of her clients' secrets. Her friends, too. That was why others trusted her with their own.

"He's seeing if he can pay for Missy's medical bills," Sheridan whispered, glancing around to make sure no one was listening. "Jenny mentioned insurance from the military, but in case that doesn't cover everything or if any special treatments are needed, he wants to make sure she gets it."

"That's very generous of him."

"He can afford it." Sheridan's gaze softened. "He also knows how much she's done for me. I wish there was something I could do for Jenny. She's so upset."

Jenny wasn't just upset as Sheridan called it. Her sweet husband was doing all he could, but she was a hot inconsolable mess.

Time for Selena to take action. For all their sakes. "I'll see what I can do."

"Thank you." Sheridan rolled her shoulders. "I'm going to keep walking for now."

Everyone handled stress differently. There was no one right way. Only what worked for oneself.

Selena kneeled between Bria and Jenny, touching each of them. "Hey, it's been a long night. What if you go home, shower, and change clothes? You don't have to be away long, but you might feel better. I'll be here. Juliet and Nell, too. I bet Sheridan and Michael can stick around. I'll call you if anything changes."

Bria bit her lip as if contemplating it.

"That's a good idea." Dalton didn't hesitate to stand, pulling her up with him. "I'll drive you."

A slight nod was all it took for him to grab her purse and lead her to the exit.

One down… "What about you, Jenny?"

Jenny shook her head. "Missy might wake up. I need to be there if she does."

"The doctors will examine her first before they let anyone see her," Dare chimed in. His concern for his wife was evident in his eyes. He dragged a hand over the stubble on his face. "I'd love to shave, and you can see Briley for a few minutes. You need to feed her or pump."

Oh, Selena had forgotten about their baby. She pulled out her phone. "Text yourself from this. You can check in as much as you want."

Jenny hesitated, but Dare took the phone.

"I'll put in both our numbers. Thank you." As he returned the cell phone, relief shone in his eyes. He helped Jenny stand. "Let's go, babe. Just for a few minutes. We'll come right back."

Jenny nodded. "Briley is probably wondering where we are. And I want to see Mario and Peach. They must miss Missy."

"I'm sure they do." As he walked with his wife to the exit, he glanced over his shoulder and mouthed "thank you" to Selena.

Her work was done.

For now.

She sat on the couch and stretched out her feet. It was her turn to take a break.

The double-glass doors opened.

Charlene rushed in, red-faced as if she'd been running in her heels and was out of breath. "Where's Nell?"

"With Gage." Selena stood. "Is something wrong?"

"I had a meeting at Brew and Steep." Charlene smoothed her hair. "Everyone was talking about the fire. The police asked for all video camera footage from the businesses on Main Street. Where the fire started and how it spread so quickly appears suspicious."

"Suspicious?"

Charlene nodded. "They think someone set the fire."

Arson? Selena couldn't wrap her mind around it. Why would someone do that to the cupcake shop? Or to Bria and Missy?

Someone must have wanted to hurt them badly to do this, but who?

chapter twenty-one

AFTER A SHOWER and putting on clean clothes, Bria sat in the hospital cafeteria with Selena and Sheriff Royal Dooley, a bald fifty-year-old man who had once dated her aunt. She missed having Dalton with her—he'd been such a support today—but he had a call with his boss and whatever the sheriff had to say didn't involve him.

She only wished she had an excuse to get out of this conversation. Thinking about Missy lying unconscious in a hospital bed was pushing Bria to her breaking point. But having to talk about the fire was enough to make her head implode. Especially based on what Selena had told her.

"You say the fire is suspicious." Bria couldn't believe people claimed arson when the fire had just happened, but she'd forgotten how fast information flew in Berry Lake. "What does that mean exactly?"

"Whenever there is a fire, commercial or residential, the chief calls in a fire investigator. That person is on the scene at the cupcake shop now, looking at the site and collecting evidence. It's all routine," Royal explained. "But during Missy's call to nine-one-one, she told the dispatcher the fire started in the dining area. That's highly unusual."

"That surprised me, too." Still, Bria didn't want to believe someone did this on purpose. "But there could be another explanation."

"There could be many other explanations," Selena agreed.

The sheriff nodded. "But the fire spread quickly. According to the chief, that's usually the case in newer buildings, but not a structure as old as yours. That suggests someone used an accelerant."

His words didn't make Bria feel better. She was, however, grateful to discover the gas had been turned off before the fire reached the line. Still, it was all too much to take in, given everything else. But one thing didn't make sense to her. "If the fire investigator is in charge, why are you here asking questions?"

"It's Friday. You're leaving town this weekend. And I wanted to do this for Elise. She and I were"—he shifted in his chair—"close. I'm not out of my lane on this. I have authority."

"I'm sure you do. It's just that this doesn't make any sense. Not you being here. My aunt would appreciate you being involved in this. She always spoke fondly of you. But the fire." Bria rubbed her aching temples. "Why would anyone want to set fire to my aunt's building? Everyone loved her and the cupcake shop."

"Yes, they did." He rubbed his eyes. "Must be dust in the air."

Bria was having the same problem, but it wasn't dust. This big gruff man must miss Elise Landon. And he was doing what he could to help her. She rubbed her wet eyes.

Selena put her arm around Bria. "I know this is difficult, but people who want something get fixated, and many want that building. Or at least they did before the fire."

His eyes narrowed. "Can you tell me who?"

"The list is long." Bria's joke fell flat. "Do you want the names?"

"Yes." The sheriff readied his pen.

Bria blew out a breath. She would rather be in the waiting room in case someone had more news about Missy.

Selena squeezed her shoulder. "You can do this."

Bria didn't have any other choice. "My aunt left me fifty percent of the bakery. It won't be mine, though, until the assets are distributed. I suppose you could say Missy wants the bakery, too, since she runs it and made plans with Elise for the future."

"Juliet, Nell, and I should be on the list, also," Selena said. "Okay, I'm kidding, but the cupcake shop means a lot to all of us."

"This isn't a joke, Miss Selena T." Royal's nostrils flared. "Is there anyone else, Bria?"

"My dad, Brian Landon. He'll inherit the other fifty percent. Though he wants to sell the business and the building. He hired a consultant, Dalton Dwyer, to help him decide the best path." Bria hoped mentioning Dalton was okay. He was part of this, but maybe she should clarify more. "Dalton works for a real estate development firm in Portland. They or their investors are interested in purchasing the building."

"Not sure I'd hire someone with a conflict of interest, but Brian always did things his own way." Royal wrote more. "Anyone else?"

"No, but those people I mentioned would never set fire to the cupcake shop." Bria was sure of that. "They want the building, not..."

A wave of nausea hit. She had no idea what remained of the cupcake shop.

"I understand why you believe that. But never say never, Bria." The sheriff wrote in his notebook. "Over the years, I've seen people do strange things for unbelievable reasons."

"You must have stories to tell," Selena said.

He winked. "Including a couple about you and Nell Culpepper from twenty years ago."

Selena blushed, not something Bria had seen before. "So, any other questions for Bria?"

Bria nearly laughed. She now had a press secretary.

The sheriff turned to another page in his small spiral notebook. "Who has a key to the cupcake shop?"

"Good question." Bria tried to remember if she'd seen a list, but she came up blank. "Off the top of my head: me, Missy, Heidi Parker who opens sometimes, Bentley Strauss who closes on the weekends, and Charlene Culpepper, so she can pick up orders when the shop's closed. There's a spare upstairs in the office in case someone takes a different shift and needs a key."

The sheriff read over his list. "Any others?"

Bria shook her head. "Those are the ones I know. Missy might know others. Why?"

"Firefighters said the front door was locked, and that's where the fire started. It was something the investigator mentioned, too."

"The back door must have been unlocked." Bria wouldn't think otherwise. "No one with a key to the shop is an arsonist. Trust me on this."

"I'm not accusing anyone of anything. As I said, the investigation has just started. It takes time, and there's much to uncover." The sheriff tucked his notebook into his pocket as if to signal the end of the questioning. "This is such a difficult time, Bria. First, losing your aunt and now the fire. I appreciate you answering my questions. The fire investigator will be in touch."

"That's fine." Bria wanted this over.

"Before you go"—Royal wrote something on the back of his business card and handed it to her—"if you need anything, and I'm not talking about the fire, my cell number is on the back. I'll have officers keep an eye on Elise's house while it's empty."

The sheriff's gesture overwhelmed her. The familiar sting at the corners of her eyes returned. "I appreciate that, and I know my aunt would, too."

"I'm taking Bria back to the waiting room." Selena handed a card to the sheriff. "If you need anything else, please don't hesitate to call me, and I'll relay the information to Bria."

Relief flooded Bria for Selena taking charge. Emotions kept crashing into Bria like monster waves, and she struggled to stay upright. Bria had no doubt she would snap if one more thing happened. But she wasn't ready to give up and sell. She couldn't. Natural fire or arson, Bria was committed to her aunt's vision of the bakery.

No matter what.

In the hospital's atrium, Dalton found the privacy he wanted to talk with his boss. But even though it was quiet, other than soft instrumental music playing, he must have misheard Tanner. "Wait. What did you say?"

"I'm cutting our offer for the cupcake shop by fifty percent," Tanner repeated. "Consider it our personal fire sale. The building will appraise lower now, and the estate might not have many choices other than to sell if the insurance deems this as arson and doesn't pay out."

This wasn't the first time Tanner had gone from choir boy to shark when he wanted a piece of property, but unease knotted in Dalton's gut. He didn't want Bria to lose money if she and her dad had to sell. This should be a win-win-win for the three parties involved. "I'll talk to Brian, but he was set on that original amount."

"Much has changed since then. The guy was desperate enough before the fire, he'll accept it."

Tanner's confidence wasn't a surprise to Dalton, but that didn't stop him from balling his hands. He didn't like this.

"What about his daughter?" Dalton needed to stay neutral. Conflicts of interest could cost him his job, but he wanted to stop anyone from hurting Bria. "The cupcake shop has a sentimental value to her. But right now, she's too upset about her friend to be concerned about the business."

Which was why he wanted to get back to her as soon as possible. He'd hated leaving her, but Selena said she would watch out for Bria.

"There's no need to go all white knight, Dwyer. Nothing's happening right away. Especially after the fire. I'll see you in the office Monday morning." Keyboard clicks sounded in the background. "I want to update the timeline for the Berry Lake two point oh project. A little birdie told me another commercial property may come on the market soon, and if that's true, I want to make a preemptive offer."

"See you on Monday." After he spoke, Dalton's mouth tasted like sand. It shouldn't matter when he left Berry Lake. There was nothing here. Or wouldn't be, after Bria flew home. And what was she to him?

An ex-girlfriend.

Yes, but he wanted to forget about that.

The daughter of his client.

Yes, and that put him into a gray area he didn't want to dwell on.

A new friend.

Sort of, especially since he arrived at the hospital earlier this morning.

But that felt like… more.

It was too early to put a label on it, but he wasn't ready to say goodbye. He knew that for sure.

A text message lit up his phone. Bria's name appeared on his screen. Talk about perfect timing.

> **Bria:** *Missy is still unconscious.*
> **Bria:** *Jenny's afraid she'll never wake up.*
> **Bria:** *After you went to make your call, the sheriff arrived.*
> **Bria:** *He wanted to know who was interested in owning the bakery.*
> **Bria:** *I mentioned all the names, including yours.*
> **Bria:** *Not because I think you set the fire. I don't.*
> **Bria:** *But because you work for two people who want the building sold.*
> **Bria:** *I just wanted you to know.*
> **Bria:** *Thank you for coming to the hospital.*
> **Bria:** *It meant a lot.*
> **Bria:** *I'll shut up now.*

Dalton's smile seemed to spread through his entire body. Nothing she'd said was untrue, yet she'd wanted to explain to him. That had to be a good sign. Especially her trust in him.

Warmth spread through his chest. He texted her.

> **Dalton:** *I'm glad I could be there. Call is over. I'll find you shortly.*
> **Dalton:** *And don't ever try to shut up around me.*
> **Dalton:** *I like hearing what you have to say.*
> **Dalton:** *Unless I'm sleeping.*

As he walked to the waiting room, his phone rang, playing the Wicked Witch of the West ringtone. Dalton stopped. He didn't want any of Bria's friends to overhear the call, given their friendship with Sheridan DeMarco, who'd been dealt a horrible hand by his mom. "Have you filed for divorce already, Mother?"

"Hello to you, too, Son." Sarcasm dripped from his mom's voice. "I'm surprised you remember me since you failed to let me know you've been in town."

"I'm here for work. Besides, when was the last time I called you?"

People in Berry Lake hated Deena DeMarco. What most didn't know was she treated her children worse than her husbands. She pushed her kids to do things most parents wouldn't because it benefited her. Some called his sister and brothers Deena's minions. They weren't too far from the truth.

Dalton dreamed of having a mother who handed out warm cookies from the oven and big hugs, but his mom was nothing like that. Still, he'd done what she demanded of him. But being told to get Heather Young pregnant at eighteen had been the final straw.

Oh, he hadn't told his mother that then. But he'd stopped coming home on holidays and summers during college, waiting until he graduated to tell his mom he wouldn't be back, and he stopped calling her, too. Dalton hadn't been much different from her, taking what he needed before walking away. But she hadn't cared because now the only time she called him was when she wanted something from him… which reminded Dalton.

"What do you want, Mom?" he asked.

"I want to know if you did it?"

"Did what?"

"Set fire to the cupcake shop?"

The wind rushed from his lungs. "Why would you ask that?"

"In case I need to find a bail bondsman if you're arrested. I'm assuming that will be the one time you call me, and I wouldn't want to disappoint my eldest son by leaving him in the slammer overnight."

"Very funny, Mom. And disturbing."

"When have I been anything but? So, tell me, oldest child of mine." Her tone turned curious. "Did I raise an arsonist? Because, hon, I would be so proud to know you stuck it to those idiot Landons."

Dalton couldn't believe her. "You shouldn't joke. Missy Hanford is injured. She's still unconscious."

"Yeah, that sucks. But there's never been any love lost between me and Elise. I never understood why your father was friends with that loser Brian. And I still have no idea what you saw in his fat daughter."

Dalton's muscles tensed. "Her name is Bria, and she wasn't fat."

"Touchy, touchy, but if you want, we can go with big-boned." His mom crowed. "Guess the rumors of you getting cozy at her place last night are true. But I suppose that gives you an alibi for the fire."

He gritted his teeth. "I'm not an arsonist. You might consider setting a fire an option, but don't forget, I take after Dad more."

"That's true, except you have some of me in you, too."

Dalton didn't like being reminded of that. His shoulder muscles bunched.

"When I finally own the art gallery, your boss will want to talk to me since I hear he's interested in purchasing every store-front on Main Street," she added.

She sounded so confident. But he remembered the fear in her eyes, selling things around the house or taking them to a pawn shop, so she could pay the utility bills. The bleak situation had hardened her out of necessity. At least that was what he told himself.

"Are you planning to poison Sal?"

"Heavens, no. I'm not a black widow. That man is so crazy for me that he wants to retire early to spend more time together. Owen will take over, become a partner, and own the entire gallery soon after."

That would take her a year or more to pull off. "You have it all planned."

"I always do."

Dalton shouldn't ask, but he was curious. "What about Remy?"

"She's working at the gallery, but that's only temporary. She has something bigger on the horizon. She's a mini-me, following in my footsteps. My little girl makes me so proud."

"The years of indoctrination paid off."

Mom laughed. "What can I say? I have a gift."

That wasn't what he would call it. "Was there another reason you wanted to talk to me?"

"Nope. I wanted to know if you might be arrested, but I guess not."

Unbelievable. "Don't sound so disappointed."

"I know you don't believe me, but I love you, Dalton. I'd do anything for you kids. I have."

"I know you have. And it might surprise you to know I love you, too." He might be as bad as her for not cutting his mom out of his life completely, but despite everything, she was still his mom. "I just can't stand being around you."

She snickered. "You're not the only one, baby."

🧁 🧁 🧁

Something beeped.

Missy had no idea what it was or where she was, but each sound hurt like a jackhammer on her head. She heard voices but didn't recognize them. A few words cut through the dense fog in her head, but they were multisyllable ones like a doctor or professor used.

Suddenly, the fog became brighter.

So bright, but her head didn't hurt as much.

"Hey, babe."

Her heart slammed against her chest. She knew that voice, but it couldn't be him. It couldn't be—

"It's me."

"Rob!" She squinted but couldn't see him through the fog. "Where are you?"

"Wherever you are."

He was such a jokester.

"I'm not a jokester."

"Wait. You read my mind." As she moved toward the sound of his voice, she felt light as if her feet skimmed the ground.

Something appeared in front of her.

Hazy, until the soft edges hardened and defined and…

"Hey, beautiful."

Rob. It was him. She threw herself into his arms and leaned into him. He was familiar yet different. The same body and muscles beneath her palms, but he no longer smelled like sweat after a day in the field or his Irish Spring soap after a shower or the many variations of smells in between.

But she didn't care. He was with her again. Something she hadn't thought would happen. "Am I dead?"

"No, not yet."

She remembered the beeps. Everything was quiet now. "Am I dying?"

"That's up to you."

"Can I stay with you?" Missy clung tighter. They'd loved each other from the age of thirteen. She belonged with this man. It didn't matter where. "Can we be together again?"

"That's not how it works." He raised her chin with his finger. "It's not your time."

No, she wasn't buying that. "It wasn't *your* time, either."

"Babe." His eyes locked on hers. "It was."

"Oh." She hadn't expected him to say that.

"But for some reason, you seem to think it's your time now." His voice was full of affection—of love—for her.

It was hard enough to lose Rob once, she didn't want to lose him all over again.

"I miss you." She buried her face against him. "It's not the same without you."

"This isn't what we planned, and I know it's been hard, but I'm so proud of you." He brushed his lips over her hair. "Mario and Peach are so spoiled and loved. Jenny would have never gone to San Antonio and met Dare if it hadn't been for you."

Missy sighed. "I also set her up with Josh Cooper. That was a disaster."

"But you tried because you knew it was time for her to get on with her life. Now, it's time for you to do the same thing."

"No." Missy shook her head to emphasize the point. "I love you. You're the love of my life."

"I love you, but I'm not there anymore. I'm not coming back."

"But you're here. I'm here." Wherever this might be. "We're together. That's enough."

"It's not enough. You have a whole life to live." Rob cupped her face. "All those things we dreamed about together. They're yours for the taking. But you have to believe they can be yours."

No! She had everything she wanted right there. Her eyes implored him. If he could see into her heart, he would know the depths of her love. "I want to be with you."

"Promise me you'll try." His voice was steady, the way he'd always been.

She dug her fingers into him, wanting a firmer grip so nothing would tear her away. "I don't want to be without you."

Concern flashed on his face, followed by a soft smile. He kissed her forehead. "You're never alone, Missy. I'm always with you."

Her breath caught. She'd known him her entire life and loved him for most of it. She recognized that tone. He was saying goodbye.

Maybe she could convince him to change his mind. Missy touched his face, running her fingers up his jawline, over his cheekbones, and down to his lips. "You haven't been with me like this. I like it."

Rob gave her a look. The same one he'd given her when he said two cats would be better than one. "Please try for me."

He'd been right about the cats. She sighed. "Okay, I'll try."

Rob's smile lit up his face. He kissed her softly on the lips. "I have to go."

Her breath hitched. "Will I see you again?"

"Yeah. You will."

He'd never lied to her, so she didn't think he would start now. Still, she had to ask. "Promise?"

He chuckled. "Yes, I promise. But it won't be for a long time."

He'd been gone a long time already. This might go faster. She smiled. "I can live with that."

"Live is the operative word. You need to wake up, okay, and live for both of us." He kissed her again. "I love you, babe."

She hugged him. "I love you, too."

Suddenly, the fog thickened. The light dimmed.

"Rob?"

He didn't answer, so she reached out, but her hand only touched air.

Everything went black.

Missy didn't know how long she was in the darkness, but slowly light appeared again. She was no longer standing but lying down. Her head hurt. Oh boy, it *really* hurt. And that annoying beeping had returned.

"Open your eyes."

She recognized Jenny's voice and wanted to tell her to be quiet.

"Please, Missy." That was Bria, and her voice was softer, thank goodness.

"Briley wants her aunt Missy." That was Dare. He was way too loud.

Missy tried opening her eyes, but it took a couple of tries. Finally, her eyelids unstuck. She blinked.

Jenny, Bria, and Dare were there.

Missy's throat hurt. She tried to talk, but nothing came out.

"I'll get the nurse," Dare said before disappearing.

She had no idea where she was. It hurt to move her head, so she couldn't look around.

As Jenny held her hand, tears gleamed in her eyes. "You're in the hospital, but everything will be okay now. It's going to be okay."

"It will." Bria touched her other hand. Tears fell down her cheeks. "Just get better."

Missy didn't remember anything except Rob.

His touch.

His kiss.

Had it been a dream?

Being held in his arms and having his lips pressed against hers had felt oh so real.

He'd wanted her to wake up, and she had.

For him.

She didn't know how to live without him, even though she'd been doing it for nine years, but this…

Today… she would try.

chapter twenty-two

S ATURDAY NIGHT, JULIET sat with the other Posse members in Missy's hospital room. Ezra was at a business gathering in Seattle—golfing, a whiskey tasting, and cigar lounge, which didn't sound like work—so she was thrilled when he allowed her to stay home. Not that she could have gone when she had to work tomorrow, but he hadn't mentioned her job.

Not once since she'd told him on Wednesday.

But that would soon change.

Their first marriage counseling session was a week from Tuesday in Hood River. Ezra hadn't wanted to see a local therapist, stating privacy reasons. She would have thought he understood about HIPAA laws, but he'd agreed to go. That was all that mattered.

The room lights were dim and no music played because of Missy's concussion. Juliet would be mindful of that when she opened the champagne and sparkling cider. She removed the bottles from her tote. "It's time for a toast."

"The world is still here, and so are we." Nell grinned wryly. "That's cause for celebration."

Selena nodded. She'd been quieter than usual tonight. "There's always something to celebrate."

Bria nodded. "Especially since Missy is improving."

"I am." Missy's voice was hoarse but getting stronger each day. The bruises on her face would heal but were still an ugly purple color. She seemed different, but Juliet couldn't put her finger on what it was. Almost dying and having a concussion might have something to do with it.

"Gage asked me out again." Nell blushed, but anticipation danced in her eyes. "I promised I wouldn't fall asleep on him again until the fourth date."

Everyone laughed, except Missy. Her eyebrows drew together until she grimaced and stopped. "Who's Gage?"

"A hottie who is also a comfy pillow," Selena joked. "A-K-A Nell's new boyfriend."

Nell sighed. "He's not my boyfriend, even though my mom calls him that. We've only been out once, and unfortunately, I was only awake for about five minutes of that coffee date."

Selena shook her head. "More like two."

"Sounds like I missed a lot." Missy sipped her water.

"Not that much." Bria touched Missy's arm. "We'll get you caught up."

"For sure. In the meantime, there's bubbly to drink." Selena side-eyed Juliet. "Does anyone else have news to celebrate?"

"I do." Juliet took a deep breath. She didn't know what she was worried about. These women were her friends. They would support her. "Missy and Bria know already, but you're looking at the newest employee of Events by Charlene."

Nell hung her head. "I'm excited for you. Event planning is a perfect career for you, but I can't believe you're choosing to spend time with my mom. That's just… wrong."

Selena gave Nell a half hug. "Charlene's easier to take when she's not your mom."

Juliet nodded. "She hasn't yelled at me once."

Unlike Ezra, but the upcoming counseling appointment was Juliet's beacon in the stormy seas of matrimony, lighting the way until they reached their destination—marital bliss. Now that they had a map and were headed in the right direction, everything would change. She was sure of it. "I'll open the bottles in the hall."

"Stay here." Missy smiled, and a rush of thankfulness rushed through Juliet. "The pop will be short. I'll cover my ears. And this way, none of the nurses will get on you."

Nell slid her fingers across her mouth as if she were zipping them. "My lips are sealed."

Selena hugged Juliet. "I'm so proud of you for making this happen."

"Thanks, but it was your idea, and you also put in a good word for me with Charlene." Juliet wanted to thank Selena for giving her the push she needed. The alternative… Juliet shivered. She didn't want to think about that. "I'm so nervous about my first party tomorrow. I hope you're still proud of me if I mess up."

"Let's try that again." Selena wagged her finger. "Reframe your words by saying, I'm excited. You'll be so proud of how successful my first party is."

Nell grinned. "Selena T at work. I wish you could teach my mom how to do that."

"Can I take a video?" Missy asked. "I've never had a post go viral."

Nell wagged her finger. "No cell phone with a concussion."

"We're going to start calling you Mom," Bria joked.

"Don't we already?" Selena winked.

Soon, they held glasses in their hands. Missy was the only one drinking the non-alcoholic version, but hers had bubbles, too.

Juliet watched them rise in her glass. "Who wants to make the toast?"

All four of them looked at Selena, who rolled her eyes. "Fine. I'll do it." Selena raised her glass. "To Elise, for teaching us the importance of friendship and cupcakes. Two ingredients for a lifetime of smiles and laughter and pants that fit a little snug. And to the Cupcake Posse, who are stronger together than we are apart. We were brought together again for a reason. So let's make the most of it."

"To Elise and the Cupcake Posse," Juliet and the others said at the same time. Everyone drank.

"I have one more toast to add. I haven't been to Main Street, and I don't know when I'll be ready to face what's there, but…" Bria raised her glass. "To the Berry Lake Cupcake Shop, may it rise like a phoenix from the ashes so Elise's legacy will live on."

"Hear, hear." Everyone drank.

Nell's expression looked wistful. "I hope it's soon."

"Me, too, but it will take time." Bria stared into her glass, but she didn't sound upset, more resigned. "The fire investigation has to be completed before anything can happen. The insurance company doesn't want to talk to me, though it's the weekend, so I'll cut them some slack. But once things get going, we'll need everyone's help to open the cupcake shop again."

"You've got it." Selena grinned, the sparkle in her eyes suggesting she already had plans. "I can work anywhere, so whenever Logan's team is on the road, I'll be here."

"I'm in." Nell sipped her champagne.

Juliet nodded. "Whatever you need."

"Great." Relief sounded in Bria's voice. "I plan to fly up whenever I can, but Missy will need help."

"She's got it." Juliet wanted to be there for her friends.

"You guys." Missy's eyes gleamed. "Thank you."

"Speaking of Elise and cupcakes." Nell set her glass on the bed tray, picked up her purse, and pulled out what looked to be a book. She handed it to Missy. "Welles found this on you after he carried you out of the fire. He asked me to give it to you."

Missy clutched the journal. "I thought it was gone."

Juliet had never seen it before. "What is it?"

Bria handed Missy a tissue. "A journal full of Elise's recipes."

A contrite expression crossed Missy's face. "I went back into the cupcake shop to get it."

Juliet gasped. "Don't do that again."

Selena nodded. "Never, ever."

"I wasn't thinking," Missy admitted. "I had no idea how fast things would change, but now I know. Jenny, Bria, and Nell have all had *that* talk with me."

"New Posse promise," Nell announced. "If there's ever another fire, we don't go back inside. On three, everyone. One. Two. Three."

"I promise."

Selena peered over Bria's shoulder to look at the journal. "Just think, you'll have lots of time to perfect new recipes."

Missy nodded, but she had a faraway look in her eyes. "I wish we didn't have to cancel orders. We have cupcakes ordered for upcoming birthday parties and weddings, including Sheridan and Michael's, but no place to make them."

"I think it's time." Juliet glanced at Bria. "Do you want to tell her, or should I?"

"Go ahead." Bria refilled glasses with champagne. "It was your idea."

Yes, it was. That pleased Juliet. "I spoke to my grandmother this afternoon. She feels horrible about what happened, and she said the cupcake shop could use the kitchen at the Huckleberry Inn to fill special orders."

Missy covered her mouth. "Now, I'm really going to cry."

Selena stared over the lip of her glass. "Then I guess I shouldn't tell you about my idea for you, me, Juliet, and Nell to buy out Mr. Landon's fifty percent if he wants to sell."

"What?" Bria shouted. "Sorry, Missy."

"It's just an idea, but mine are usually good ones, as we all know." Selena sipped. "But I was thinking about how we all want to help. What better way?"

Juliet's stomach fluttered. That would give her two things—two jobs—to do outside of the house. She had no idea if Ezra would go for it, but anticipation buzzed through her. "I love the idea. I really do, but how much money are we talking about?"

Bria tapped her chin. "Dalton and I each calculated one and a half million dollars, but I'll be honest, the building was a significant part of the original value. Who knows what it's worth now?"

"So seven hundred and fifty thousand dollars divided by four is?" Selena looked at Bria.

"One hundred eighty-seven thousand dollars," Bria said without missing a beat.

Nell and Missy had deer-in-the-headlights expressions, and Juliet didn't blame them. That was a lot of money. She wouldn't know how to ask Ezra for that amount or if what Selena suggested was even possible.

"Don't panic or think it's impossible. We can do anything if we want it enough." Selena's face lit up as if she were speaking in front of thousands, not four old friends. "That amount is using the pre-fire value, and I'm assuming the most we'd have to pay."

Missy bit her lip. "Do you think your dad would sell, Bria?"

Bria shrugged. "I don't know, but this would get him the money he wants. I haven't spoken to him since the night of the fire. When I do, I'll see how he feels about it."

"And remember, this isn't happening now," Selena added. "But I wanted to throw it out there for… planning purposes. All in favor?"

Five hands shot up, including Juliet's. The possibilities excited her, so she would focus on those and not the obstacles in the way.

Missy hugged the journal. "Elise would love this idea."

"She would." Bria sighed, and then a smile tugged on her lips. "If this happens, it'll be hard to stay in San Diego."

Nell shrugged. "You have a house, a car, and three of your besties in Berry Lake. What more do you need?"

Juliet nodded. "Nell has a point."

"I third that." Missy grinned.

Bria laughed.

Selena rubbed her chin. "I don't live here, but Logan and I have considered building a vacation home somewhere."

"Ber-ry Lake, Ber-ry Lake, Ber-ry Lake," Nell chanted, and Juliet and the others chimed in. Until Missy covered her ears, and they stopped.

As everyone drank their bubbly and dreamed about a new

Berry Lake Cupcake Shop, a feeling of contentment settled in Juliet's chest. Things—good things—were happening to all of them. She only hoped they continued.

On Sunday morning, Bria packed the rest of her clothes and rolled her suitcase into the living room. This was her last day in Berry Lake. Her flight departed that afternoon, so even with the hour-and-forty-minute drive to the airport, she had plenty of time to close up Aunt Elise's house.

Close up.

That didn't mean the same thing as she thought a week ago. She hadn't finished sorting through the items that remained, packed more boxes, or mailed the ones she intended to send, but that gave her more reasons to return sooner. As if her four friends weren't reason enough.

Warmth pooled at the center of Bria's chest before spreading to the tips of her fingers and toes.

They were her friends, and that must be why today was so… bittersweet.

Last night had been so much fun.

Missy had tired quickly, but the rest of them had continued talking even after she'd fallen asleep.

Selena's idea about them owning the cupcake shop had been a surprise, but a good one. Sure, it was nothing more than a day-dream—like telling each other what they'd do if they won the lottery—but maybe—hopefully—they would make it happen. As Missy had said, Elise would have been all over that.

Bria emptied the dishwasher. She'd returned plates and pans to people who had brought over food and given away the leftovers. She glanced at the clock.

Almost nine.

Dalton would be here soon. Her pulse kicked up a notch. He'd wanted to see her yesterday, but she'd spent Saturday at the hospital to give Jenny a break and time to set up a room for Missy, who would stay in the O'Rourkes' house until she healed.

A knock sounded.

Bria's heart leaped. Okay, more like rose on its tiptoes, but seeing him made her happy. She never expected to feel this way again about Dalton Dwyer, but he didn't seem to be the same boy he'd been. Bria wasn't the same girl, either, so there was that, too.

She opened the door. "Hi."

Dalton wore a burgundy Henley and faded jeans. The casual style suited him. He held his hands behind his back, but then he brought his right arm around and handed her a bag from the candy store. "These aren't to share. They're for your flight."

Her chest squeezed tightly. It was a given she would see Missy, Nell, Selena, and Juliet again. But would this be goodbye for forever with Dalton? Part of her was afraid to ask.

"Thanks for the candy." She went to her purse on the coffee table and stuck the bag inside. "Now I won't forget them."

His mouth quirked. "Aren't you going to ask what's in my left hand?"

Not the most subtle hint, but Bria would play along. She cupped her chin. "Oh my goodness, Dalton, do you have something in your left hand?"

"How observant of you, and yes, I do." Amusement lit his

eyes. His left arm swung to the front. He held a plain brown bag. "What do you think is inside?"

"Do I get a clue?"

"Nope."

"Breakfast?" she guessed.

"Ding, ding, ding. You win. Now for bonus points, what kind of breakfast?" He spoke like a TV game show host.

Bagels, muffins, pastries, doughnuts, egg sandwiches. There wasn't a clear-cut answer. She decided to go with her first thought. "Bagels."

"Bzzzz." His attempt at a smirk was adorable. "Doughnuts. They had the sprinkle kind."

Bria recalled the chocolate cupcake he'd had at their meeting. It had sprinkles, too. She would leave that one for him. "You love sprinkles."

"They're fun. Sweet. And the perfect topping."

"Can I steal that to use with the cupcake shop?"

"Go for it." Dalton sat on the couch, pulled napkins out of his pocket, and ripped open the bag to show six doughnuts, each different except—they all had sprinkles. "You can pick first."

"I want sprinkles, too." A good thing since non-sprinkles wasn't an option. But she enjoyed learning he liked sprinkles. If only she had time to learn more. "I'll take the pink-frosted one."

"Excellent choice." He took the chocolate doughnut as she expected. "I'll snag this bad boy."

Like the cupcake. At least she now knew one of his favorites. Would remembering that matter?

Bria forced herself to take a bite.

He motioned to the boxes in the living room. "Still packing?"

"No." She pictured her list held to the front of the fridge with a magnet. It would be there when she returned. "I didn't check off all the to-do items, but for the first time, that's okay. It'll be waiting for me when I come back." She half laughed at the change in herself. "Selena T's podcasts are helping me."

Her friend would be amused and happy about that.

"Listen to your heart," he mumbled.

Bria inhaled sharply before studying Dalton as if seeing another side of him for the first time. "You follow her podcast?"

"I even subscribe." A faint pink tinged his cheeks. "I tuned in because I was curious how someone from Berry Lake found that kind of success. But one show, and I was hooked."

"Same."

"How's Missy?"

"Improving each day." Bria planned to stop by the hospital on the way out of town. "Smoke inhalation can have long-term effects, but the doctors are pleased with her recovery so far. I'm grateful to Welles and his partner for getting her out so quickly."

Dalton's gaze was on her, but his face was hard to read. Then, his eyes darkened, growing more serious. "How are you?"

Uncertain about what happens after we say goodbye? Only Bria didn't dare ask. She'd gone from hating the man to wanting to be friends to… Her feelings about Dalton Dwyer were a jumbled mix, as if she were stuck on her washer's spin cycle. She bit into her doughnut.

He kept staring. "I can wait."

Guess he wouldn't let this go. Bria swallowed. "I'm good. Doughnuts are like cupcakes. They make everything better. That's what my aunt used to say, and she was right."

"Cupcakes and doughnuts are two of my favorite things. I'm glad you like them, too."

"I do, but not as much as I like you."

Oh, no. Had she said that aloud?

Based on Dalton's wide grin that reached his eyes, she would say yes.

She blew out a breath and then took another bite, focusing on a speck of dust on the coffee table. How had she missed that spot?

"I like you better, too," he said.

Her gaze jerked to his.

He wiped his mouth with a napkin. "The only thing that would be better is if you came with sprinkles."

"Sprinkles might be hard to pull off, but sparkles, I can do."

Dalton's eyes softened, matching his expression. "I have fun with you."

"Me, too. With you." She eyed the remaining doughnuts sitting on the bag. The vanilla cake one with white icing and chocolate sprinkles looked yummy.

"Take it," he urged. "You know you want it."

"I do." She raised the doughnut to her mouth and bit into it. "Delicious."

As they ate breakfast, they spoke about everything except the elephant in the room—they lived in different states. At least California and Oregon were in the same time zone. Not that keeping in touch was a given. They might not be on the same page with liking each other. "Like" to her might differ from "like" to him. For all she knew, they weren't reading the same book.

Bria laughed. "I can't believe I'm sitting here with you."

"Thanks for not holding the past against me."

That wasn't one hundred percent true. "I did."

"You had a reason, but…"

She leaned forward. "What?"

"You and me. Like this. How we were at the hospital, if the circumstances were different. Better…" He wet his lips. "I want more."

A thrill shot through her. "I do, too."

As his head fell back slightly, he released a huge breath. "I'm so happy to hear you say that. Relieved, too. I hoped, but…"

Didn't they just do this? "What?"

"Can we forget about the past and start over?" He held her hand. "You need time, and I'm willing to wait."

She hadn't forgotten what happened, but she needed to stop looking back if they wanted to move forward. Yet, she wasn't ready to sprint. Dalton appeared to realize that. "Thank you."

"When you're in town next, I'll head over from Portland and take you to dinner. Or, I can pick you up from the airport and drive you to Berry Lake. Whichever. Both."

Tingles skittered across her skin. "That would be wonderful."

"And nothing against the chicken and broccoli casserole, but I want to take you out to a restaurant."

"You're on." She scooted closer to him. "There's one thing I'd rather not wait for."

"Another doughnut?" He leaned in.

"This will be better than that."

"Go for it."

That was the only encouragement Bria needed. She leaned toward Dalton, closed her eyes, and kissed him on the lips. Soft. She soaked up the taste of him—chocolate and warm and… There was something else, but her mind blanked. It would come to her.

For now, she wanted to enjoy the moment with her lips against his.

Enjoy him.

Almost believing she were dreaming and he might not be there in the light of day, Bria drew away and slowly opened her eyes. "Thank you."

Wide-eyed, Dalton flashed a charming grin at her. "That should be my line."

"Next time." It wasn't a question because there would be one.

"Next time will be dinner and a kiss." He sounded as confident as she felt.

An unfamiliar peace—a strange contentment—settled over Bria.

Once upon a time, Dalton Dwyer had been the reason she'd left Berry Lake. Now, fifteen years later, he made her want to return. "Dinner and kisses."

Dalton laughed. "Your plan is better than mine."

"I thought you might agree." Plural kisses were better than singular ones, especially when he tasted like... And then it hit her. "Buttercream icing."

"What did you say?"

His kiss reminded her of that. "I remembered something my aunt said to me."

You know what I always say. Cupcakes are better than men, but a few good ones are out there. You might find one who's as sweet as buttercream icing.

Dalton wrapped his arm around her. "You okay?"

Nodding, Bria smiled. "Aunt Elise knew what she was talking about."

🧁 epilogue 🧁

S UNDAY AFTERNOON, JULIET'S feet hurt, but the rest of her body smiled. She turned onto the main highway headed for home. Oh, she was tired from partying at the hospital with her friends last night, staying up late and getting up early this morning to prepare for the party, but it was the most satisfying tired she'd been since her theme park days.

When Charlene mentioned Juliet's first event would be a birthday party, she'd pictured a luncheon or brunch, not a tea party for a cute eight-year-old named Petra. Thank goodness the details had been in Juliet's inbox last night, or things might not have gone as well. With the party behind her, she realized that was part of the sixty-day trial period—work under pressure because event planners had to think on their feet and come up with quick alternatives in some situations.

Running a tea party for ten little girls took energy and patience Juliet hadn't realized she possessed, but Petra claimed it was the best birthday ever—her guests agreed—and Juliet received a fifty-dollar cash tip. Charlene told her to keep the entire amount, even though Juliet tried to give her half.

Of course, tea was lacking from this tea party. It turned out kids preferred pink lemonade to chamomile. Charlene was aware of this thankfully, or the day might have turned into a disaster. Juliet missed serving Berry Lake Cupcake Shop cupcakes—since the bakery was… not open—but the girls didn't mind the ones from the market. They ate and drank everything, including the cookies and triangular sandwiches Juliet made. Her favorite part was giving an etiquette lesson like her grandmother gave her and the Posse.

She couldn't wait to tell them about it on the group chat. Bria and Selena were in airplanes, flying home, so Juliet wouldn't have to rush messaging everyone.

Excitement buzzed through her. She'd found herself in a magical groove that nothing except being a princess had ever brought her. Not even acting. She didn't know how often Charlene did birthdays like these, but Juliet hoped another was on the calendar soon.

"Yes!" Juliet turned onto her street. She'd discovered something she was good at. And she wanted to tell Ezra, no matter what he might say. Until their marriage counseling appointment, less than a week and a half away, she could handle anything.

As she parked in her driveway, her cell phone rang. She turned off the ignition and then glanced at the phone. Charlene Culpepper's name appeared on the screen.

She accepted the call. "Hi, Charlene."

"Three people have called about scheduling children's birthday parties. You're magic, Juliet. Pure magic."

That was how she felt. "Thank you."

"One person asked if you did princess tea parties. Is that something you'd consider?"

"I… I could do that." At least Juliet thought so. "I have an old costume that Ezra had custom-made for me one Halloween. I'd have to see if it still fits." She'd lost weight since then. Ezra's weekly weigh-ins made her paranoid each time she stepped on the scale.

She would bring that up in counseling, along with the list of things she wanted them to discuss.

"Wonderful." Charlene sounded like she was smiling. "You must role-play as a princess, so I'll pay you a higher hourly wage."

Juliet forced herself not to scream. Instead, she wiggled all over. "Thank you."

"Are you home yet?"

"I'm in the driveway."

"Wash your tea set and then rest," Charlene ordered in her no-nonsense tone that no doubt drove the Culpepper sisters crazy. "Don't cook dinner. Order or go out."

"That sounds like a great idea. Ezra is in Seattle and won't be home until later."

"Well, you deserve an afternoon of self-care, so pamper yourself. See you on Monday."

Juliet's body thrummed with excitement. She put her phone in her purse.

She wanted to call Ezra, but he might be busy, and she didn't want to disturb him. He would arrive home soon enough.

Juliet had been trying so hard to make him proud. This might do it.

Things were better between them since she'd brought up counseling and made the appointment. That gave her hope the relationship would not only improve, but she'd also have the marriage she dreamed about.

She removed the rolling cart containing one of her tea services. That had been a last-minute addition, but she'd thought the floral teacups with a gold rim were a better fit for a kids' party than Charlene's statement-making white with silver trim.

Inside the house, she rolled the cart through the foyer. Thai food sounded good. Or tacos. Those were tasty on Tuesdays—and every other night of the week.

A movement in the living room caught her eye. Ezra sat on the couch with a glass in his hand.

She let go of the cart's handle. "I thought you'd still be in Seattle."

He said nothing.

That was odd. Juliet had never seen him so still and quiet. "Ezra."

His face was pale, and the lines around his mouth appeared deeper. Strange given how hard he worked so his wrinkles wouldn't show.

Juliet sat next to him and touched his hand.

He stiffened, his muscles tensing beneath her palm.

"Are you sick?" She felt his forehead with the back of her hand.

Ezra jerked away. "Don't touch me."

She flinched but remained seated. "What's wrong?"

He gulped his drink. "*You* are what's wrong. I give you every-thing, and you do nothing."

Juliet swallowed, sorry she'd asked. But she wasn't about to be the timid wife he expected. Not today. What had Selena told her? Oh, right. Juliet deserved… better.

She lifted her chin. "I take care of the house and you. Whatever you tell me to do, I do it. Everything I do is for or about you. I even got a job for you."

Ezra sneered. "What you do isn't a job."

"Have you been drinking?"

"Yes, Juliet. I have." He picked up a bottle from the floor and refilled his glass to the top. "When a man's wife can't do anything right, whiskey is a big help." He downed a quarter of his drink. "I should have realized you only married me for my money."

Her mouth gaped. "I didn't. I fell for you long before I knew you were wealthy."

His lips curled. "No wonder you never made it as an actress. You possess zero talent."

His barb hit hard, but she kept her shoulders pushed back. He must be drunk because his words were harsher than usual.

"Ezra." She held her voice steady. "Whatever has happened, I love you."

"You love my money." He hung his head, something she'd never seen him do in twelve years of marriage and one of dating. "This is all your fault."

It usually was. Juliet squared her shoulders, preparing herself to face the onslaught of incoming fire. "What did I do this time?"

"You weren't enough." He raised his glass. "I had to find another way to cope."

"I don't understand."

"Remy."

Ezra made no sense. "What about Remy?"

"I was with Remy today." He spoke quickly, so it came out like one word.

"In Seattle?"

"There was no trip or any late-night hours or dinner meetings," he jeered. "You drove me to her. You. That's why it's your fault she's…"

"She's what?" Juliet's voice sounded shrill. She didn't care.

Ezra downed more whiskey before slamming the glass on the table and sending droplets of amber liquid everywhere. His accusing gaze met Juliet's. "Remy's pregnant."

If you want to know what happens next to Juliet, Bria, Missy, Nell, Selena, and the Berry Lake Cupcake Shop, read Tiaras & Teacups, the second book in the series. For more info, visit: https://melissamcclone.com/blcp2

If you want to know more about Jenny and Dare, Hope and Josh, or Sheridan and Michael check out my Beach Brides/Indigo Bay miniseries which contains prequels to the Berry Lake Cupcake Posse series, visit: https://melissamcclone.com/blcp_prequels

Join Melissa's newsletter to receive a FREE sampler collection, and hear about new releases, sales, freebies, and giveaways. Visit: https://melissamcclone.com/join

about the author

USA Today bestselling author Melissa McClone has written over forty-five sweet contemporary romance novels. She lives in the Pacific Northwest with her husband, three children, a spoiled Norwegian Elkhound, and cats who think they rule the house. They do!

If you'd like to find Melissa online:
melissamcclone.com
facebook.com/melissamcclonebooks
facebook.com/groups/McCloneTroopers

other books by
melissa mcclone

All series stories are standalone, but past characters may reappear.

The Beach Brides/Indigo Bay Miniseries
Prequels to the Berry Lake Cupcake Posse series…
Jenny (Jenny and Dare)
Sweet Holiday Wishes (Lizzy and Mitch)
Sweet Beginnings (Hope and Josh)
Sweet Do-Over (Marley and Von)
Sweet Yuletide (Sheridan and Michael)

One Night to Forever Series
Can one night change your life…and your relationship status?
Fiancé for the Night
The Wedding Lullaby
A Little Bit Engaged
Love on the Slopes
The One Night To Forever Box Set: Books 1-4

The Billionaires of Silicon Forest
Who will be the last single man standing?
The Wife Finder
The Wish Maker
The Deal Breaker

Mountain Rescue Series
Finding love in Hood Hamlet with a little help from Christmas magic...
His Christmas Wish
Her Christmas Secret
Her Christmas Kiss
His Second Chance
His Christmas Family

Her Royal Duty
Royal romances with charming princes and dreamy castles...
The Reluctant Princess
The Not-So-Proper Princess
The Proper Princess

Quinn Valley Ranch
Two books featuring siblings in a multi-author series...
Carter's Cowgirl
Summer Serenade
Quinn Valley Ranch Two Book Set

A Keeper Series
These men know what they want, and love isn't on their list. But what happens when each meets a keeper?
The Groom
The Soccer Star
The Boss
The Husband
The Date
The Tycoon

For the complete list of books, go to:
melissamcclone.com/books.com